To

Thanks for the
hard work!

Sam

GUNSHOT Heart

Gun Shot Heart
By Sam Destiny

Copyright © 2019 Sam Destiny
Cover Copyright © Jay Aheer of Simply Defined Art
Photographer: Reggie Deanching of RPlusMPhoto
Model: Blake Sevani
Edited by Kim Young of Kim's Fiction Editing Services
Formatting by Aimie Jennison
All rights reserved. No part of this book may be copied or reproduced without written consent of the author.

This is a work of fiction. Names, characters, places and incidents are the product of the author's imagination. Any resemblance to actual events, places or people, living or dead, is coincidental.

OTHER BOOKS BY SAM DESTINY

Standalones
AJ's Salvation
Call Me Michigan

Tagged Soldiers Series
Tagged For Life
Forever Girl
Tagged For A New Start
Forever Try
Tagged Soldiers Boxed Set

Finding Single Dad's Series
Single Dad's Nightmare
Single Dad's Mistake
Single Dad's Loss
Finding Single Dads Boxed Set

*He that cuts off twenty years of life
Cuts off so many years of fearing death.*
-
William Shakespeare

PROLOGUE

"THAT IS MY HUSBAND!"

The screams... They never get old, never hurt less, will never cause me *not* to flinch.

I turn to the woman struggling behind the police tape while they load her husband into an ambulance, the latest casualty in a gang war in the slums of New York.

The sobbing gets stronger as I walk over to the woman and nod at the uniforms to let her go. This is usually the worst part. The questioning gaze, the hope, then the despair.

"I'm Detective Atwood, ma'am. Your husband is a hero," I say, then help her slip under the police tape.

Tears stream down her face. I see signs of exhaustion in every line, dark circles under her eyes. She's probably the one who has to take care of the kids while her husband protects the weak.

"Donald saved a life tonight," I continue. "The EMTs are positive he'll make a full recovery. He caught the bullet in the shoulder. Before you know it, he'll be sitting at your table, demanding food, hoping to catch a Lakers game." I wink at her, but the tears don't cease.

"I know…" She sobs as we stop near the ambulance. "But there'll be that call one day. *The* call. I'd never ask him to stop doing what he loves, and I love him too much to walk away, but—"

"Moira, stop annoying the poor detective. Are you coming or not?"

The officer's demand from the back of the ambulance causes his wife's breath to catch. She smiles and pats my shoulder before climbing in.

My partner, Will, steps up to my side as the ambulance pulls away. "It ended better than it could have," he says, as if I need the reminder.

I nod. "I know. This time. What about the countless times it doesn't? We've been there too many times, Will. Why do people even get into a relationship with somebody in this profession?" I gave up on finding love when I became a detective for the NYPD. "You saw her. It takes a toll on the spouse's emotions. Each time he's gone and the phone rings, she expects…" I wave my hand through the air. "You know what? It doesn't matter."

Hearing a shrill whistle, I look to see our boss waving us over to where the rest of our team stands.

Wolfe is as tough as they come, and I cannot remember him ever losing his cool.

"Forensics is collecting all the evidence, which we'll look over tomorrow. Right now, go home, have a drink, watch some TV. I'll see you in the morning."

I raise my head and stare up at the sky for a moment. How has this city become so riddled with gang violence that we push investigations to the next day?

"Home or bar?" Will asks. I shrug, wondering the same.

"Bar," I decide, then arch a brow at Will. "I'll go with or

without him, but when he just nods toward my SUV, I know that at least tonight, someone will distract me from all those thoughts of loneliness.

CHAPTER ONE

BLAKE

I SHIFT UNCOMFORTABLY, my tux straining across my shoulders. Or maybe it just feels like it because, technically, it had been fitted to me.

"Just promise me you won't mess with the wrong woman, okay? I know you hate social functions, but seriously, Atwood. Don't stick it where it doesn't belong."

I nearly roll my eyes, but know Gordon Wolfe, my sergeant, wouldn't appreciate the gesture. Instead, I clear my throat. "I don't know what you're talking about. I always behave. People love me."

"It's not love that women feel for you, buddy," my partner, Will Hawkes, mutters next to me. I bump him with my shoulder, grinning.

Nikki Bates, the only woman on our team, rolls her eyes. "I swear, sometimes I think I'm stuck in the boys' locker room at school."

I grin. "I happen to like that feeling. You know, when everything was still possible and the world was your oyster."

Back then, I hadn't yet seen what I've seen now and never experienced what I do these days. I won't lie. High school was easy, perfect in comparison to what I'm doing now.

Then again, I assume high school is easy in comparison to *everything* you have to do as an adult.

"All I'm saying is, if you have to hook up with someone, make sure it's a waitress," Wolfe announces over our bickering.

Declan Jones and Jim Davis, the last ones of our team, aren't here. I have a sneaking suspicion they will be a no-show, probably making some excuse.

Can't really blame them.

We're standing at a masquerade ball for some charity or another. Each of the districts sends a team every year, rotating the duty. This year, it's our turn, especially because we're not currently working on a case.

It's not that I like having to investigate murders, but they sure make for a nice excuse to get out of things like this.

"Stop twitching, Atwood," Nikki scolds.

I pull at the collar of my shirt. "I hate wearing a tux. I'll mingle, talk to people I should know, but will probably make a fool out of myself," I hiss, and she links her arm through mine.

Nikki's been part of Intelligence even before I'd joined. She's always been one of the guys, and I wouldn't want it any other way.

"Stick with me. I'll make it fun," she promises.

"Atwood, the commissioner is over there. You're coming with me to distract his wife," Wolfe orders and grabs my arm, pulling me along.

I grit my teeth. Wait... I'm not allowed to flirt, then am needed for exactly that? "Why? Do you need something from him you know she'll oppose to?"

The commissioner's wife is his conscience. It's why he's still one of the only good, trustworthy politicians.

You know, the ones who aren't easily persuaded.

Wolfe shakes his head. "I just have some questions about accessing case files we might need." He smiles when we reach the group. "Adalbert!"

Wolfe shakes hands with the commissioner as I grasp his wife's hand, pretending to kiss it. "Juliet, you look incredible," I tell her, although it's a lie. She wears a brightly colored dress in various shades of blue, paired with yellow heels and red lipstick that is more on her teeth than her lips.

Her dyed hair is such a light blonde color, people think she's sixty instead of thirty-four. For how sharp her brain is, she sure has no taste when it comes to style.

She flutters her lashes and giggles. "Detective Atwood, you're always such a charmer. And you actually have manners, unlike your sergeant."

Her eyes go to Wolfe, giving him a disapproving glance. He acknowledges her rebuff with a tilt of his head.

"I apologize, Juliet, but I figured you'd prefer Atwood's company over mine anyway." When he pretends to kiss her hand, making Juliet grin, I bite my cheek to not roll my eyes.

"You might be right about that, but don't let my husband know."

The commissioner chuckles, patting his wife's shoulder awkwardly. "You know, Wolfe, I'm jealous Atwood can take over the hard tasks for you." He winks. "I wish he could do the same for me."

I hold back a grimace. I can't help but think he's talking about his wife.

Clearing my throat, I look around, glad when I don't spot a waiter near us. There's no way I'm standing here any longer, worrying the conversation could turn into something I'm not comfortable with.

"I'm going to get us something to drink," I announce, walking away.

I shiver at the thought of sleeping with the commissioner's wife. I can't think of any duties that—

"Detective Atwood, it's so good to see you."

Layla Storm, the NYPD's poster woman for equality and female rights, crosses over to me. I force another smile. In her forties, she's well-built and lean, but there's something very…masculine about her.

God, I need a stiff drink.

"Miss Storm," I start, giving her a smile. "I'm sorry, but I'm going to have to find you later. I promised the commissioner and his wife I'd get them something to drink."

She laughs, which sounds rehearsed. It's meant to be cute and flirty, but I find it obnoxious. "You can always find me, no matter how late it is." She flutters her lashes, making sure there's no chance I'll misunderstand what she means.

I wink at her, trying to squash my nausea. "I'll remember that." I walk away, wondering if anybody would notice if I left.

TIA

I tug on my midnight blue gown, feeling uneasy. Chloe slaps my hand away.

"You look great. Stop tugging on it. Thank you so much for doing this for me," she says, pushing me toward the door. I know the cab's waiting downstairs, yet I don't want to go.

I told her I'd stand in for her tonight at some social function she's supposed to be at on behalf of the agency she works for. She pulled the *I-hardly-see-my-children-as-it-is* card. That might be true, but Chloe usually doesn't mind going to these things.

I glance into the mirror in the hallway as we pass, realizing that while the gown would look incredible on Chloe, I am too skinny for it. It's not that I don't eat enough, but rather that I'm always stressed. I have no idea the last time I'd just relaxed.

My sister, her three kids, and I are barely making it. We can pay rent and put food on the table, as well as pay a babysitter every now and then during the day, but there's hardly any room for luxuries. Not that I would actually have the time. If I'm not watching her kids, I'm working at the bar.

I think about having my first free evening in months. "I don't think I can go, Chloe." I brush my hands across my hips, which are basically non-existent in this dress.

She pushes me toward the door again, opens it, shoves the invitation into my hand, then spins me around to face her. "You'll be great, Tia. Just smile, have a few drinks, and don't talk to anyone important. You don't want me to look stupid, do you?"

Anger surges through me, but I swallow it down. I'm not dumb. The only reason I work in a bar is because I can't take any shifts during the day so we don't have to pay a babysitter consistently. I'm not incapable of holding a decent conversation, but don't try to convince Chloe of that.

I guess getting out of the house tonight will be a good thing.

She finishes tying the Venetian mask around my head. I touch it gingerly. I can see okay and breathe freely. I guess I can handle it for a little while.

"Bye."

I make my way downstairs and slip into the cab, tell the driver the name of the hotel, then settle back, watching the lights of New York pass by. It's only in the solitude of the cab that I start to worry. I can't remember when I was last among people wearing their finest clothes and had to prove that the area I lived in didn't define who I was.

"We're here, ma'am," the driver announces.

I lean forward and glance out of the front window, mouth dropping open. "I... What? It can't be," I mutter. I'm not prepared, not ready to step inside.

"Yes, ma'am. The Regency."

I grab money from the clutch and pay him before slipping out. I gather my dress in my hands as I make my way up the stairs. I know I'm technically late, but since I hadn't planned on being here for the announcements and thank yous, I'm practically right on time.

When I walk into the hotel, someone directs me to the ballroom. My breath catches. There are easily two hundred people inside. The men all wear tuxes and simple black masks, which I'd rather be wearing because the small feathers of my mask tickle my forehead.

The only thing I enjoy about the masquerade already is that you can't tell what people look like. Everyone is equally mysterious. God, how would it feel to act like those women in movies? You know, take a stranger into a dark corner, have our fun, then just part ways again. No names, no numbers.

I'm not the type for one-night stands...I don't think. I've been taking care of my sister since she turned sixteen and I had just turned eighteen because our parents chose to abandon us. I didn't have many serious relationships after that.

Actually, I never had *anything* serious because even if

something went on for a few months, we hardly ever crossed into serious territory.

It's also kind of hard when you watch your sister's kids during the day and work nights because I have no free time. Besides, not many guys like their girlfriends working at bars.

"Turn that frown into a smile and you'll shine like the sun," a guy says, stepping toward me and grasping my hand, pretending to kiss it.

I roll my eyes, but still can't help the small smile playing over my lips. "Does that really work? You know, a pick-up line like that?" He's taller than me, which isn't exactly hard with my five-foot-five, but I must look up quite a bit to meet his gaze.

He laughs. "Well, if my lines don't work, I just tell the ladies I'm a detective with the New York City Police Department. That usually does the trick." I see him wink behind the mask. "Name's Will Hawkes."

I shake my head. "I'm flattered, Detective Hawkes. Honestly. But whatever your aim is, you'd be better off directing your attention to someone who might make you happy at the end of the night."

He's about to say something else when a woman behind me calls out to him. I don't even bother turning around as I make my way over to a waiter holding a serving tray and grab a glass of Champagne, hoping no one realizes how much I hate that stuff as I down the whole glass.

This is going to be a long evening.

BLAKE

I grin to myself when I see Will being turned down by a woman in a midnight blue dress, her blonde curls reaching down her back. I wish she'd have pinned them up because the gown is backless.

My eyes stay on her even as the woman in front of me, whose name I can't remember, drones on about her gardener and the pool boy, who aren't doing a very good job anymore. I long for some relief, yet haven't found anyone who has piqued my interest. Although, I must say, I feel a little tempted to walk over to the woman who turned down my partner.

"God, I need to find someone pleasant," Will mutters as he joins our group.

"Sunshine didn't want you, huh?" I tease. He glances over his shoulder, but she's already gone.

He sighs. "She has pretty lips. Full and tempting. She was also frowning, which makes me think she didn't want to be here in the first place. Figured she and I had something in common, but I didn't even get far enough to tell her that."

I nod. "Did you try a cheesy line?"

"Of course. Told her to turn her frown into a smile and she'd shine like the sun. Didn't appreciate that, or my job title. Man, women today..." He shakes his head. "I swear, they are only impressed with uniforms, and we aren't patrol cops."

"Have you ever tried telling a woman how pretty she is? That might work," I suggest, raising a brow, but Will only shrugs.

"I've moved on. Anything else that looks good to you?"

I spot Nikki standing a few feet away. As if she knows what we're talking about, she shakes her head, reminding me of the fact that she compared us to teenage boys. I can't help but agree.

"There are a lot who look as if they could be nice, but let's face it. More than half of these ladies are older than you and I combined." It's not quite true, but he gets my drift.

"Atwood, Hawkes, come over here for a minute."

We nod to the rest of the group we've ignored and walk over to our boss.

"There are some judges here. We should talk to them. Can't hurt to have someone like them on our side, you know?" He glances around, a frown on his face, obviously realizing how hard it will be to find someone among all the guys wearing tuxes and masks.

God, I just want to leave.

"I have a better idea, boss. How about we get out of here and go to a real bar? You know, one with hard alcohol?" I suggest. Seeing a hint of indecision on his face, I press on. "Come on. You don't want to be here any more than we do. First round's on me."

Nikki walks over and growls, "If one more guy grabs my ass, I'll break his wrist."

Will links their arms. "Stick to me. Anyone who touches you will get a death glare from me. I'm sorry you need a man to keep the others away, but it'll be the most peaceful solution."

I hide my grin behind my hand, pretending to brush my scruff. I am pretty sure Will doesn't mind being Nikki's protector/company.

If there wasn't a rule against relationships between team members, those two would've probably hooked up at some point. As they walk away, Will gives Wolfe an apologetic glance over his shoulder.

I'm sure he's *very* disappointed that he can't schmooze the judges.

Truth be told, most of the judges are douches who you

could easily catch with their pants around their ankles while some Domina whips them. Not that I care what they do in their free time, but I *do* care when they have a wife and kids at home.

I look around. "Is that Benson over there?" I ask, spotting a tall guy with white hair who's the right height. When he turns, not wearing a mask, I can see it's the judge.

Wolfe slaps my back. "You're up, Atwood. Remember, he's a conservative, so keep your opinions to yourself."

I roll my eyes and nod, then start to make my way over, stopping a server who's handing out Champagne. I hate that shit, but it's the only alcoholic thing close to me at the moment. Before I can reach the judge, something seems to catch his attention and he glances around, probably checking for his wife, before he walks forward. I decide to keep my distance. Sometimes it's easier to have something incriminating in hand rather than having to be nice.

When he stops in front of Sunshine, who's standing a little off to the side and nibbling on canapés, I shake my head. "Dirty old man," I whisper.

He says something and she covers her mouth, trying to quickly chew her food. He leans in, whispering. I wish I could see her reaction behind the mask, but when she suddenly leans back a little, I know whatever he'd said didn't amuse her. When she shakes her head sharply, Benson shrugs.

I can't help but move closer, trying to be inconspicuous about eavesdropping.

"Just because I'm here alone doesn't mean I'm looking for somebody," Sunshine says, indignation in her voice.

Benson laughs softly while she crosses her arms in front of her chest, a small, sliver bracelet with shining stars and other trinkets on it flashing in the light. No idea why it catches my eye, but it makes her wrist seem fragile, elegant.

"Come on, pretty lady. I—"

"Atwood."

I swing my head to the right, seeing a woman walking up. How the fuck does everybody recognize me? I give her a smile when she stops in front of me, even as I look over her shoulder at Sunshine. She's talking furiously now, and I can't help but think I love the way her cherry red lips purse with each and every word.

A certain part of my body thinks that lipstick would definitely look good on my skin, and the rest of me can't help but agree.

TIA

I'm seething. It suddenly makes so much sense why Chloe refused to come here tonight. She knew she would be the center of attention for every freak in the room. The douche in front of me rubs his impressive belly, then leans in again.

"Five hundred. That's my final offer. It won't even be that long. We'll find a nice little corner, you ride me and show me your tits, then it's over and you're much richer than you were before coming. Lennard always has a few of you ladies at these events because, well...sometimes we need entertainment." He waggles his brows at me.

I place my hand on his chest and push him back. "Listen, buddy," I say very slowly, "if you suggest that I'm a hooker one more time, I'll tell everybody here things I'm sure you don't want people to think of you. I'm here on behalf of Clarke's Finances and Holdings. If you wanna confirm that, call my boss. Now, if you'll excuse me..." As I'm about to walk away, something else strikes me. "Make another move on me, I promise you'll regret it."

I stride away, the need for a stiff drink nearly killing me. The bar at the back of the room is unexpectedly empty. With all the idiots running around, I figured there'd be a lot of lonely wives or desperate men standing here.

"Vodka on ice," I order, and the bartender eyes me.

"You can have beer, white or red wine, or Champagne."

I hold his gray gaze. "Vodka. Straight. On ice."

When he just arches a brow, I curse. I know there's a bar in the front of the hotel, but I'll have to pay for the alcohol there, and vodka will be especially expensive.

"Wine. White," I order on a sigh.

"See? You're a good girl," the bartender taunts, and I grit my teeth.

I never speak to my patrons like that, do I?

"Turn that frown into a smile and you'll shine like the sun."

I've heard the line before, but the voice delivering it is different.

I turn. "How many detectives run around trying the same line?" I ask.

He grins. His hazel eyes sparkle through the eyeholes of his mask, I can see freckles on his cheeks where the black satin doesn't reach, and his lips are full. Even without seeing his whole face, I know he's too freaking handsome for his own good.

"How do you know I'm a detective?" he asks.

I shrug, accepting the glass of white wine the bartender places in front of me. "Wild guess. I also assume you're buddies with Detective Hawkes."

He smirks. "You should be on the force. Yes, I'm a detective, and yes, I am. Will is my partner. I'm Blake." He holds out his hand. When I just glance down at it, not moving, he shakes his head. "I just said that line because he thought he could win you over with either that or his position. Being the competitive guy I am, I wanted to try it to see if it would work for me. It wouldn't usually be my style."

I arch a brow, somewhere between annoyed and intrigued. "And how would you *usually* try to win a lady over?" I can't believe I said those words, knowing he'll take them as a challenge.

"Well..." He reaches up and takes off his mask before giving me a slow once-over.

I was right. He's off-the-charts handsome.

"With you, I'd say midnight is your color and only the stars can rival the sparkle in your eyes." The side of his lips quirk up. I know he is aware of how cheesy that line is, but it somehow works. I feel my cheeks heat beneath the mask.

"I'm..." *Chloe. It's easy. Just say the word.* I've uttered it a few times over the evening and it never once bothered me, but somehow, the word just doesn't come over my lips, "charmed," I finish. His lashes lower, hiding his hazel eyes from view.

I watch his Adam's apple bob as he swallows, clearly considering his next words. "If you don't want to tell me your name, I can handle that. I'll just keep calling you Sunshine, like I did in my mind."

I cock my head. "You know, that almost sounds mysterious. Like Cinderella. I'll take it. Tell me, Blake. What does a guy like you hope to find at an event like this?"

I sip my wine, watching him glance around the room. There are a few people on the dance floor now, following whatever classical piece is playing. I took a dance class in high school, and as much as I'm not sure I remember all the steps, I wistfully wish someone would waltz me across the marble tiles.

"Honestly?" he finally asks.

I arch a brow. "No. Lie to me."

He considers my answer for a moment, then grins. "I hope to find never-ending love. You know, hearts and rainbows."

My heart speeds up, then settles back into its normal rhythm. I didn't come here hoping to find anything of the sort, but hearing him say he's here for some simple fun—because, ultimately, I assume that's what he's implying—does something to me.

I wonder if *I* could be that simple fun for him. I have nothing to lose, and with me not even having given him Chloe's name, neither does she.

Suddenly, he holds out a hand to me. "Sunshine, would you mind giving me this dance? Or maybe two?"

Seemingly on its own, my hand touches his. He grins, knowing he's partly won me over.

"Maybe you should put on the mask again," I suggest, which clearly startles him.

He coughs, putting his hand on his chest in mock hurt. "Okay... I didn't realize I was that ugly."

I suddenly feel flirty and brave, so I place my hand on his chest and lean in until my lips touch his ear while I whisper, "I just think less people will stare at what's mine for the next few minutes if you put the mask back on."

I feel his heart race underneath my palm. I can't help but think that maybe, just maybe, I don't have to be me at all tonight.

CHAPTER TWO

TIA

THE EDGE of the dance floor seems to be the crossing line for something I cannot name or place, and I feel like he deserves to know what he's getting into with me.

"You know, I need to be honest here. Unless you are a dancing god, we'll probably make fools out of ourselves because my last dancing class was, well... It's been some years back. Like in high school."

He grins, then leads me in a wide circle on the dance floor before drawing me in and placing his free hand on my lower back.

"Trust me to lead us, Sunshine. I'll try to make sure we keep our faces masked." He winks behind the black satin as we start moving.

It's funny how my body is hyperaware of his fingers pressing into my back, the tips dancing across it as if he's actually playing along with the tune.

I lean in a little, conscious of people watching us. I smile at them, then focus back on my partner. "Can you play the piano, Blake?"

He pulls back to look at me, his fingers stilling, and twirls me around the dance floor before shrugging. "I can't believe you felt that. Yes, I can. My parents considered it a necessary social skill. You know…" He rolls his eyes, "because it can save lives and pay the bills."

As much as he sounds bored with the fact that he can play, I can't help but think he enjoyed it or he wouldn't be playing the notes on my back. "It might not save lives, but I assume that's why you became a cop," I reply. "Playing piano is for the heart—or to win ladies over." I smirk. "Just imagine how sexy it would be… You playing a heartfelt tune, the lady losing more clothes per stanza until she sits at your feet, naked, begging you to forever claim her."

Thanks to movies, I can almost see us in that scene, the bowtie around his neck undone, the jacket off, his bare feet on the pedals of the piano while haunting melodies flow through the air.

He thinks for a minute. "I don't do forever, but I like the part where the woman loses the clothes," he states, his voice sounding amused and serious at the same time.

I wonder why he'd never do a lasting relationship, but I also can't help but be glad because, hell, I couldn't commit.

Not that I'm interested in him.

Much.

"I bet you can coerce any woman to get naked for you, Blake. After all, your pick-up lines are smooth…like jagged glass."

He laughs, the sound warm and tempting, then leans in, his cheek brushing mine. "You are so nice to me, Sunshine. Careful, though. You might inflate my ego to epic proportions."

He smells good. A hint of sweet, yet male, then something that's probably all Blake. Tender and sinful at once.

"I think you manage to do that all by yourself. Tell me something. I feel a lot of death glares on me behind the masks. The women here know you, don't they?"

He sighs, the smile vanishing from his lips. "I hate social functions, but I won't lie... I like ladies. As long as they're beautiful, I'm not really picky."

"I like how unapologetic you are." Only after the words are out do I realize how true they are. He doesn't hide the fact that he spends only a few hours with a woman or pretend to not know how handsome he is.

My words seem to surprise a laugh out of him. "I don't think anyone ever complimented me on that. Besides, if you ask Nikki, the only woman in our unit, she'd tell you I'm like a high school boy. All hormones and screwing on my mind."

I snort. "I bet she's wrong."

He furrows his brows, confused. "What do you mean?"

I give him a slow grin. "I'm sure you also think about breasts. Guys always do."

He shakes his head, a wide grin on his face. "Damn, Sunshine, you're something else. Man, now I'm thinking about breasts."

I move a little closer, making sure he feels my chest against his. His breath hitches. "Okay, let's see if I can distract you from that *horrible* thought," I whisper, letting my hand wander up to his neck, my fingertips brushing along his collar. I feel the skin prickle underneath my hand, a shiver running through him.

"Keep going, Sunshine," he growls, "and we won't be dancing much longer. Also, you're not distracting me much. More like...heightening my focus."

I don't stop my wandering fingers, but pull back enough

so I can hold his gaze while teasing him. His grip on me tightens, his lips slightly parted. I stare at them, not sure if he can see it under the mask or not.

His tongue darts out to wet them. "God, woman. Stop looking at me like that."

I smile, but can't look away. I'm suddenly dying for a taste. I force myself to meet his eyes as he brushes his thumb over the back of my hand, quickening my pulse.

I know we're playing with fire, but I don't care. If he'd ask me to follow him, I'd gladly go, not caring where he led. If somebody asked me to climb him like a tree, I'd probably merely demand some kind of privacy.

"Oh, Blake..."

I only realize I whispered the words out loud when he exhales quietly, as if trying to steel himself against something —or prepare himself for something entirely unexpected.

BLAKE

Despite what she'd said earlier, we move smoothly over the dance floor. It's strange how much it bothers me that she won't tell me her name. I mean... I usually don't mind, couldn't care less if I know the name of the woman I'm with, but Sunshine intrigues me. She's funny, smart, different. I can't help but think she's out of place in this crowd.

The music turns softer, slower, and I draw her closer, our joined hands resting against my shoulder. I want to remove her mask, see what she looks like. Her lips are full, red, and beautiful, especially when she smiles shyly, but that's about all I can really tell about her. Even her eyes are somewhat hard to make out. I can't be sure, but they look like a dark blue or brownish color.

She hums softly and rests her head against my shoulder, the feathers from her mask tickling my cheek.

"You know, I think you and I should get out of here," I whisper, hoping I said it quietly enough that if it's not what she wants, she can pretend she didn't hear me.

She tilts her head up a little. It takes me a second to realize her lips brushed against my neck. "Agreed," she replies. "But... I'm not going home with you, and I'm not taking you home."

There are a million things I want to reply, most of them my standard answers, but I don't say any of it. Instead, I clear my throat. "I can introduce you to my boss if it makes you feel safer."

What the hell are you doing?! You don't take women back to your place because you don't want repeats or to risk stalkers. In fact, there are a lot of reasons no woman has ever made it into your apartment.

She pulls back to look at me. There's something in the way her lips tilt that makes me think she's quirked her eyebrow. "No quickie, Detective? Isn't that what you were hoping for? A dark corner, just—"

"I need to get you naked, Sunshine, but I also need to take my time with you. You can't tease a man the way you do, then want to finish him off with a quick fuck, one that probably won't satisfy you much."

She giggles. "Would that hurt your ego? Knowing you didn't get me off?"

She's way too smug. I need to change that. I lean closer, touching her ear with my lips. "I just really want to bite your nipple, knowing I can make it hard. Tease it with my tongue, then move lower and tease something *else* with my tongue," I whisper.

She gasps, her grip on me tightening.

"I bet your panties are soaking wet, aren't they? You didn't come here to leave alone, did you?"

She brushes her mouth across the pulse in my neck and up my jaw, nibbling on my earlobe before whispering, "What panties?"

I pull back and blink at her. She's bluffing. She has to be, but that doesn't change the fact I'm getting hard as steel inside my tuxedo pants.

I step back and grasp her hand. She laughs, but follows my hasty steps. Seeing Will standing near the door, I can't help but mess with him. Pausing briefly, Sunshine steps up to me, her hand still in mine, the other one wrapped around my arm.

"I don't know what your problem is, Hawkes. I used the same line you did and scored the girl."

He cocks his head, ready to say something when Sunshine leans forward. "Don't believe it. He gave me fifty bucks to walk past you with him."

Hawkes bellows out a laugh as my jaw drops. "I can't believe you just said that," I huff.

She shrugs. "Aren't we out the door yet? My bad. Forget what I said, Detective Hawkes." I can all but see the way she probably flutters her lashes at him.

"You're something, Sunshine," I mutter. She presses her lips against my shoulder in a peace offering I'm happy to accept. I need to get out with her, *now*.

"Call me if anything pops up," I tell my partner, then pull Sunshine out the door. "Did you have a coat?"

She hands me a ticket. Gentleman that I am, I stand in line at the coat check. Subtly, I watch her, expecting her to get nervous and bolt. I have a feeling she usually isn't a one-night stand kind of girl. As much as I am sure she came in the hopes of experiencing something extraordinary, I'm not sure she really knows what that means.

"Sir? Your ticket?" I spin around and hand it to the young kid. He walks up and down the racks, then returns with it in his hand. "I'm sorry, sir. This coat—"

"It's a lady's coat." I point over my shoulder. "It's Sunshine's." He stares at her for a very long moment, his eyes nearly popping out of his head. I clear my throat impatiently.

"Yes, sorry." He rushes to hand over the simple black coat.

I help Sunshine into it, then just stand there and stare at her for a brief moment. I still can't see much of her face, but now that the lighting is much brighter, I notice how pale her skin is. Almost exquisitely so.

She wipes at her lips, as if worried she's smeared something. That might be the case in just a few minutes. "Already regretting the decision?"

I reach up and brush my thumb under her mask. "Take it off." I'm not sure if I'm ordering or asking, but she just cocks her head and winks.

"Certainly not. I won't let you get out of taking me home that easily."

I grin, although I feel a slight pang. I need to know what she looks like, the curiosity almost killing me, but it seems that I have to wait just a little longer.

TIA

I can see the disappointment in his eyes, but for some reason, I'm confident he won't be disappointed when I finally show my face.

We walk outside, seeing a few cabs waiting. A driver gets out as Blake walks over, but he instantly shakes his head, making it clear he'll open the door for me. I hesitate before getting in. He reaches out to brush his thumb across my bottom lip, then gets in first, holding out his hand.

I take it and slip in next to him. He tells the driver an address that's really close to my place, yet is a whole different world. There's a park between our neighborhoods. He lives on the pretty side. A fence runs through the middle that you cannot go through unless you have a key, and no one from our side has one. It's like I live on the wrong side of the tracks.

He takes off his mask, his face contemplative in the relative darkness of the cab. I take his hand. "It's Tia, by the way," I whisper. He looks at me, then leans in.

His lips are soft, yet demanding, dominating a kiss that doesn't even last longer than two minutes. He pulls back, leaving me wanting more.

"Nice to meet you, Tia," he says with an endearing smile.

I cup his cheek, brushing my thumb across it, feeling the slight stubble against my palm. "You're too handsome, you know that?"

His eyes search my face, although he cannot see much of it. "I've been told that a time or two, yes."

Funnily enough, he sounded all cocky when he answered my questions before. This time, that was absent.

The space in the back of the cab is tight, yet I shift, making it pretty obvious that I want to crawl into his lap.

There's indecision on his face as he makes room for me and shifts my dress so I can straddle his hips. "You should be buckled up," he mutters, his fingertips brushing across my bare back.

They are soft, making it obvious that he doesn't do manual labor, yet I remind myself he definitely doesn't have an easy job.

"Hold onto me and I'll be fine," I assure him.

His lips draw into a tight line as he lowers his eyes. "I'm not sure I'm your safest option."

My hands frame his face, but he still he refuses to look at me. I nudge his chin up to look into his eyes. "What could be safer than a police officer?" His hands on my hips dig into the skin. I wish we were already at his place because I want everything he promised back at the hotel.

When he doesn't smile, I hesitate before reaching up, untying the mask, letting it drop to the floor of the cab. Blake bites his lip. I hope it's too dim in here for him to notice the dark circles under my eyes. By the time we reach his place, I expect he'll be too needy to watch me closely.

"God, Tia..."

He cups my cheeks and kisses me, his lips hungry. I wrap my arms around his neck as his hands wander down my arms and over my back. I feel him hardening, his erection pressing into my thigh. I groan into his mouth.

"Tia...," Blake whispers against my lips and rests his forehead against mine. "You need to get off my lap. I've taken a lot of women in a lot of weird places, but if you grind against me once more, it'll be in the back of this cab, and that's the last thing you deserve."

"I don't care," I whisper. Right at that moment, I honestly don't. I want to do something I'd never do, and I want to do it with Blake.

He gently lifts me off his lap and sets me onto the seat. I

huff and cross my arms in front of my chest, pouting. He scrubs his hands over his face.

"Don't, Tia. You're a good girl. You deserve so much more."

I look at him, eyes narrowed. "What in the world makes you think I am a good girl?" To prove my point, I slide my hand up his thigh and across the erection straining against his zipper. He bucks, but I have a feeling it's involuntary.

"You were honestly outraged when... Benson earlier... I..." His breath grows heavy.

When he doesn't stop me, I feel emboldened. I cup him and squeeze a little, making him moan. It's been years since I've fumbled around with a guy. My cheeks heat, my lips drawn into a somewhat guilty grin.

Suddenly, a warm hand covers mine, his large palm stilling me. "No. Not now, Tia... Please... When the hell are we going to be there?" he calls out to the cabby, but the only answer we get is a chuckle and him muttering something about being glad to give a cop blue balls.

I have to bite my cheek to keep myself from chuckling, and when I glance at Blake, I can tell he does, too.

BLAKE

When Tia slips out of the cab as I pay the cabby, my heart beats in my throat.

"Girlfriend?" the cabby asks. He's probably in his fifties, his face lined with laughter, his temples graying.

"Nope. Just met her." And if it goes the way one-night stands usually do, I won't ever see her again. Then again, I don't usually take those home.

He shrugs. "I see."

It's funny how you can sometimes tell when people want to say more. I'm impatient, but for some reason, I want to know what he thinks. Cabbies are much like bartenders. They sometimes act like therapists.

I cock my head. "You see what?"

He meets my eyes in the rearview mirror. "Nothing, man. Just... You know."

No, I don't know. That's why I fucking asked. "Spill."

He glances out the side window, watching Tia hug herself as she waits. Her mask dangles from her fingertips, and her expression is somber, yet clearly filled with something positive, too, because her lips are pulled into a small smile.

"Girls like her? You might get them into your bed, but they won't ever leave you fully again."

"Are you saying she's a stalker?"

He waggles his brows. "I'm saying she's a life changer. A girl you cannot forget. Unless you plan to seriously work toward a relationship, you might want to...I dunno...not take her up."

For a second, I'm startled, especially because this is already so much different than my usual MO, then I shake my head. "Thanks for the advice, but I think you're wrong. Anyway... Have a successful night, man. May you get a hundred more fares." I hold out my hand and he shakes it, giving me a knowing smile.

I get out and walk over to Tia. She looks up at me as I close in, wrapping my arms around her. I capture her lips with mine, feeling her melt against me. Her arms come around my neck, fingertips tangling in my hair, nearly making me groan. I never knew I liked small touches, but with Tia, it couldn't be more obvious to me how much everything she does turns me on.

"Ready?" I ask against her lips, wanting to give her the chance to leave if she's having second thoughts. Maybe I should've asked that when the cab was still stopped at the curb. "You can still leave."

She peeks up at me. I cannot wait to get her somewhere I can see her eyes. In the streetlights, they are just as dark as they were behind her mask, but at least I can see her features. Her face is elegant, finely cut. I can't help but think that even if she were a little more plain, I'd have still taken her up on her offer.

There something about her that touches me in a way I've never experienced before. While it should have me worried, I suddenly crave the feeling—even if for just a few hours.

It's as if she holds the reins to all my demons, and as long as she keeps them leashed, I can breathe more freely than ever before. I don't know when I last felt this...light.

"You cannot get rid of me that easily." She places a soft kiss on my lips. "You promised to get me naked and tease my nipples until I moan. Wasn't that what you said? I want you to kiss your way over my skin, to tickle the pleasure out of me until I can hardly remember who I am. Are you up for that, Blake?"

Instead of answering, I take her hand and press it against my erection. I cannot wait to have exactly what she just offered. "Come on." I wrap my arm around her shoulders and unlock the door, letting her enter first. She walks over to the elevators as I praise the brightly lit foyer. Walking up, I turn her to me, my gaze taking in her features. Her eyes are blue like the ocean, and just as deep. Her lips shimmer as she looks up at me and smiles, wrapping her arms around my middle under the tux jacket.

I wonder if that means I should kick her right back out because she might have a hard time keeping this a one-time thing. Deciding to test the waters, I say, "Maybe I should take you out before taking you to bed. You know, like—"

She shakes her head. "No, Blake. If that's what you want to come out of this, maybe I *should* leave. We have the next few hours, but after that..." She swallows. "There won't be more. You said yourself that you don't do relationships, so..."

I jab goes through my chest, making me want to rub away the pain. She picked me because I made it obvious there'd be no repeats? While it is exactly what I wanted to hear, I suddenly don't like it.

Her face softens and her hand comes up to cup my cheek. "Come morning, the magic will be gone and you'll be glad when I leave."

I force myself to grin. "I was just testing you anyway. You know, you looked at me kinda hopeful there for a minute," I tease, hoping to lighten up the situation. The elevator behind us dings.

She winks. "You are quite enjoyable to look at, so I feel privileged to have the chance to follow you...for tonight."

I back her up into the elevator until her back hits the cold, mirrored wall, then I blindly fumble to press the right button. After pressing the four, I brush her hair back, then kiss her shoulder.

"Fine," I decide. "You can look at me like that all you want."

She laughs, the sound soft and feminine. I grin, wondering why I'm so nervous to take her into my apartment—and my bed. After all, I left the awkward teenage years behind me over a decade ago, but I guess the feelings still find you sometimes.

CHAPTER THREE

TIA

THE URGENCY in Blake when we left the masquerade is suddenly gone. He's tender, sweet, making me wonder what is going on.

The building is nice, but nothing special with its faded cream façade and thick carpets leading down the hallways to the apartment doors. He unlocks a brown door, then pushes it open and lets me step inside.

"You want coffee or something?" he asks, throwing his key onto a side table by the door before turning on the lights. We stand in a small dead-end hall, just big enough for three people. Blake opens a door to his right and walks in. I follow. The moonlight streaming in through the windows hits a seating arrangement and something I assume to be shelves.

When a light flickers on, I see an open kitchen, a granite countertop separating it from the living room beyond. He hangs his tux jacket over a chair, then gets busy opening cabinets, his back to me. I slip out of my shoes and swallow down my nervousness, then walk over to him. I leverage myself onto the counter behind him, letting my fingertips trail up and down his back.

He stiffens and pauses in whatever he's doing.

"Blake," I whisper.

He turns to me, and I see his bowtie undone. I pull it from his collar and drop it onto the counter next to me. His hazel eyes on my face, he swallows when I start to unbutton his white shirt, pulling it from his pants before pushing it over his shoulders. The freckles spread over his shoulders are adorable, and I lean in, placing gentle kisses on them.

I pull back and draw my dress up so I can wrap my legs around his hips, yet as much as I try to seduce him, he's still expressionless.

If it weren't for the crotch of his pants, which seems too freaking tight, I'd say he's unaffected. I scoot forward. I feel him tremble, but he tilts his head when I brush my nose up his neck, nibbling on his earlobe.

A moan escapes and his hands grip my thighs, squeezing. "Fuck, Tia," he mutters.

I smile, but don't stop my gentle kissing. I'm not a born seductress, but I've seen enough movies, read enough books to know which steps I should follow.

How hard can it be, right?

I close my eyes as my fingertips trail down his back. He shivers, giving me a smile. "I... I didn't know I was ticklish," he explains, making me smirk.

My hands reach his waistband and I drag them around to the front. Pulling back slightly, I open the button. His eyes burn into mine, the flames between us burning brightly. I can tell he's barely holding onto his control.

Then it hits me. He isn't impassive. He's trying to take this slowly.

I free his erection from the constraints of his pants, wrapping my hands around the considerable size, and stroke lazily. He groans, his head hanging.

His lips crash to mine as he twists me until I lay on the counter, the cold granite cooling me down. He kisses his way up my legs, lifting my dress with the movement. My muscles quiver, the feeling of his scruff and soft lips unexpected, yet welcome. He nips every now and then, causing me to gasp.

"Fuck, Tia. You are so responsive."

I swallow the remark that it has been a while for me, so of course my body jumps at the smallest touch.

His fingers slide up and down my thigh before brushing over my panties. I'm glad I picked a small, elegant pair instead of something comfortable, especially when he suddenly pulls them off me and discards them.

I arch my back as his finger brushes my most sensitive spot. "Jesus, you're so wet," he mutters, and I feel a finger push inside me.

I want to reply with something flirty and witty, but the truth is, I can hardly think with his lips on my skin and finger moving in and out of me. Suddenly, his finger is gone, his tongue replacing it.

My hands go into his hair, ruining the perfect style he had for the masquerade, and he groans when I tug a little. He circles my clit with the tip of his tongue, licking and biting gently, before kissing up my thighs. When he places my legs over his shoulders, putting his tongue back on me, I bite my lip to keep myself from moaning any louder. He's definitely good at this, which benefits me immensely.

"Blake," I gasp suddenly, feeling my orgasm building. "Please. I... I'm going to..."

He softly bites my nub again, causing me to cry out as a strong wave of pleasure tries to drown the burning fire of lust inside me. I shake all over, my legs quivering as he teases every last wave out of me, then he draws me up and kisses me softly, grinning smugly.

"And now," he announces, pulling me off the counter and into his arms, "round two."

———

BLAKE

She still trembles as I carry her through the semi-dark living room to the bedroom. I know my way around in the dark, yet am glad I didn't close the curtains this morning.

The lights of New York stream through the windows of the bedroom, bathing Tia in a soft, ethereal glow as I set her back onto the floor next to the bed, then kick off my shoes and toe of my socks. She looks up at me, and I cup her cheek.

Still feeling her tremble, I squash a smile about having given her an orgasm that lasts so long. I kiss her softly, wondering if she's going to get all shy now, but her hands travel back to the front of my pants, finding what she'd been stroking earlier.

The feeling of her hand on me brings me awfully close to shooting my load, her small fingers gripping my cock, stroking expertly. To save me from embarrassing myself, I nudge her hand away, gathering her dress around her hips before pulling it over her head. For a second, I'm worried about simply discarding it onto the floor. Smirking, she takes it from me and throws it behind her, then takes off her bra and steps in so her chest touches mine. She pushes up onto her tiptoes.

Her lips find mine. I let her dominate that one kiss—until she shoves her hands into my boxers, squeezing my ass in a way that's almost rough. A groan rumbles from somewhere deep within me. She pushes my pants and boxer briefs down in one movement, following them to the floor.

I step out of the clothes, then hold my breath when she kisses up my thigh, her hands slowly following. I both cannot wait for what is coming and dread it at the same time because if she puts her lips around me—

Holy mother of God.

All thought flees my mind when she leisurely drags her tongue along my length, her fingers wrapped around the base. When she licks the drop of precum, I place my hands on her head because my legs are ready to give out.

She meets my eyes. I wish I'd turned on a lamp, but even in the semi-darkness, I can tell she's gauging my reaction as she takes me into her mouth, swallowing me down as deeply as she dares.

"Fuck, fuck, fuck," I mutter, locking my muscles to keep myself from moving my hips. I want to fuck her mouth until I come all over her tongue, but she's in charge. I want it to stay that way a little longer.

I sink my fingers into her soft, blonde hair, gently cupping the back of her head as she starts sucking me in earnest, her tongue teasing the underside of my dick while her teeth graze the soft skin. She follows her lips with her hand, the fingers creating a tight circle that has me moaning out in pleasure.

She hums her appreciation. I nearly come undone right then and there.

Hell, I've gotten blowjobs before. Some have been pleasurable, but with her, it's different somehow. So much more intense, so...

I don't know. I can't put my finger on what it is. As much as I'm sure she doesn't hookup regularly, she seems to know exactly what to do to drive me crazy. Her rhythm increases, then she slows down until there's hardly any friction, leaving me panting, ready to beg for more.

Her second hand comes up to fondle my balls, making my knees shake. If she notices, she doesn't say anything or ease the pleasurable torture.

"Tia," I rasp out, then clear my throat. "Tia, I need to…" *Come.* Funnily enough, I cannot say the word. I'm not even sure if I want to come in her mouth or pick her up and place her onto the bed.

She only nods, kissing my thighs, driving me nuts, then she takes me back in, swallowing, making me groan.

"Need to…move…my hips," I whisper, my balls tight. I'm so ready to come, it's almost painful.

She doesn't react as she sucks. I cannot suppress the need any longer, fucking her mouth the way I've wanted to since she knelt in front of me.

She takes all I give. When a tingle shoots down my spine and races through my body, I try to pull out, but her hand cups my ass, holding me in place.

"I'm coming, Tia. I—"

She takes every last drop as I fill her mouth. I don't even know why this feels so intense. I had sex just a couple days ago with a nice lady who occupied my body for hours. Still…

Tia swallows and smacks her lips, making me groan. Fuck, that's so sexy.

She slowly gets to her feet and pushes me back. I drop onto the mattress like a stone, my body quivering. When she crawls over me, I draw her in for a long kiss, tasting myself on her lips. She'd taken all I'd offered—and liked it.

―――

TIA

One minute I'm hovering over him, feeling proud of myself, and the next, he flips me so I lie on the mattress while his scruff tickles across my skin as he kisses and licks his way down my body. He cups my breasts with his hands, teasing the nipples until they pebble, painfully demanding more attention.

"You have condoms, right?" I mutter as the thought strikes me. Yes, I'm on the pill because it reduces the problems I have whenever I get my period, but that doesn't mean I'm going to risk catching anything from him.

"Sure do," he replies, not pausing his kisses. Relieved, I close my eyes and focus on the feel of him. His hands brushing down my sides and back up again make me shiver.

His tongue teases one pebbled nipple, then the other, then the first again until I feel the need to do something to relieve the pressure building inside me. I don't know if I'll be able to keep this going for hours, but man, I want to.

I want to ride him, have him take me from behind, then follow him into the shower to get cleaned up—only to start again. I've never spent a night like that, never felt the intensive need, but Blake makes it easy.

I want him, all of him, and I want him to claim my body in any way possible.

When he gets up, I am about to protest before he walks back, something in his hand. He takes it between his teeth and tears it open, making me realize it's a condom.

He climbs back onto the bed and kneels, rolling it down expertly, then hesitates for the briefest second.

I look at him, seeing the same expression of nervousness on his face that's probably on mine. I spread my legs wider, making more room for him. The tip of his erection brushes my core, causing both of us to inhale sharply.

"You would think I'd manage to last longer this time around, but I have a feeling that's not going to be the case," he says, his voice strained.

I cup his cheek and pull him down to my lips, wanting to distract him from his worries. I've come once, considering that a win, so I'm not worried about it. I wrap my legs around his hips because, damn, I want him inside me *now*.

When he slowly enters me, I gasp. He's big, or maybe it just feels that way because I haven't had anyone inside of me in a long time. I feel myself tense up as he pulls out, then pushes back into me.

Luckily, Blake seems to be able to read my body's reaction because he shifts, cupping my face before kissing me until I'm breathless.

"Jesus, Tia, you're so fucking tight. If I move my hips now..." He shakes his head. I grin.

Instead, I move my hips, biting my lip as I feel him deep inside of me, filling me so completely, it makes me tingle from head to toe. "Come on, Blake," I urge. He groans against my shoulder, then slowly pulls out and thrusts into me harshly.

I cry out in pleasure, my nails digging into his back. He curses under his breath, his hips taking us exactly where we need to be.

I don't remember the last time I had sex, but I do recall that it was *nothing* like this. He holds onto me tightly, kissing me repeatedly, our ragged breath making it obvious how close we are to falling over the edge. When he adjusts his hips a little, hitting he spot I didn't even know existed, I'm no longer worried about not coming.

I bite his shoulder, muffling the moan I'd make otherwise, and I swear I hear him laugh.

It's with his name on my lips that another wave crashes over me, the pleasure drowning out everything but the man I'm with. I throw my head back, squeezing my eyes closed while my inner walls grip him, milking him for everything he has.

"Fuck, Tia...," he gasps. I feel him pulse inside of me, and I move against his slow thrusts, helping him ride out the pleasure as long as we can.

He kisses me slowly, our hearts beating as one, then he moans as he pulls out and gets up, walking to the bathroom to discard the condom.

I stretch, then freeze. Does he expect me to get dressed and leave? Will he be upset when he comes back and finds me still in the sheets?

He answers the question when he slips into the bed, drawing up the blanket. "You're something else," he mutters, then presses a kiss to the side of my head. I shift until my head rests on his chest, his heartbeat slowing.

"I think I bit you," I state, more as a way of making conversation than me really being worried about it.

"You definitely did," he replies, amusement in his voice.

There's silence, and I feel the need to fill it. "Do you need me to, you know...get dressed and—"

His grip tightens around me. "How about you stay, give me a few minutes to gather my strength again, and we'll see where we take it from there?"

I stay where I am, grinning to myself.

I like a man who makes plans, and his plan sounds good to me.

BLAKE

Hearing Tia's steady breathing next to me, this would normally be the time I'd sneak out of the apartment, but first, this is my place, and second, I want to keep her near me. I lean over and kiss her between the shoulder blades. She shifts, sighing in contentment. I smile to myself, then climb out of bed to grab some water. I feel weird walking around naked with a stranger in my bed, so I blindly reach around on the floor until I find my boxer briefs and pull them on.

Despite being extremely tired, I feel like I have too much energy, and as much as I want to wake her for another round, I know it's more the fact that I fear the nightmares. It doesn't happen every night, or even every week, but it's sometimes like my body's warning that I'll have a shitty night.

I'm strung like a wire and linger in my living room for a few minutes, sipping on a bottle of water. Something dark lying on the floor near the kitchen catches my eye, so I walk over, picking up Tia's black panties. I grin, considering keeping the little souvenir, but I know she'll be gone by morning and there'll be no repeats. Not for her, not for me. As much as she silences something within me, makes me feel powerful and gentle at the same time, I cannot give her anything more.

In fact, I've already gone beyond what I normally offer a woman, but Tia is different.

Rubbing the back of my neck, I wonder what exactly I need to calm my demons. I consider turning on the TV, but I'm too afraid to wake my company, and for some reason, I don't want her to leave just yet. I quietly walk into my room and place her panties next to the bed, then slip out again, stepping to the windows in the living room to look outside.

I stare at the park, one I often jog in. Beyond that is a neighborhood where you don't want to be outside at night. There are worse in New York, but there are also better. I'm drawn to it because I feel as if the kids who live there have a chance. Their parents work hard, sometimes two jobs, and manage to put food on the table and clothe their children decently. The street corners are less likely to be filled with drug dealers or gangs, but still, when darkness falls, the detestable, the prostitutes and their violent pimps, invade the streets.

Warm hands wrap around me from behind. When Tia leans in, I feel the buttons of my shirt press into my back. She must've picked it up in the kitchen, and I'm almost mad at myself that I missed the sight of her wandering through my apartment naked.

She gently kisses my back a couple times, making my heart slow. I hadn't even realized it was racing in the first place. "I should get going," she says softly, her voice thick with sleep.

I grab her hands, pulling them up to my lips to kiss her fingertips. "It's the middle of the night, Tia," I mutter. "Stay just a little longer. I promise. I'll come back to bed."

Neither of us moves. She rests her cheek against my back, arms wrapped around me, while I close my eyes. Her fingertips dance across my stomach and up my chest, before going back down again, lazily tracing circles across my skin. When I twitch, she giggles softly.

Turning in her arms, I see only two buttons fastened in the middle, the sleeves rolled up. "You look good," I whisper. She grins up at me, then leans her head against my chest. I search for the anxiousness and restlessness inside of me, feeling nothing.

"Are you okay?" she asks.

Because we won't see each other again, I figure I can give her a little something.

"I sometimes have nightmares," I start in a low voice. "I can occasionally feel them coming on and get all restless. I was worried I'd wake you with tossing and turning."

She nods against my skin, kisses my pecs, then meets my eyes. "Nightmares about what?"

It's funny how that question is still hard to answer, although I can't help but think about it each and every time I wake up, bathed in sweat. I blow out a breath. "I'm a police detective. That means saving people, yet sometimes there are those you can't save, those you have to stop from hurting others. That's partly what I dream about. I often run in my dreams, as if searching for something I can't find, and am crushed with guilt. There are featureless faces, sometimes just voices, and I start running toward them, but then a new one appears and I can't reach the first one anymore. It's..."

"Exhausting," she finishes. I nod, resting my lips against her forehead. "Come on." She steps back and tugs on my hand. "If you start tossing and turning, I'll wake you up and stop the nightmare."

"Just be careful. I might wake up and start swinging," I only half joke. She smiles as she walks backward, leading me to the bedroom. "However, I don't feel restless right now. I think it's going to be okay."

"Good."

There's something in her voice, but I can't see her face. I try to place her tone, but I don't know her well enough to define it. I'm also not sure I want to ask. We've reached my limit on deep and meaningful conversation for the night.

Hell, for an entire month, yet I hardly said anything.

She slips out of my shirt as we climb back into bed. I wrap my arms around her, holding her tightly, her head on my chest. It feels right. God, Kelly Watts, my best friend, would have a field day if he knew how touchy-feely I am with her.

"Good night and sweet dreams, Blake," she whispers against my skin. I grin to myself. I think the last person who wished me sweet dreams was my mother when I was a kid.

"Good night, Tia," I reply, already feeling my eyes getting heavy. She starts humming, as if trying to calm me. I think how funny it is, but for some reason, it lulls me to sleep faster than anything ever has.

WHEN I WAKE in the morning, I reach over to the other side of the bed. Empty and cold. I check the clock on the bedside table. Not even six. I know she's gone, yet I still climb out of bed. Her dress is gone, my apartment silent.

"Tia?" I call out, reaching the kitchen.

There's nothing. No note, no number, no trace she's ever been here—except for red lipstick on the collar of my button-down. She placed the tux over a chair neatly, obviously having collected all the pieces from where I dropped them.

I comb my fingers through my hair. *So this is what it feels like*, I think to myself.

I'm the one who usually slips out, but somehow, even knowing we won't see each other again, I can't deny that it feels weird. Of course, it's way less drama this way. But, man, I thought I'd be waking up with her next to me, would have seen her sexy smile one more time after offering coffee, then I could've sent her off with one last kiss.

Get a grip, my mind tells me. *It's exactly what you wanted. No strings attached.*

Maybe it is, yet this time, it feels as if something is missing.

CHAPTER FOUR

BLAKE

I WALK into the office and see Will at his desk. He looks up and grins at me. I already know what's coming. Frankly, that causes me to grin, too.

I hold up a hand to stop what he's going to say. "Yes, she and I left together, and I guess I can thank you for that."

There's no one else around, which I'm thankful for. I don't need Wolfe or Declan to hear this, and Nikki even less. As much as Tia wasn't just like any conquest, I'm going to talk as if she were because if Nikki knew the truth, she'd have my balls.

"She would've looked better with me. Would've looked better *on* me, too," he replies as I take my black leather jacket off and throw it over the back of my chair.

I lean against my desk and cross my feet at the ankles. "She looked fine kneeling before me...and lying under me... and with her hand on my crotch in the cab."

For a moment, he watches me, then cocks his head. I

wonder if he can sense that things aren't as superficial as I make them out to be. "You're full of shit, Atwood," he mutters.

I shrug, lowering my eyes to make him feel as if I have something to hide. "Whatever you think, big boy. You're just upset because she turned you down, yet I only needed to show my pretty face to get the girl."

"She was probably just desperate and hoped you wouldn't follow her like a love-sick puppy. There's no other reason a woman as pretty as her would've taken you home," Nikki announces as she walks in.

Will snickers. "Morning."

I glare at her. "I'll have you know that I've taken many classy women home."

"If she went home with you, she didn't have class to begin with," Wolfe interrupts, walking in with Jim and Declan.

"Thank you, boss," I growl, seeing him wink at me.

"You're welcome. You can deal with that better than Hawkes can with knowing his ugly mug isn't enough to draw a woman." Wolfe grins, then walks into his office. If he's joking around with us first thing, there's no special case to work on. Nothing big we needed to get started with before returning to our small criminals, like drug dealers.

"Not everyone can be as pretty as you, Atwood. Man, I went jogging this morning and—" Jim starts, but Nikki snickers, cutting him off. He narrows his eyes at her. "What?"

She shrugs. "Nothing. I just doubt that you even know what jogging is." She points at his belly and the way it strains against his shirt. We all know it's not fat stretching the material, but muscle. Jim has picked up boxing and weightlifting the past few months and has gotten pretty big.

He rolls his eyes. "Aren't you a funny one, Bates?"

"It's the only thing she has left since her cat ran away," Declan announces.

Nikki's jaw drops. "That was private, jerkface!"

I look at her, brow raised. "You had a cat?"

She glowers at me, then sits behind her desk, clearly letting us know the conversation is over. I arch a brow at Jim, who just shrugs.

"It was a beastly old thing," Declan whispers conspiratorially, but not low enough that Nikki doesn't hear.

"He had character," she protests.

Smirking, I sit behind my desk, going over the files sitting there. I have some reports to make corrections on because some person who has never been out on the street thinks my report isn't "detailed enough".

As if writing that I killed the guy who threatened me isn't detailed enough.

"Atwood, do you remember the Olson case?" Jim asks.

That was a case of reported domestic violence. Jim had been the first responder when the wife called for help. It was a mess, filled with preconceptions and false accusations, until we eventually discovered the woman was the aggressor.

"Sure do. Why?"

He sighs. "I have to appear in court. I feel as if I read the victims' reports so often, I don't remember what I thought anymore. But my file is gone..." He shrugs.

I roll my eyes. "You took it home the day you met your brother for a beer, then drove his ass home and stayed there because he was drunk. I assume that's where you left it."

As good a cop as Jim is, he's hopeless when it comes to paperwork. When he had a girlfriend, he was a little better organized, but...

Well, in this line of work, relationships don't last that long. I haven't tried to have one in years, but I know Nikki dates on occasion, as does Declan. I don't remember when they were last with someone more than a few months, though. The only one who's ever actually wanted something more is Will, who now watches me. I try to ignore him, inwardly groaning when I hear him scoot his chair back and walk over.

He perches his hip on the edge of my desk. "What's up?"

I lean back in my chair. "What are you talking about? You seeing ghosts?"

"What were you thinking about just now? Your face scrunched up, as if regretting something."

That list is fucking endless, but I don't say that. "Relationships and how a girl kept Jim in check there for a while," I say loud enough to taunt the other man.

"No woman keeps me in check. They just sometimes make sure I'm better organized," he snaps, then flips me off.

I chuckle, focusing back on Will, whose brows are arched. He's like a brother to me. We don't share blood, but we watch out for each other. Him more than me sometimes. He seems older than he is, and I can't help but think it's because he has seen things nobody should have to. I appreciate his friendship more than he'll ever know, but at that moment, with his inquiring gaze on me, I can't help but think he pisses me off.

"I don't plan to get into a relationship, just like I don't ever plan to date. I like scouting the bars with Watts too much," I explain, knowing it sounds as if I'm trying to justify myself.

It doesn't matter. The rest of the team thinks I'm wild and wicked. I'd rather have that than them knowing I'm mostly just haunted and broken.

TIA

First one-night stand, first time sneaking out, first time getting home utterly giddy since before high school graduation... Today is a day of firsts, and I wouldn't change it for anything.

At ten minutes to five this morning, I tiptoed into the apartment, discarded my dress, and slipped into bed. Blake's cologne still clings to me, and as futile and stupid as it is, I hope it'll rub off onto my pillows. I don't go back to sleep, too high on what had happened, suddenly feeling lonelier than ever before.

I don't regret much in life, especially helping Chloe when she got pregnant at sixteen, giving birth to my niece at seventeen. I was nineteen when Olivia was born, and I worked odd jobs to support my sister and make sure she finished high school. After all, our parents kicked her out when she'd decided to keep the baby. I left with her because she is my little sister and I'd do anything for her.

Two years later, she finished high school—and gave birth to my second niece, Paulette. Things got harder after that, so we decided to move from the country to the city. The chances to find a job were higher here, especially because Chloe had the possibility of a job through someone she knew.

Back then, I had the sneaking suspicion she was sleeping with a businessman who occasionally came to town, but when I asked her, she denied it. I opted to believe her because, well...it's none of my business.

She started working at Clarke's Finances and Holdings, while I worked at the odd diner. We'd been living in a tiny one-room apartment, but after two years, we managed to afford something bigger. I had my own room, she had one, and the girls shared one.

A little over a year ago, Chloe came home crying, and I knew instantly what it meant.

We're still in the same apartment, but I now have the

smallest room, the one Chloe occupied before, because she has a toddler.

It's barely six when my bedroom door bangs open and Pauli runs in, jumping onto my bed.

My high from having been with Blake is long gone, my situation trickling back in. It's one of those mornings where I can't help but think that had I not gone out of my way to help Chloe and her children, she'd probably not have gotten pregnant with Neo. I love my nephew, just as much as I love both of my nieces, but I know my life would be much different had they not been around.

Shaking my head to rid myself of these thoughts, I grab Pauli and tickle her. She laughs in delight, then cuddles next to me.

"You are awake," she states.

I nod. "Seems like it. So, what are your plans for the day?"

I try to remember what Chloe told me yesterday about what would be going on today, but I have to admit, I didn't listen, too busy worrying about what the evening at the ball would bring and how I'd look.

Weekends are usually the two days I have time for myself, and I cherish it.

My niece shrugs. "I don't know. What do you wanna do?"

I blink. "Me? It's Sunday, sugar. You're gonna hang with your mom."

Pauli shakes her head, sitting up again. "No. She told you yesterday she has to work at least half a day, remember?"

"So, I have to go to the office, but I promise I'll try to be back as soon as possible. Hopefully before two."

That was what she had told me yesterday, but with having to prepare for the ball, it must have slipped my mind.

I bite my lip angrily. It's not Pauli's fault, so I smooth a thumb over the frown on her forehead and give her a wink. "She did say that. How about we take a walk."

For me, it's the easiest way to make sure Neo falls back to sleep, but the girls hate taking walks. While that can be remedied for Pauli with a stop at the playground, Liv won't like that very much.

We don't have much money to go anywhere, so we could do some crafting at home.

Yeah, exactly what I wanted to do today.

Pauli drops back onto the bed dramatically, throwing up both arms. "I hate walks."

"I do, too," Liv announces from the doorway.

I sit up, cocking my head. "Well, what about making some fall decorations?" We have pens, markers, and scissors. Things that will keep the girls occupied for a little while.

They are amazing children, quiet and sweet most of the time. I have a feeling Pauli would probably be a bit more bubbly if Chloe wouldn't constantly be short-tempered with her. I try my best not to be, but I already know when I go back to work tonight, I'll be the same. Most days, I'm exhausted, especially since they cut Chloe's pay and I left the bar I'd been working at. It led to us not being able to pay a babysitter regularly, so I have Neo at home more often than not.

No sleeping in for the bartender. Ever.

"Decorations sound fun," Liv decides, then leaves the room. Chloe walks up, already dressed and ready to leave.

I eye the clock on my nightstand, thinking I must not have looked at it correctly when the girls came in. "Chloe, it's shortly after six," I say as she sets Neo onto my bed. I reach for him before he topples off the side as my sister turns away.

"I have to be at the office by seven. I promise, I'll be back as soon as I can," she calls while walking away.

A few seconds later, the apartment door closes behind

her. She didn't even kiss her kids goodbye, say "thank you", or ask how yesterday evening went.

She just assumed I did everything exactly the way it would benefit her. Damn, I suddenly wish I made a fool out of myself last night.

Sighing, I slide to the edge of the bed, Neo in my arms, and nudge Pauli, who's staring up at the ceiling, counting things I cannot even see.

The child is weird, but damn, I can't help but think she's sometimes my favorite.

BLAKE

I appreciate days where we have no new cases, but I won't lie. Those days are boring as fuck. I don't want bodies, but a little shooting somewhere on a street corner, no one injured, can't be bad, right? It gives us a chance to walk around, talk to people, instead of sitting behind a desk, fixing reports.

When my day finally ends, I walk out, seeing Kelly standing outside the station. He's a firefighter, a damn good one, but I know he's been through some tough shit, as well. I check his face carefully as I greet him, just to judge what kind of day he had, but he just gives me a beaming smile, easing my worries a little. We give each other a bro hug.

"Watts. Ready for Gun & Shot?"

The bar we most frequent is owned by a cop and usually filled with cops, doctors, lawyers, and firefighters a lot of the time, but we love it because, well...because it's familiar.

When he shakes his head, I arch a brow at him. "I need something..." He sighs. "I mean, I want to find someone nice, so let's try a different hunting ground tonight."

Kelly is looking for love, but usually ends up with a woman who won't let things go that far. He sucks at picking them, but that doesn't keep him from trying.

I also believe, if you hope for something that lasts, it might not be the smartest idea to sleep with them right after meeting, but he doesn't want to hear that.

"Well, I'm not out to get laid, but I'll take one for the team," I tease.

He arches a brow at me, then grins and punches my shoulder. "You get laid at that charity thing?"

I shrug, and he shakes his head. I'm itching to mention Tia, to explain I took her home against everything I normally do, but suddenly, am no longer sure what it means.

We get into his truck, and I briefly wonder if maybe I should drive myself. After all, if he finds someone, he'll go with her and I'll be stranded. "If you pick up a woman, I'm taking your truck home," I say, and he grins, but then sobers.

Worry rears its ugly head. "Man, what's up with you? Seriously, Watts. I'm getting all soft here, thinking something's up."

He flashes me a wide grin, but it doesn't reach his eyes. "I'm good, Atwood. Just exhausted. It's been a long shift," he says, and I nearly roll my eyes. They always are. I don't think there are ever easy days at the station, not when you have to help put out fires, save lives, then deal with the memories.

"Okay, fine. What if I tell you I think something is wrong with me?" He looks at me, a worried frown on his face. "I didn't get laid at the ball. I took the woman *home*." He jerks the wheel, just to be dramatic, and I chuckle. "Come on. Say it."

He laughs, then shakes his head. "You're joking, right? You *never* take them home. Privacy and all that. No repeats and shit."

I clear my throat. "Honestly? I don't even know what it was. And..."

I don't know how to end that sentence. I don't know what went on in my head when Tia was around. It's as if she mutes everything that usually screams in my head, especially all the warnings I always tell myself when it comes to my one-night stands.

Kelly parks the truck in an alley next to some hole-in-the-wall we've never been to before and turns in his seat. "And?"

I glance at the simple brick wall and nod toward it. "Wanna talk about it inside with a beer, or would you rather freeze our asses off out here?"

"Now," he says, which I hate because he'll watch me the whole time. I have no idea what my expression will say about that night.

Opening the door, I groan. "Actually, I don't think there's anything to talk about. Come on. Let's go inside."

I don't wait for Kelly to protest. Just walk around the corner and into the bar. It's bigger than it looks from the outside, and packed for a Sunday night.

I push my way through the bar and catch the bartender's attention, ordering two beers. She's raven-haired and flirty, even with dull brown eyes. I can't decide if it's the color or the job, but she isn't really pretty in my eyes.

"And?" Kelly prompts again when I place the beer in front of him on the table he found in the corner.

Knowing he won't drop it, I sigh. "When she suggested in the middle of the night that she should leave, I told her to stay. I could've kissed her goodbye and gotten her out of my apartment, but I didn't. Instead, I took her back to bed and spooned."

For a long moment, my best friend sips his beer, then

looks at me. "Tell me you at least have her number, because clearly—"

"Don't even finish that sentence," I interrupt. "I don't know what it was, but trust me, there won't be a lapse in judgment again."

He licks his lips. "Maybe it wasn't a lapse in judgment, but a lapse in heart, Atwood. You can't keep women at arm's length forever."

I snicker. "I actually let a lot of them very close, you know."

Kelly rolls his eyes. "I don't know why you refuse to look for someone to go through life with."

I close my eyes. "You of all people should know that our lives aren't made for that. We run the risk of dying each time we go to work. Not many women can live with that."

I know it's a low blow, but when Kelly just grits his teeth and swivels on the chair to take in what the bar offers, I know he understands.

A few years back, a girl he loved enough to make a go of it just up and left in the middle of the night with no explanation. It's one of the things that makes me extremely cautious.

I don't want to ever go through that much heartache, no matter the benefits.

TIA

Gun & Shot is like any other bar I worked at, yet different. The mood feels more intense, but I recognize the lost souls, the tortured ones, and those who only come here to forget.

"Whiskey, neat," a guy orders.

I look up. Although I hadn't served him before, I know he has already had four of those.

"Are you drivin', handsome?" I ask pleasantly. I don't want to cause trouble, but I certainly won't let him get anywhere near his car.

He cocks his head. "It's been a while since someone called me handsome," he mutters.

I give him a wink. "Well, people clearly haven't been looking. If you want another shot, hand me those keys." I place my hand on the bar. He passes them over without much discussion. I smile. "Good decision. For that, this one's on the house." I pour him two fingers' worth and hand the glass over before hanging the keys under the bar on the designated spot for that purpose.

"My name's Colson," he says before emptying the glass in one long swig. I don't know if it's a first or last name, and don't really care. I write the name down on a pad to remember whom I took the keys from.

Donna, my new colleague, leans close to me. "You can tell the hard days. Some come in together and down their shots." She nods toward a couple who has been holding onto their beers since they walked in. They look companionable and at ease. "Then you have those who have no life to go back home to, which is why they walk in together. That's one of the Intelligence units from the station nearby. You won't see Wolfe, their boss, with them often, but Hawkes and Davis are here quite a few times. And then…" She cranes her neck, clearly not spotting the person she's looking for. "Hawkes' partner isn't here. He and a firefighter friend are regulars."

I nod, then see Colson waving me down again. I walk over to him and angle my head, knowing guys like it, then sigh.

"Want me to call you a cab?" I ask, and he arches a brow in surprise.

"Already cutting me off? I only have a slight buzz going." His words are soft around the edges. I have no doubt he's being truthful, but I can't help but think that as a police officer —or whatever position he holds—he shouldn't wake up with a hangover tomorrow.

Leaning over the bar, which I hate doing because guys tend to look down my shirt, I smile. "I bet you have to work tomorrow and should probably get home. We want you in one piece and sharp as a knife, don't we? You cannot do your job if you have a hangover."

He holds my gaze. Out of the corner of my eye, I see someone trying to get my attention. I slap the bartop. "Think about it. I'll be right back."

I move down the bar. "Lemme guess. Two beers and two tequilas?" The guy stares at me, taken aback. I wink. "You ordered that from Donna earlier."

He blushes, then rubs the back of his neck. "Didn't think I was that predictable, but yes, please."

He is predictable, but only because he didn't escalate his drink orders. Some people start off light and go harder the next round, but he and his friend have downed the shot, then nursed their beer for a while. It's funny how easy it is to keep an eye on everyone, even though there are quite a few people here.

"You got a good one there, Warrick," Colson suddenly says.

I look up to see my boss walking in from the back. It's my first night, my first shift, and after I'd proven I knew what I was doing and didn't need training, he left me alone with Donna, probably expecting me to come running within the first hour.

He watches me for a long moment, then nods at Colson.

"I saw she took your keys. Must be good since there was no fight."

I'm not surprised he has cameras out here. I actually feel better knowing that.

Colson laughs. "I don't know. She has charm."

I grin and wink. "She also expects a hefty tip for being such a charming person, but I bet I don't need to tell you that." This time Colson chuckles. I glance at my boss, seeing a soft smirk on his lips.

After Colson pays his tab, leaving the tip I hinted at, and stumbles out of the bar to the cab I called for him, Warrick nods at Donna, silently telling her to cover for a few minutes, and leads me back into the office. I glance at the two screens sitting on his desk that show almost every angle of the bar, thinking this is finally a job I'll keep.

"When you said you knew how to handle a bar, I didn't think you were serious. You have no idea how many people come in and lie about having experience."

Oh, but I can. It's hard to find a job, especially if no one trusts you.

I wait, not saying anything as I watch Donna on the screen, flirting. I swear, that woman has to make her wage in tips. She's just too cute and too nice.

When Warrick doesn't say anything, I nod toward the screen. "I'm not like her. I do flirt, but that's a minimum. I'm not cute-as-a-button and definitely get pissy if someone grabs or degrades me, but I won't let minors drink in your bar and will make sure no one drives drunk. I promise to work my ass off to make this place feel like home for the patrons, and I also will jump in to help wherever needed. I can handle myself, as you saw, so... What's it gonna be? Am I going to be here regularly?"

Finally, I pull my eyes from the screen to meet my boss'

gaze, seeing him smirking. "We're opening together tomorrow. Be here at three thirty to help me clean and get everything ready. Three more hours and your first night is over. How does that sound?"

I exhale slowly, relieved. "Perfect. I'll be here. Thank you."

With that, I walk out of his office and make my way back to help little Miss Flirty behind the bar, my heart a lot lighter than it had been when I got here earlier.

CHAPTER FIVE

BLAKE

THINKING of Kelly going home with a cute little redhead last night, I almost smile to myself as I enter the station. I don't get far as Will and Nikki meet me in the door.

"New case," Will snaps. I turn, following him out again. "We're heading to the crime scene."

I nod as we get into his car, Nikki climbing into hers. I wonder if Wolfe will already be there or if this one is on us.

"What do we know?" I ask

He shrugs. "Female, early twenties. That's all we know, but it's not too far from here."

And he's right. Not even fifteen minutes later, we park by an alley already closed off with police tape. We flash our badges to the officer standing there. The medical examiner, Dane Saxton, spots us and walks over. He's in his fifties, decent, and straight to the point.

Will stops next to him, while I make my way over to the body, half-listening to them. Someone hands me gloves, which I blindly grasp as I squat down.

"Didn't get much chance to look at her yet. Just got here right before you guys did. Seems she was strangled from behind with the strap of her own bag."

I glance at her neck and see the ligature marks. The bag isn't close by, so I turn slightly and spot it behind me.

I focus back on the victim and brush her blonde strands back from her face, seeing her soft features, unable to keep myself from thinking of Tia.

The hairs on the back of my neck stand on end, unsettling me. Why do I feel like I'm missing something? I'm tempted to rub the spot when I remember the gloves on my hands.

"I can't tell much else. She was surprised, that much is clear, but other than that..." Saxton shrugs as I stand. The way she looks—jeans and jacket still in place—it doesn't look as if she's been sexually assaulted.

Will thanks the medical examiner, then joins me, taking the wallet an officer hands him. He flips it open, then shows it to me. All her money's still there, so it wasn't a robbery.

"Purely bored killer?" I ask. That possibility is most likely. He didn't come here searching for a kill, but seized the opportunity when it presented itself. Otherwise, he would have used a weapon.

Will grunts, focused on the inside of the wallet, then sighs. "Let's hope it was just an ex with a vendetta."

That would mean it would be a one-time thing, whereas a bored killer could lead to a lot more bodies.

"Her name was Molly Savannah and she was twenty-six," he reports.

I glance down at her, brows furrowed. I shift a little to move my shadow from her face, then cluck my tongue. "I would've guessed much younger. I mean, look at her." She's not wearing much make-up, making it easy to see her flawless skin.

Will turns toward the girl as Nikki walks over, having just talked to somebody behind the police tape.

"That was her boss. She worked at a bar," she reports, then nudges me with her shoulder to move over, looking at the body. "She's young," she states my thoughts from a second earlier. She's quiet for a moment, then sighs. "I'm gonna go back and talk to her boss again."

The zipper of her jacket is only half-closed, so I slowly push it aside to check the green shirt underneath. "Paddy's." I look up at Will. "That pub right around the corner?" We passed it coming here, but there's something about bars that makes them unassuming during the day, yet seem to be the center of attention at night.

"Maybe he waited for her here."

We both look around, trying to figure out where somebody could've hidden. Then again, it most likely would've been dark by the time she entered the ally. "The half-closed jacket implies she didn't come far."

I stand and nod at the door behind Hawkes. "Wanna bet this is the side entrance to the bar? She probably locked the front, then walked out this door. But... Why the alley?"

No girl in her right mind will walk into an alley in the middle of the night. Not even seven feet from her body is a fence, and I don't see a gate in it. I also doubt she would've scaled it at night.

Will scouts the area as I walk around the victim, wondering what we're missing. I stop, noticing her fisted left hand. Seeing a watch on that side, I know it's her non-dominant hand. If she were trying to defend herself, she would have fisted the other one. Also, if she was being choked, I'd assume she would have tried to slip her fingers under the strap, so her hands wouldn't be curled like that.

I crouch down, taking a closer look before waving a crime

scene technician with a camera over. He takes a few pictures from every angle, then I slowly open her hand. There's something written in red on her arm. I push up her sleeve a little, careful not to disturb it.

Lipstick? It's slightly smeared, but I can still make it out. My heart skips a beat when I see the whole message.

"Hawkes?" I call.

He walks away from the fence, something in his hand. He holds it up for me to see. "Lock. Wanna bet she had a bike and the guy took it?"

I shrug, shaking my head. "I don't think he planned to kill her, not intentionally, and I bet after he realized what he'd done, he wanted to get away as quickly as possible." I point to her hand.

Will crouches down. "Is that..."

I nod. "A message for us."

I KILLED THE WRONG ONE.

―――

"TELL ME ALL YOU KNOW." Wolfe strides in.

I look up from my desk, watching our boss shrug out his jacket, his eyes on the whiteboard that we use to solve cases. I glance down at my notes. "Victim's name is Molly Savannah. Her ID says she's twenty-six. However, I wouldn't be surprised if it comes out that she's younger. She works at a pub called Paddy's and always rides her bike to and from work. She lives maybe ten minutes away. Her boss, Patrick O'Mally, had to leave early last night, but it wasn't the first time she locked up."

Nikki leans a hip against her desk. "She was likely strangled with a strap of her bag, so it's easy to assume he used what he could get his hands on. He also stole her bike, but since O'Mally couldn't tell us what it looks like, we cannot exactly keep an eye out for it. We're still trying to contact her family. It seems she moved to town three years ago with a boyfriend, who has since become her ex. He hasn't seen her in months, or so he says."

Wolfe nods, his eyes still on the victim's photograph. "Check the boyfriend, Davis. I wanna know all about him."

Jim clears his throat. "I did that when the name came through. His name is Aaron Lanchester, but he seems to be on the straight and narrow. Works as a mechanic, has a new girlfriend and a baby. Phone records show he hasn't contacted our victim in a while. Uniforms went over to his place to bring him in for questioning."

Wolfe snorts, and I can't help but feel bad for the ex. I mean, we know he most likely didn't do this, but because Wolfe's still missing some important intel, he considers him the most likely suspect. Crazy how quickly you can be judged just for dating somebody at one time.

I rub my chin, wondering where that thought came from. I've never thought about it like that before. If you keep spinning that thread, I'd be on a *lot* of lists.

Damn, that suddenly puts one-night stands in a whole new light.

"I want to talk to him. Just because he has someone new doesn't mean he's over his ex. Who knows? Maybe there was a fight between the current girlfriend and him that made him seek out our victim."

I clear my throat. "Possibly, but there's more."

Wolfe turns to me, leaning against the wall next to the whiteboard. "Okay..." He sounds impatient.

I stand. "Victim had a message on her arm. 'I killed the

wrong one' was written in what seems to be her own lipstick. While it could be a distraction in order to cover his tracks, I'd say chances are high the words were serious. She wasn't harmed in any other way, and using her own bag as a weapon?" I spread my arms out. "Had he been gunning for her, he would've brought a knife or something. Strangling someone isn't easy, no matter how small she was."

Wolfe cocks his head. "If he caught her by surprise and from behind, I don't think there's much she could've done. Still, it's important we look into that, too. Was anything stolen?"

Nikki shakes her head as the desk sergeant walks into the room. That woman is tough, doesn't take any crap, even though I have a feeling she's only as old as I am.

"An Aaron Lanchester is downstairs, guys," she reports, then turns and walks back out.

Declan, silent until now, jumps up from his desk. "I'm gonna go and talk to him, boss."

Wolfe just nods. I wish I could go with him. I like interrogation much more than research.

"Anyway...," Nikki continues. "Nothing stolen, her clothes weren't touched. We're waiting to see what else the ME finds, but I gotta be frank here. This is all kinds of weird. And attacking from behind... I think if it would've been a planned hit, he would've wanted her to see his face, make her fear grow.

"Also, let's assume she got into a fight with a woman. Most wouldn't be able to kill someone that way. Considering they'd probably have equal strength and height, it would be just too hard. Unless our victim was drugged."

Wolfe nods and thinks for a minute. "Okay. Hawkes, Atwood, I want you to go to the bar and check it out. See if you can find any video that we might be able to use. Davis, go and talk to the ME. If this really is just the start of a streak until our guy finds the right one, I want all the information he can give us. Bates, you and I will go check our victim's apartment and talk to the neighbors. Maybe she had a stalker we know nothing about."

As I grab my jacket, Will grins at me. I roll my eyes, knowing he's thinking that it's barely ten and the bar will be open before long.

I jab my elbow into his ribs when we're on the stairs. "This isn't a fun trip."

"I know, but you know how it is with interviews. It might take a little longer and—"

I shake my head. "If he's a decent human being, you know he'll close the bar tonight."

His smile vanishes. "Yes, but this is New York and people, such as the other waitresses and bartenders, need to earn a living, so..."

I sigh, knowing he's right, yet wishing people on this planet wouldn't care so much about money and could properly grieve someone they've lost.

TIA

Neo sits and stares at me, babbling, so I hand him the teddy he's reaching for. Liv and Pauli are in school and preschool, which I'm kind of glad about. As much as I love having them around, I'm drained, although I didn't spend more than six hours at the bar last night. But I'd been out of work for three weeks, and it's incredible how quickly you can get used to being lazy.

My mind's on everything and nothing at the same time,

Blake's face appearing in my thoughts every so often. I knew I wasn't cut out for one-night stands, but I'm still glad I went through with it. Despite the fact I'd gotten all the cuddling and sex I'd been missing for years, knowing he didn't want me to leave in the middle of the night gave me the confidence I've been lacking.

Granted, it might have to do with him being a detective, but I like to tell myself it was because he didn't want me to go. I hum as my phone rings. It takes me a moment to realize I should answer. I don't even know why I'm so absent-minded when I'm normally rather controlled.

"This is Tia."

"Hey, it's Warrick. Would you mind doing a double shift today? Donna has to leave early, and she was scheduled to be on the later shift with me. If not, we can have her come in later."

Hell yes, I can do extra hours. In fact, I'm going to work as many extra hours as I can so I can afford a babysitter for Neo. As much as I love him, it would also give me the chance to sleep in and do my own thing in the mornings.

The thought makes my heart skip a beat. "Of course I can. I don't mind at all. Seriously. How many hours are we talking?"

He sighs. "Ten, possibly eleven. The good part? You won't have to share tips since guys don't usually tip me," he jokes.

I smile. "It's Monday, Warrick. How many people frequent a bar until past midnight on a Monday?" As much as I hope for extra hours, I doubt I'll get them very often during the week. Weekends, though? Maybe.

"A lot, Tia. Police officers, firefighters, doctors... Some work twenty-four-hour shifts and sometimes need a drink when they get off."

"Okay." I pause for a moment. "Are most of those guys who come in people you've worked with?"

He blows out a breath. Maybe this is something we should talk about later. I don't know him very well.

"Ah, you know what? Forget I asked. I'm just gonna—"

"Do you have any idea how people react when cops walk into a bar, Tia? And I'm not just talking uniforms. If they have the slightest inkling you're on the right side of the law, people are hostile. It's hard for us to find a place we don't get judged. It's why I opened the bar, and it's been going strong for years because patrons change and more districts come in. It's a little out of the way for some, but it's a rather safe spot to have a drink and unwind."

I smile. "And a place you'll probably always find a designated driver or someone who'll make sure you get home safely."

I hear the grin in his voice when he replies. "That, too. Plus, it draws the ladies. And not just a few, although it's a little slower on that front during the week."

No need to tell me that. I caught a couple having sex in the bathroom last night. I wanted to bleach my eyes. "Well, uniforms are sexy, even when they aren't worn." Neo started to whine next to me, slapping my knee with his small hand to get my attention. "Okay. I have to go."

"I'll see you in a few hours. Wear flats and make sure you get some more sleep. It will come in handy tonight."

I laugh. "Trust me, I know. See you later." I hang up and pick up Neo, who's all grumpy, making me assume he's hungry.

I shift him on my hip, mad that as little as Chloe sees her son, she still manages to spoil him rotten. He hates being put down unless you sit down with him. Even then, it's sometimes not good enough.

Walking into the small kitchen, I place him into his high chair and strap him in. He fusses loudly until I hand him a carrot to nibble on. Almost instantly, he quiets. I turn on the radio, hearing a news report about the police finding a body. I change the station. I know there's crime in New York, your chances of getting raped, beaten, robbed, or killed are extremely high, but that doesn't mean I need to be reminded of it over and over.

I like being naïve, being ignorant of what can happen to me. Otherwise, I'd start being scared of going to work. I have to walk to the subway, take the train for a little more than half an hour, then walk to the bar. I wish I had a car, but there's no money for that.

God, the list of things I wish I had is long, but luckily, I can usually justify not having a car because public transportation is often faster and more handy. After all, New York traffic is hell.

Unless you drive in the middle of the night, which you would. Then the streets are empty and you'd be safer, a voice in the back of my mind whispers, but I ignore it, as always, knowing that I cannot change a single thing now anyway.

BLAKE

After talking to the bar owner and the victim's colleagues, we're no closer to answers. They don't remember anyone standing out or being overly interested in Molly. We make our way back to the station.

"What are you thinking?" Will asks.

I take a deep breath. "I just wish it would've been a stalker, you know? Someone who sticks out. Hell, I'd even take the ex." When we showed his picture, no one recognized his face, which I wasn't surprised about. "Thinking that there could be someone else out there who might be killed..." I shake my head.

Especially because the list of possible victims is basically endless. The fact Molly was blonde and worked at a bar isn't anything we can go by...until there's another victim.

"Sucks that we'd need a MO for a serial killer. I mean... Yes, we could go and check out every single bar, but let's be serious. Maybe for him, she was merely a blonde crossing his path."

A blonde crossing his path... Just like Tia.

I push the thought away, but Will arches a brow at me. "What?" he asks.

I look at him. "I didn't say anything."

He shakes his head. Working with a detective sucks sometimes. We notice too much, even in the small gestures. He clicks his tongue. "You winced a little bit. Did I say something wrong?"

We're close, but not that close, and usually avoid drama. Hell, Nikki was right. We excel at locker-room talk. Still, I say what's on my mind.

"Remember the blonde from the ball? When you said 'crossing his path'... She was just a blonde crossing my path. I mean, how do you see someone and just think, *Let's kill her?*"

He fake coughs and shoots me a troubled glance. "You're thinking about a woman *after* you sleep with her? What's wrong with you?"

I playfully punch his shoulder, grinning for a moment before getting serious again. "I don't know." And that's the truth. I have no idea why she's still on my mind. Normally, I cannot even recall the faces of the women I sleep with.

He sobers. "Our victim looks a little like her, doesn't she?"

I shake my head before even thinking. Besides the blonde waves, there was nothing on Molly that reminds me of Tia. "I don't know. I mean, yes, she's blonde, but that's it. It's not even the same shade of blonde. And her face was too round, and..." I shrug. "Well, I don't know. I just..."

Will parks in front of the station, then turns to me. "Too bad you don't know her last name. I'm sure we could find her address or her number so you can check on her. Maybe just knowing she's okay will wipe her from your mind."

For a second, I search his face, trying to figure out if he's making fun of me or not, but there's nothing but sincerity in his eyes. "That would be stalking. Besides, I'm not worried about her. I don't know her enough to be worried about her." That should be the truth, but I'd love to just be able to shoot her a message, even if it's just a quick "hi". I slip out of the car and touch my phone in my pocket, wishing I knew her number.

Will follows. Before he can say more about Tia, I stride into the station. The desk sergeant calls my name and waves me over.

"There's a girl over there who asked for you. She had your card," she says, nodding toward the little office by the door. I wonder if maybe Tia stole one of my cards, but when I finally turn to see the person in the room, she's a little ginger-haired girl, skittish. I'm certain I've never seen her before.

"Did she say what her name was?"

The sergeant shakes her head, then nudges me forward. I tell Will I'll meet him upstairs.

I've handed out my card twice today, and a lot more times before that. Sometimes people show up long after I've forgotten I even gave them my card, so when I push into the room, I have no idea what to expect.

She instantly stands, her pale green eyes wide and her expression incredulous. "You're Atwood?"

I nod. "Yes, ma'am. Now, I know I didn't give you my card, so we haven't met before." I need a clue, even as I try to remember if maybe she's one of the girls I took home at some point.

"I... I worked with Molls...Molly. She was friend. A good one. When I started at Paddy's, she took me under her wing. I..." She trails off as tears streak down her face. I walk over to her, pointing at the chair.

"Hey, I'm sorry. Sit, take a few deep breaths, then tell me what's on our mind." I make a mental note to ask for her name, but experience taught me that you get more out of people if you let them talk first before making them feel like suspects. This girl is too weak and too small to be the murderer, but that doesn't mean she's innocent.

I hand her a box of Kleenex from the table, then listen while she gives her statement.

CHAPTER SIX

TIA

I YAWN, watching Pauli on the playground. She was supposed to be at preschool, but since she had a minor cough, they told us she had to stay home. There was no fever, no sneezing, nothing, yet I'm stuck with her this morning. For some reason, I have less patience than usual. Even sweet Neo is annoying as hell today. To make sure I get some peace and quiet, and maybe a chance to properly wake up, I decided on a playground visit.

Pauli is shy, but once someone starts talking to her, she won't shut up. So far, she's still sitting by herself in the sand, singing and playing as if she doesn't have a care in the world.

And she doesn't. I've picked up as many extra hours and I can, and her mother has taken on more work in her company. Money's still rather tight, but I won't lie. I think we're better off than some of the others around here.

"Tia," Pauli calls and waves happily. I wave back and smile, although I'm exhausted. I slept less than three hours last night. Gun & Shot was open longer than expected, and the trip home had been excruciatingly long because the subway was stopped for some medical emergency. When it felt like I had just fallen asleep this morning, Pauli had jumped onto my bed.

God, it's going to be a very long day.

I rub my hands across my face, sighing, leaning forward on the bench. Neo fell asleep in his stroller on the way here, which I'm grateful for. I know it won't last, but I'm just glad for the reprieve.

A pair of black Nikes steps into my view. I lift my eyes just enough to see unassuming gray sweatpants. However, since I now no longer see Pauli, I tilt my head to the side, not looking up any farther.

"Move it, buddy," I say, not caring how angry or bitchy I sound.

"Is that any way to greet a one-night stand?"

My eyes snap up to hazel ones, my heart skipping a few beats. Blake Atwood, wearing a gray hoodie, looks at me with something akin to suspicion.

I clear my throat. "Unless said one-night stand has a caramel macchiato, I don't exactly feel like talking to him." I long for the concoction, but in my rush to get out of the house, I forgot my wallet.

"Maybe he wants to talk to you," Blake replies, but I don't even dignify that with an answer.

I had a one-night stand with the intention of never seeing the guy again. With me staying away from crime scenes...and crimes, in general...I'd been sure Detective Atwood and I wouldn't ever cross paths again, yet here he stands.

My heart's utterly happy, while my mind is on the verge of panic. When I try to stifle a yawn, Blake sighs and walks away.

I close my eyes, caught between regret and relief.

In a book or movie, this would turn into a romantic scene where he shows back up holding coffee. The truth is, I don't know where I'd fit in a boyfriend. My family is my life. They are all that matter to me.

Still, I can't help but press my hand to my chest because my heart cracks right down the middle. The feeling of Blake holding me through the night just... I don't know. I guess it reminded me of what being happy felt like. I'm not a virgin, I've had previous relationships, but sometimes I think I'm turning into a nun.

A small boy approaches Pauli. They start playing together, which means I'll get to sit on this bench a little longer. I cannot find the motivation to clean the apartment or entertain the kids. I just don't have the energy.

A red cup appears in front of my eyes. I look up. Blake's holding out a cup of coffee, and judging by the smell, it's my favorite poison.

"I... Thank you, but that wasn't necessary," I say, accepting the cup. It would be a shame to let it go to waste, right?

He sits down next to me, holding his own cup, and shrugs. "You look like you need it."

I give him a small grin. "Still a charmer, huh?" I want to be as flirty and as pretty as I was that night, because he sure as hell looks handsome, but I'm just not.

I'm probably pale, my hair is a mess, and I assume I look like a homeless person in my leggings and oversized hoodie.

He doesn't react to my comment, so I look at his face to see him watching the playground. I can't help but feel a little safer right now with him sitting next to me.

"Which one is yours?"

None, but because his tone sounds strange, as if he's

upset, I don't say that. Instead, I nod toward Pauli. "That wild one over there came with me."

His gaze follows mine to where Pauli and the boy play quietly. She's wild when at home, but in public, she's the sweetest thing ever.

"Wild?" he echoes.

"Just like her mother," I say, thinking of how Chloe used to be, always sitting in the library until she decided to be daring one day.

My oldest niece is the result of that adventure.

"Huh." It's all he says as I lift the cup to my lips, sipping carefully so as not to burn my tongue. I groan when the first sip of caramel goodness hits my soul, and Blake chuckles.

"I remember that sound," he whispers. I glance at him. He's leaning forward, elbows on his knees, staring at his hands. I lift the coffee again, sneaking glances at him. Every once in a while, his eyes flicker up to Pauli, then back to his hands.

I remember those hands on my body, and it's then I realize that while I thought the morning couldn't get worse, the universe clearly took that as a challenge—and proved me wrong.

―――

BLAKE

Should I demand an explanation? She doesn't have just one kid, but two, and somehow, I cannot stop thinking she also has a guy to go with it. I'm jealous as hell, my heart hammering inside my chest. I should just tell her goodbye, yet I can't get my feet to move.

She looks exhausted, her skin pale. I'm tempted to ask her

what she does for work, but she made it more than clear that she never expected to see me again. It fucking hurts, even though I usually hope for the same.

"So...," I start.

She looks at me, tilting her head back and emptying the cup. It took her less than five minutes to finish it, even though I'm pretty sure it's hot as hell. I hold out the second cup.

"What's that?" she asks, brows furrowed.

I grin. "A second one."

She blinks, then beams. "You are freaking perfect," she exclaims as she takes it. My cheeks heat with the compliment, although I know it's not meant seriously. "So?" she echoes, and I glance up at her little girl again.

She is cute, smiling all the time, and even though none of this relates to me, I can't help but feel proud of Tia. "So, this is what it feels like," I say quietly. I can feel her gaze on me, but I can't meet her eyes.

"What what feels like?"

Her voice is like I remember, and so are her lips. Her hair's pulled into a ponytail, but not even the oversized hoodie can detract from how pretty she is.

"This is what it feels like to help someone cheat," I explain.

She exhales slowly and leans forward, pulling the stroller closer. The boy inside is asleep, but turns into her hand when she touches his cheek. "What it feels like to help someone escape their life, you mean? Must be about the same as you feel when saving a person's life," she replies quietly, thoughtfully, and I search her face, wondering what she's saying.

I didn't see any marks on her body, so all I can think is while her husband, boyfriend...significant other might not be abusive, she seems to be unhappy. It makes my heart squeeze.

You couldn't make her happy even if you tried, my mind snarls.

I close my eyes for a moment. "You can walk away," I suggest, although I imagine that's hard with two kids.

"I can't. The happiness of these kids is all that matters to me. I'll always put my life second because, hell, it's not their fault they were born." I swear I hear her mumble, "It's mine," but because it's not clear, I don't comment on it.

"You can find help," I insist, then wonder if I'm talking about myself. I don't know what it is about Tia that makes me feel different, but as much as I tell myself I need to walk away, I can't.

She shakes her head, then stands to dispose of both empty cups. I stare after her and grin. Just by the coffee consumption, she could almost be a cop, although we are less spoiled.

"I don't need your help, Blake. I've been managing my life alone since I was nineteen. I can deal with it. I don't need a savior."

I grit my teeth, angry. Why did she have to do it alone? It should be a two-person task. Before I can say anything, the little girl comes over, inching toward Tia while looking at me.

"Who are you?" she asks.

I glance at Tia, but she doesn't meet my eyes. "I'm a friend of your mom's," I say. Tia closes her eyes as the girl beams.

"Isn't she pretty? I love my mom!"

I nod, giving her a smile. "She is."

Tia clears her throat. "Are you done playing, Pauli? Ready to go home?" she asks, but Pauli shakes her head and hurries away without another word. Tia rubs her palms across her face.

I wonder what guy managed to score her and where she lives. Couldn't be far from here if they visit this playground.

"It's crazy how close you and I live," I comment.

She gives me a brief smile that doesn't reach her eyes, then shrugs. "Funny how there's still a world between your life and mine, your apartment and mine. I could easily fit us all into yours, while Pauli shares a room with her older sister, Liv."

Three kids? No wonder she calls our one-night stand her escape from life.

As much as I hate people who cheat, I'm no longer mad at her. Still, I feel like I need to clarify something.

"I wouldn't have slept with you had I known there was someone else."

She laughs. The sound is cold and bitter, cutting right through me. "You didn't ask, Detective Atwood, and I didn't really get the impression you *cared*."

I didn't, and I realize it's the first time this has ever mattered. Whenever I pick a girl up, I couldn't give a damn about what she has at home. Truth be told, I probably really didn't care that night...until she wrapped her arms around me in the living room. After that, I wasn't ready to let her go.

TIA

I should tell him these aren't my kids, but maybe if he thinks I'm involved with somebody, he will leave me alone. It hurts that he believes I could be that heartless, or that desperate. If there's one thing I hate, it's cheaters.

"I assumed you were a decent woman," he finally says, and I laugh. I can't help it.

I arch a brow. "Explain to me how a decent woman would have a one-night stand, then sneak out in the morning. A decent woman wouldn't have done that, Blake. You don't fuck decent women. You fuck the desperate ones, the ones out for trophies. All the others want serious, lasting relationships. A man makes love to those women, and it certainly wouldn't be after barely exchanging names. I think you need to seriously consider if decent is what you're looking for."

He stands and starts to pace as Neo begins to fuss inside the stroller. Before I know what's happening, Blake picks him up and holds him as he continues pacing.

"I never looked for... I always look for decent. I don't fuck everyone, Tia, no matter what you think." His voice has risen, so a mom sitting on a bench nearby clucks her tongue and points at all the children.

He apologizes softly. I can't help but smile. With him distracted, I glance briefly at Pauli, then allow myself to soak up his presence, his good looks, the way he makes me feel.

Would his mood be different if I had welcomed him with a big smile when he'd showed up?

"I didn't mean to cheapen what we had, or ruin your day by being here, Blake," I whisper, feeling guilty. He doesn't deserve to be caught up in my drama. I was at the ball as a stand-in, and I had already tired of it by the time I got there. He was handsome, flirty, and took me home so we could have some fun. It should've ended there for him. "I know you never expected to see me again, and maybe I should've mentioned how close you and I lived to each other, but..." I shrug.

"A whole different world," he repeats what I had said earlier, and I nod.

"I couldn't have known you'd show up here, Blake. People from your side of the park never come over to ours. There's a reason there's a gate only your side has keys to." I wish it were different, and maybe if he and I would've met in another life, we could've had something more. "I promise, if I see you, I'll walk the other way."

It's the last thing I want because I hardly ever have discussions with someone besides my sister. When I'm at work, there are patrons who try to talk to me, but it's different, less personal. I miss having friends, but again, with the life I have, where would I make time for them?

He finally pauses his pacing, Neo happily babbling. He looks good with my nephew in his arms. My heart is ready to open up to him, but my mind comes and beats it down until it's nothing more than a crumbled mess.

I can never have someone like Blake Atwood.

"I don't want you to walk the other way, Tia." He walks back over and sits. I reach for the boy cuddled close to him. He releases Neo, albeit reluctantly, but keeps his eyes on me. "It is what it is, and maybe that's a...a sign."

I smirk. "Hurts saying that, huh?" I tease.

He grins, rubbing the back of his neck in embarrassment. "You're something else. I don't know what it is about you that makes me feel more open, and no, it wasn't hard to say." He's quiet for a moment. "I thought about you yesterday, Tia. It was weird and unexpected."

I snort. "Thinking of me is weird?"

"Not what I meant. It was more about *when* I thought about you." He clears his throat, then continues. "We have this case I cannot tell you much about."

"Naturally."

He grins. "Naturally. Anyway, my partner said something about the killer just seeing the woman and deciding to murder her, so...yeah."

For a brief moment, I cannot believe he just said that, then I burst out laughing, startling Neo, who starts to whimper. I kiss the top of his head, still giggling. "I hadn't realized I was so bad you wanted to kill me just because you saw me," I tease. His horrified expression makes me giggle even more.

"Not what I meant at all. God, Tia... Don't twist my

words around." He groans and rubs the back of his neck again, something he seems to do when embarrassed. "I meant, I...I thought about how easily it could've been you."

It's then I realize that he was worried about me. I'm speechless. I can't remember the last time someone I wasn't related to cared about me. I make sure Neo can't topple off my lap, then stretch my arms out and give him a wide grin.

"Still here in all my comfy glory."

He nods, his lips tugging into a smile. "And I'm glad about that." He suddenly stands.

Funny. I didn't want to have him close just a few minutes ago. Now I can't stand the thought of him leaving.

―――

BLAKE

I stand in front of Tia, looking down at her with the toddler on her lap, and my heart does things it's never done before, while my mind gets increasingly angry that this is another man's baby.

I don't think I ever thought of having children. As a detective, there's always the chance you won't make it back, which is why I stay away from relationships.

That, and because you are a fucking murderer, even if all those people deserved what they got.

The thought, even though it's not a new one, hits me in the chest, stinging more than usual.

"What?" Tia asks, concern edged on her pretty features.

I force a smile. "What what?"

She shrugs, cocking her head. She watches me for a second, then checks on Pauli before looking at me again. "You had a funny expression, as if you thought about something...unsavory."

"You didn't see that," I mutter.

She laughs. "It's part of the job."

I assume she means in the corporate world because the ball we met at was big on those. I bet she needs to watch businessmen like a hawk to make sure they don't screw her over.

"Well, I have no doubt you're good at your job."

I debate on saying my next sentence. Although I know I'll probably seek her out here more often, I don't have much hope of us being in the same place at the same time.

"I don't date. My job doesn't allow it. Who would want to be with someone like me?"

She snorts, then sees I'm serious. "Yeah. Who would want to be with someone hot, reliable, and tender?" she mumbles.

I kneel in front of her, smiling softly. "That's not what I mean, but thank you. It's more that with my work, I can get killed at any time." *And kill people on occasion*.

She blinks, her expression thoughtful, then she lowers her lashes. "Anyone would be stupid not to date you, Blake. Risks or not, I think you're worth it. I mean..." She shrugs. "Time with...someone you love should be worth it, and if we always shy away from things because we could end up being hurt..." She trails off, as if she fears she's said too much, and as much as I want to reach out and touch her, I don't.

"What?" I know what she's saying, I think, but I want her to voice it, even though I won't go down that road with her.

I won't go down that road with anyone because it won't be long until the cuffs click around my wrists. My shooting the wrong person is bound to happen eventually. One wrong decision and it could be me facing trial for having shot someone innocent.

"Nothing. It's stupid. I should listen to my own advice,

but I can't even fit in time to read, so where would I..." She sighs. "You know what? Never mind."

Her unfinished sentence will probably haunt me forever. Does her significant other make her so unhappy she wishes for something new? Why doesn't she walk away from whatever this is, whatever is hurting her, and try to start over?

"You can find help, Tia. Start over with the kids. I mean..." I glance over at Pauli. She waves, beaming. Smiling, I wave back, my thoughts a jumbled mess. I have no idea why I even care. I lean forward and grasp her chin, forcing her to look at me. Her skin is cold and soft against my fingertips. For a second, I itch to trace her cheek, but I refrain. "You deserve to be happy, Tia, no matter what you think. There's a whole support system—"

She jumps to her feet so quickly, I nearly fall back on my ass, but catch myself in time. "You don't understand, Blake, and I'm not your responsibility, either."

Explain it to me then. Tell me everything so I understand and can tell you the same thing again!

The thoughts bounce around my head, but I can't allow them past my lips. I should be going, should have breakfast and jump into the shower, prepare for the day, maybe think up another angle we can try on the case. Instead, I stand, looking at Tia.

"You're right. I'm not responsible for you..." *But I want to be.*

I freeze at my thought, my eyes glued to her face and the way indecision mars her pretty features. Her eyes are closed, her lips drawn into a tight line, as if she can't decide whether to reach for what she wants or run the other way as quickly as she can.

"I'm not responsible for you, Tia, but I can be your friend, and friends tell each other things they're going through." My voice is rough. Whatever it is about this woman that has me all twisted, has me throwing my principles and everything else out the window, it terrifies me.

"Friends," she spits. When her stormy blue eyes focus back on me, I can see she's decided. "You and I had an amazing night, Blake, but that's all. It was never meant to be anything else, and I don't need any more friends." She runs a hand through her hair, pausing for a second as she looks at Pauli. "I need a guarantee that these three kids get the best chance in life because none of this is their fault. Which means I need to work hard whenever I'm not watching them. I don't have time for friends, myself, and even less for...for..." She grits her teeth, "*love*. This is goodbye, Blake. Maybe *you* should walk the other way when you see me."

When she turns away, calling for Pauli, I know I'm dismissed.

TIA

The kids and I make our way home, heart hammering in my chest. I didn't get the impression Blake wanted more, yet I could tell by his tone that being friends wasn't what he wanted, either.

Shaking my head, I swallow down all these unwanted and unexpected emotions. It doesn't matter what I want, what he wants, what any of us wants. I cannot commit, and he cannot open up. I didn't give birth to these children, but my sister knows I have her back, no matter what.

I nearly cry with self-hatred when I think that Pauli and Neo most likely wouldn't be here had I only made it clear that Chloe had my *support*, but not my *life*. Instead, now I'm like a live-in servant because I wanted to make it right for my little sister when my parents didn't.

"Aunt Tia, why are you crying?" Pauli asks as we make our way up the street to our apartment.

I wipe at my cheeks and give her a big smile. "It's the wind. It doesn't do well with my contacts," I lie, and she eyes me dubiously. Sometimes she knows how I'm feeling better than my own sister does.

I glance over my shoulder, knowing Blake wouldn't follow me, yet somehow hoping he had. We'll probably never go to that playground again. There is another one in the other direction. It's smaller, and I don't know anyone there, but at least I won't run into Blake.

Once we reach our building, Neo fusses in the stroller and Pauli has been singing some nonsense song, nearly making me scream out loud because I want just a second to sort through everything I'm feeling. If I had a best friend, maybe I could talk this through with her. There'd been a time Chloe and I were very close and I would've told her everything. However, that changed a long time ago. She's no longer the same person she was back then, and neither am I.

I guess that's what happens to you when your own parents cut you out of their lives. They reached out to me a few times because I wasn't the one with the baggage—their words, not mine—but I can't go behind Chloe's back. Either they take us both back into their lives or we'll make do on our own.

As I clean the apartment while constantly yawning, Pauli makes a sudden comment along the lines of liking me more than her mother. That's when I know it's time to make changes here at home.

Now all I have to do is figure out what those changes are.

CHAPTER SEVEN

TIA

THREE DAYS LATER, the bar is buzzing...and so is my head. I've almost been late to work for the second time this week because Chloe didn't make it home on time. Also, the mood in the bar seems different, more subdued.

"What's going on?" I ask Donna. She opened the bar with Warrick today, so I'm sure she's already been informed. She looks up, her eyes wide and confused. Sometimes she seems to be quite sharp, but other times, her hair color defines her state of mind.

"I don't know what you mean," she finally says.

I arch a brow, wondering why she doesn't feel the tension running through the room. There are many groups huddled together, the guys talking in hushed voices, the beer sitting in front of them, untouched.

"Never mind," I tell her, then pull a few beers for one of the tables in the back. I don't mind serving occasionally, and I know Donna definitely prefers it that way. Funnily enough, that is perfect for me. I rather know no one else is in my way.

"Hey, guys," I say, beaming at the group sitting at the table.

Five pair of eyes turn to me, and they sadden as they take me in. I let my smile fall away as I set down the glasses, then cross my arms in front of my chest.

"All right. Who died?"

One of the guys clears his throat. "No one."

That's a lie. "Okay... How about we try the truth this time? What happened? Was it an officer?"

I haven't been here long enough to know many of them, but I've seen some of the faces a few times. I recognize the lonely souls that have nothing besides work—souls like Blake Atwood, even though he lets loose every once in a while—so I do a quick sweep of the room, seeing most are here. The rest are probably on shift.

"It's just a new case Intelligence is working on. It's all over our district, so..." The guy, who is probably close to retirement, lowers his eyes. "You know we cannot talk about it."

Yes, I do. I also know that somewhere during the evening, when alcohol sits in empty stomachs and guys forget to whisper, I'll find out everything. I won't lie. I'm feeling itchy. Crimes happen all over town every damn minute, but so far, none have made the bar feel like it does tonight.

Donna rests her hip against the counter, turning to me when I walk back behind the bar. "Why do you think something's going on? I mean..." She nods toward the patrons. "They're acting like they always do when there's a hard case."

Aha, so she *does* realize something's off. "What are hard cases?"

"Two tequila... Better make it a double," a guy says as he walks up and takes a barstool, sitting with a heavy sigh.

"Same," the second adds, sitting.

The first guy looks at him. "One was for you, but come to think of it, maybe two each *is* a smarter thing."

I nod and grab the shot glasses, pouring two for each man. I watch them throw the first shots back quickly.

"First one at the crime scene?" I ask, while Donna walks around the room, collecting empty glasses.

Both nod, downing the second shots. "Never seen a murder victim before," the second guy mutters and pales even more...if that's possible.

So my assumption was right. Then again, it's not really hard to guess with everyone's attitude here tonight. Although... "I'm sorry. I've never seen one, either. I guess it's not like in the movies. I'm sorry. Seriously."

They both shrug, then lower their heads. "I hate that uniforms are always the first to arrive. I mean, I get that someone needs to make sure the crime scene is secured and all, but..."

I lift the tequila bottle again, refilling the glasses. "The police have psychologists you can talk to. Please, make sure you utilize them." As much as I want more information, I cannot stand the thought of them suffering from this.

For some reason, my thoughts drift to Blake. I wonder which district he works for, hoping he doesn't have to see murder victims very often.

I start washing some glasses while the men talk among themselves. I'm only listening with half an ear until...

"...Atwood was. He's a decent guy. Took me away from it, gave me a new task. I don't think I could've been around that. I..." Guy number one shakes his head, gritting his teeth so hard, I worry he'll hurt himself.

"Have you guys caught the game stats? I missed them," I say loudly. They both look up. It's a shitty distraction, but I can't help myself. Maybe distraction is the best thing here.

"You watch baseball?" they ask in unison.

"I'm Tia, and yes, I do. I do prefer football, but gotta take whatever's on."

Guy number one leans forward. "Jackson. Nice to meet you. I prefer football, too. Which team?"

I arch a brow. "College or NFL?"

"I'm Landon," guy number two announces, color slowly returning to his cheeks. "NFL."

"The Saints. I've always wanted to go to New Orleans. I guess I dig the golden and black." I wink.

They both shake their heads with a grin. "Wrong team, lady. So wrong. Let me teach you about loyalty," Jackson teases. I breathe a sigh of relief.

Glancing around, I see Warrick at the other end of the bar, watching me with an expression I cannot place, curiosity and pride mixing with suspicion, but decide to not worry about it. If I learned anything about him it's that you'll hear what's on his mind the moment he wants you to hear it, and not a second earlier.

BLAKE

He's looking for a blonde barkeeper.
He killed the wrong girl again.

My chest aches, thinking about what that means. I'm bent over my desk, my focus on the paper in front of me. We found prints on the woman's wallet and ID, yet those prints aren't in the system. A recheck on the first wallet comes up with the same.

Our assumption is the suspect knows *something* about the woman he's looking for, but it cannot be what she looks like.

It would be too easy to walk into the bars to see if she's in there.

"Too many fucking bars," Jim mumbles from his desk across from mine. I look up, seeing him pouring over the list of possibilities. I don't need to see that list to have a vague idea of how many bars we'd have to check for someone strange.

It's going on ten pm. I've been here since we returned from the crime scene at ten this morning. There wasn't anything new around the second victim, yet I felt as if I hadn't seen any of it before.

The wide, surprised eyes.

The sentence written on her arm with a pen.

The ligature marks around her neck.

I wonder what he'll do if he ever catches a woman whose handbag can't be used as a weapon. He's still an opportunist, even though this was his second victim.

Art, who studies all the videos we receive, walks in. "They have video surveillance because the club has an outside camera, but there's nothing to see. Same goes for the ATM across the street. Guy wore a hood and a ball cap pulled low. I tried to turn it, enhance it, anything that could give us a vague idea of what he looks like. Nada."

He pins a picture to the murder board anyway. I stare at it for a long time, seeing nothing but shadows and clothes.

Nikki cocks her head. "Do you think it's an accident that he wore nondescript clothes?"

There's no logo, nothing visible to discern what type of clothing he wears. It's all black and one big shadow.

"If he wears clothes like that, my thought is he's going out with the intent to kill," Declan points out.

I stand, holding my arms out. I wear black jeans, a shirt that's equally as black, and a dark jacket. I've worn them for years. I spin in place. "*I* didn't leave the house planning to murder somebody this morning, and we look the same." Except he seems to be smaller and rounder than I am.

Art nods. "I wear the same sometimes, to be honest. That won't get us far. However, since I was able to pull up his picture, I calculated height and weight. He's five-five, five-six at most, and I'd say about two hundred and ten pounds. Based on his size, I'd say he never killed before. Too unfit."

He's also small to be strangling women, but I guess he can make up for that with strength. Besides, the first two victims barely made it to five-foot-three. It would still be easy enough for him.

Donna comes to mind when I think of tiny bartenders, and I feel the urge to pick up the phone and warn Warrick. The thing is, until we have the official okay, I cannot say a word. There's still hope of keeping a panic from spreading, but we need to find the fucker before there's a whole string of dead women.

Blowing out a breath, I start reading the crime scene reports, jotting down anything strange, but there's not much—just like the other four times I read it.

Will stands next to the board, looking at the meager info we have. The suspect is a damn ghost. I have a hard time believing he went from a contributing member of society to murdering people. There has to be a ladder he climbed, his crimes escalating the longer he's gotten away with it.

Wolfe walks in. He's been with the ME and the second victim, and his face says it all.

"Nothing new. Victim wasn't raped. Wasn't even touched, besides being strangled. I wonder why she was in the alley."

Contrary to the first victim, the second girl didn't have a bike in the alley, as far as we know, or a car parked there. She didn't even need to be there, but the video of her and the attacker makes it pretty obvious she went there of her own free will.

My head buzzing, I sit back in my chair. Tia's smiling face at the ball appears in my mind. It's not that I want to have her naked in my bed again, although I wouldn't mind. I just long for a moment to talk to her.

I can't help the smile slipping over my face, but then I remember that she has three kids and no support at home. I don't know why else she went and had an affair.

Fuck, I'm not even that. I was a one-night stand she clearly never wants to see again, and I can't figure out why that pisses me off so much.

"Okay, listen up," Wolfe calls. I look up, pulled from my thoughts. "Go home and get your minds off the case. Get a beer, watch trash TV, and go to bed. Tomorrow, at eight sharp, we're back here. Maybe we'll see something new, or think of someone to talk to that we haven't yet."

It's almost funny how quickly everyone stands, grabbing their shit, worried Wolfe will change his mind. Will catches my eye.

"How about we catch that beer at Gun & Shot?"

I smile. "Hell yeah."

Somehow, I'm not ready to be alone just yet.

TIA

It's half past ten when the door of the bar opens and I look up, seeing Blake walk in. My breath catches. Before I even know what I'm doing, I place the tray I'm carrying on a table and hurry to meet him halfway, suddenly remembering he and I didn't part on good terms.

"Blake, I... Hey," I stutter, wanting to tell him that I heard about what happened, but the words don't come out.

His hazel eyes widen as he searches my face, as if he can't believe I'm standing here.

"Miss Ball," Will says.

I give him a brief smile. "Mister Unlucky. Sorry you weren't as handsome as this one here," I tease, and Will laughs.

Blake, still watching me, brushes a blonde strand over my shoulder. "What are you doing here?" he says softly.

I notice a lot of eyes on us, so I nod him over to two empty spots at the bar. "Have a seat and I tell you."

"We'll take a booth." He turns and catches Donna's eyes. "Make it two beers, pretty girl," he calls out to her. I can practically see the happy hearts in her eyes.

"Okay."

I turn and grab my tray, picking up a few more empty glasses on my way back behind the bar. Once Donna pulls the beers, I start to grab them.

"Oh, I'll do it, Tia."

Jealousy courses through me. I know Donna and the patrons sometimes disappear for a bit, and I can't help but wonder if she wants to land Blake...or already did.

"You stay here, sweet cheeks. All the men walking up need your smile to cheer them up," I say sweetly. She's really nice, and maybe we can be friends eventually, but when it comes to Blake, I just can't stand the idea of her flirting with him—and him taking her up on it.

I grab the beers and am off before she can say another word. "Here you go, guys."

I set Blake's beer in front of him. When I start to pull away, he grabs my hand, his eyes full of fury and...fear?

"You're a bartender?"

I don't know why, but I get defensive. "And that makes me a worse lay, right?"

He gets up, leaning on the table and coming so close, I could kiss him easily. "You shouldn't be working here, Tia. Do you have any idea how dangerous it is?"

I glance around the bar and snort. "With all the cops here? Yeah, I'm shaking like a tree in the wind."

Blake takes a deep breath, but before he can say something, Will touches his arm. "Take it somewhere else, Blake. You're drawing way too much attention," he hisses. I step back and look around, realizing he's right.

Blake straightens and blows out a breath, then grabs my wrist and pulls me into the back hall, proving he knows his way around. There's no reason he'd know this door, this hallway, if he hadn't vanished in here with someone before.

Once we're out a sight, I pull free. "What the hell do you think you're doing? I'm at my job and—"

He steps toward me, furious. I step back until my back hits the wall. "You cannot work here anymore," he snaps. My jaw drops. "Along with the fact that this place is so fucking far away from your home, it's a bar. You have three kids to take care of and…they cannot lose you."

I blink up at him. "I'm here *because* of them, Blake. Someone needs to watch them during the day. And, trust me, this bar is better than many others I've worked at. I left my last one because they were serving minors. This is the best job I've had in a long time."

He shakes his head, punching the wall next to me, making me flinch, before resting his forehead against mine. "Tell me you have a car," he pleads, his voice soft, gentle, in complete contrast to his expression. "Tell me you don't take the subway in the middle of the night."

I stay quiet, which tells him everything he needs to know.

To my surprise, he frames my face, searching my eyes. His thumb brushes over my cheek, then my lips. If his hands would move a little lower, he'd feel the way my pulse hammers in my neck. I want him to kiss me. I want it with everything I am, even though I swore to myself there wouldn't be a repeat.

He quickly steps back, combing his fingers through his hair, almost tearing at the strands as he paces the hall. "When do you usually leave to get here? And how long does it take you to get home?"

I swallow past the lump in my throat. "I don't know." My voice is raspy. I cough to clear it. "I mean, it's really none of your business, Blake. You can't come in here and boss me around."

He shrugs, hopelessness in his eyes. "I... Seeing you here caught me by surprise, that's all. I didn't... I thought..." He sighs. "I don't know where I thought you'd be working, but I'd been sure it was something during the day."

I snort. "Something that still allows me to be at the playground at nine in the morning? Must be a fantastic job." For a detective, he sure as hell didn't combine the pieces well.

"You need to stop working here, Tia. Promise me. I can only imagine how long it takes you to get home on the *subway*, and I... It's dangerous."

I meet his eyes. There's nothing I can say, and as long as I don't know what the hell is going on, I think it's best I start guarding my heart against Blake Atwood.

―――

BLAKE

Tia's a bartender.

Tia's a blonde bartender, in the same district the guy seems to be targeting, and is the right height.

I have no idea what to think because the only thing on my mind right now is to throw her over my shoulder and drag her out of this building.

I cannot believe her significant other lets her work at night. Even if things were tight, I'd still make sure my girl worked safer shifts, the ones during the day, and not so far from home. Although I can agree on this being one of the safest bars around.

Just the thought of some drunk asshole laying a hand on her...

I shake my head, then lean against the wall across from her, watching her in silence. She's not pale like she was before, although the light in the hallway is bright and white, and her eyes are framed in black, drawing my attention to the way she's watching me. She has her hands behind her back, as if to keep herself from touching me. I wish that were true.

"How long have you worked here?" And how in the world had I missed her?

"The night after the ball was my first shift. I didn't know this was your district. I knew it was a cop bar, but—"

I close the distance between is in less than three steps and frame her face with my hands, gently touching my lips to hers. They are as soft as I remember, and for a moment, the panic inside me eases.

She pulls away, albeit reluctantly. "Blake," she whispers. "We can't. I can't. No repeats, remember? It was one night."

I don't know why she keeps saying that because it's

suddenly no longer what I want, although what that would be isn't clear in my head, either.

Relationship?

Affair?

Just one more night?

I don't know what I want, yet I know I need something. "Let me be your friend, Tia," I whisper against her lips.

She gently grasps my wrists. "Friends don't kiss. Friends don't try to keep other friends from earning a living, no matter what way that is."

Friends also don't let friends get killed, I think. I should let her go, but I can't.

"I'm worried about you. I couldn't stop thinking about you all day." Yes, this is something friends shouldn't say, but I don't care.

She pulls my hands from her face and steps toward the door that leads back to the bar. "Don't, Blake. Don't worry about me. I'm tough. And don't think of me. I'm undeserving. And, please, don't ever kiss me again, okay? If you truly want to be my friend, do what friends do. Ask about the children, joke around..."

"Friends exchange numbers." And I need hers so I can check up on her.

She gives me a soft smile. "If you prove to me you're nothing more than my friend, maybe I'll give it to you. For now, I need to get back to work before people think you and I had a quickie. I'm not like Donna." She winks.

"I didn't fuck Donna, if that's what you're implying."

"Huh." She forces out a smile.

I close the distance between us again, stopping when she straightens. As much as I want to touch her again, I'm going to respect her wishes. "I know my way around because Warrick had some trouble a couple months back and we took a guy away, that's all. You can ask him if you want."

The tension melts from her face, although her eyes remain wary. "Okay." And with that, she opens the door and walks back into the bar.

I linger a few moments, not caring what anyone thinks. The door to the office opens and Warrick walks out.

"Atwood, going after my waitress?" he asks, and although his tone is playful, his eyes are serious.

"No. I met Tia at the ball. I didn't know she worked here until today. I'm just… It was a weird day and I had her on my mind…" I shrug.

He nods. "Heard it was a hard one. Another murder victim."

I wonder how much he knows. It's his bar, and cops sometimes forget that there are civilians around.

He smiles. "Tia dealt with Jackson and Landon earlier. They were pretty shaken up, but they didn't say much. She was good with them."

I have no doubt about that. I nod. "I bet. They were… I remember my first."

Warrick nods. "So do I. I don't think you ever forget that first. However, I also remember a lot of those that followed."

I'm tempted to warn him about the recent victims, but I know I shouldn't. "How much do you know?"

He shrugs. "Girls found in alleys. That's about it. They've been pretty tight-lipped with this one." Then he smirks. "If I say that it pisses me off a little, are you gonna tell me to get back to the NYPD?"

I shake my head. "We need you here. This bar is the safest haven we've ever had, and you know it. Just… Make sure to watch your girls, okay?"

He arches a brow, expression hardening. "Are Tia and Donna in danger?"

"Bartenders always are. Creeps hide everywhere. Tia is pretty, and you know how we cops get over pretty things."

He chuckles. "She'll have you by the balls if you grab her ass. I don't think she's the type to just vanish into the bathroom with anyone. Truth be told, her life is tough enough. I doubt she'll start anything with someone anytime soon."

He gave me a perfect opening to ask about Tia, to find out more about her, but I refrain from doing so. Warrick was one of us. He'll catch the signs immediately.

"If she's a good one, all the more reason to watch her."

I walk back into the bar, hoping we find the murdering fuck even faster now.

CHAPTER EIGHT

BLAKE

A WEEK HAS GONE by with no murders. We're all on edge, just wondering when he'll strike next. We've gone over each of the cases again and again, finding nothing new. Unless someone comes forward with more evidence, we can't do a fucking thing.

"Ready?" Kelly says as I approach a building across from the park entrance.

We decided to hang out today. Wolfe gave us off, which I hate and love at the same time. Being idle sucks, but at least running and beer are on the agenda. Luckily, Kelly's off today, as well.

"Have you been to Gun & Shot lately?"

Tia is so his type, and I wonder if he's been in there.

It's been a week since I've seen her, although I know she has worked every night. For some reason, my whole team has found a new appreciation for that bar, but because I cannot just be her friend, I decided to not go back, but appreciate them feeding me the current status on her.

I keep wanting to beg her to work somewhere else. Hell, I even considered talking to a few bar owners myself to one, see the bars, and two, find someone who has an opening for her that's closer to her place, but I can just imagine the wrath that would bring down on me.

"I have, actually. There's this new bartender. She's feisty. You should see her."

I turn to him, watching him stretch. I just want to get this going to see if she's at the playground. The weather has sucked the last few days, but today is bright and sunny, albeit a little cold.

"Her name's Tia." I don't know why I felt the need to say it.

He cocks his head and grins. "Anything I should know?"

"She's the one I took home after the ball."

He blinks slowly, then starts chuckling. "No way in hell. Your one-night stand turns out to be a bartender at the bar you like to frequent most? Tough luck, man."

I shrug. "Honestly? It's worse *not* seeing her. The case we have, the one that's stalling?"

Kelly's my best friend, and as much as I shouldn't tell him about cases, he always gets information. Today, I need to talk to someone about what's behind the lines I shouldn't cross. I know there's no need to tell him to keep it to himself. I trust Kelly more than I trust Will, and that guy's my partner.

He nods. "Murder victims and the apology written on them."

"Yeah. Blondes. Pretty." I pause, making him arch a brow. "Bartenders."

His jaw drops. "You're *worried* about her? That's a first."

There are so many firsts with her, yet I cannot voice those because it would make them too real. "I'm worried about *all* those women. Donna looks like that, too. We've known her since she started there, Kelly. It's been... What? Four years?"

"Yet you mentioned Tia first." He sits down on the steps leading up to the apartment complex. Seems he realizes we won't be going anywhere.

"Coincidence. Besides, you brought her up."

He grins. "Because you've been aiming for exactly that. So, does she know?"

I startle, my eyes wide. "Does she know what?" My heart jumps into my throat.

Kelly's grin widens. "I was talking about the case, but your reaction makes me wonder... Is there more between the two of you? Damn, I should've looked at her closer."

I close my eyes, taking one deep breath after the other. *I will not hit my best friend. I will not hit my best friend.*

"I'm not going to touch her, Blake," he says.

I open my eyes, focusing on him again. "I didn't say anything."

He stands and shrugs. "You didn't have to. It's written all over your face. I assume she doesn't know. Did you tell Warrick to keep an eye on his girls?"

I'm still waiting for permission from Wolfe, but it hasn't come yet. With no other victim yet, he's decided to not cause a panic. "No, we're waiting."

"For another body?" Kelly prompts.

I shake my head, turning my attention toward the park. I don't know exactly where Tia lives, but ever since realizing it's so close, I can't help but extend my running routes around the buildings there. No idea what I'd even do if I knew where she lived, but that doesn't mean my heart's not set on finding her.

"I'm hoping he's got it out of his system. I imagine making one mistake is hard, but two? That has to eat him up. Maybe he's gonna do something to himself to get rid of the pain and guilt."

I swallow hard, hoping Kelly doesn't hear just how much I longed for that a few years back. It's eased up considerably since then, but there are still times I can't get over everything I did, even if it was in the name of the law.

"Suicide?"

I nod. "I check the news reports closely, just hoping for something that stands out, but… I don't think there'll be a clear way to know. There are too many dead people on a daily basis in a city like New York." And it's terrifying to think about.

"I don't know what to tell you about the girl, man. If she's important to you, maybe you should try something scary, like *date* her."

I don't tell him that she nixed that idea before I ever even got there. I also don't tell him that maybe I'll just be her friend because… I like her so much, I don't know where to go with these feelings.

―――

TIA

Chloe got home early. I hardly know how to act around her, but part of me is relieved because I need someone to talk to about Blake.

"Hey, Chlo." I join her in the living room where she's playing with Neo. Liv sits at the kitchen table, doing her homework, and Pauli is off in their room doing…something.

"Tia." She smiles tightly, something in her expression I cannot place. Shaking off the uneasy feeling, I grin.

"I met someone at the ball, and... God, I can't remember the last time my heart skipped a few beats when seeing a guy."

She looks up from her son, her expression somber. "You're thinking about dating? Does that mean you'll take on less shifts?"

I bite back a comment about picking up *extra* shifts and sit down on the couch. Neo struggles in her lap, stretching his little arms for me, and I reach for him without even thinking about it. She tightens her arms around him.

"Chloe I—"

"When I'm home, I can take care of my children," she snaps, and my jaw drops.

I'm doing everything to make sure she doesn't have to work two or more jobs, and she talks to me like that? "It's not my fault your kids see more of me than you lately," I reply through clenched teeth. "I just wanted to—"

She stands, placing Neo onto the couch. "I'm sorry I'm working longer hours to make things better for you and the kids. Clearly you don't appreciate it."

I gape at her. "Don't appreciate it? We can switch, you know. You can do all the night shifts and watch the kids during the day, being sleep-deprived, and I'll work a nine-to-five. How do you feel about that?"

I don't know how this has escalated, but suddenly, I don't see my little sister anymore. I see a stranger.

"So you think I have the easy job?"

I know there's no reason for her to explode like this, but isn't there a saying about people who protest too much?

"I don't think either of us has it easy, but I think you should appreciate all I've done for you. I've wanted to get back to a daytime job for a few months now, but all you do is tell me that—"

"That no one would watch the children? That I'd have to

step back from my hours to take care of them? That it would be incredibly selfish? Yes, I've said all that."

Her expression softens as she steps toward me. "Tia, the way we're doing things now works, doesn't it? And you enjoy working at the bar, so why do you want to change things? I promise. Should you no longer enjoy working at the bar at some point, well find a way, but I know you like it. We've talked about that often enough."

I close my eyes. "Yes, but I have to travel so far and—"

She waves me off. "That was your choice. You worked around the corner and decided to leave that job, so don't bring that down on me. You didn't want to work there anymore."

I have explained that to her numerous times, so I take a deep breath. "They were doing illegal business. It could've landed me in prison. What don't you understand about that?"

Chloe reaches out and brushes a hand across her son's head. "As long as you didn't do anything illegal, they wouldn't have taken you in."

She doesn't get it. I rub my forehead, exhaustion making me more irritated than anything else. I glance at the clock, seeing I have a few hours left before I need to get back to the bar.

"I'm gonna go lie down for—"

"I have to grab some papers from the office and deliver them to a client in about an hour, so it would be really nice if you could just watch the kids."

I stare at her. "I really should get some sleep, Chloe. I haven't gotten more than two or three hours lately because you work so much more than you used to, and—"

Her eyes blaze. "What in the world are you saying?" she shouts.

I rub my temple. "Nothing. I'm just saying that you work a lot more than you used to. It isn't only hard on you, but on me, as well." Especially because she usually gets at least eight hours of sleep.

I don't know what's going on in her head, but the truth is, I don't even recognize her lately.

Her lips tilt up into an evil smirk. "Too bad you're not pretty enough to be a hooker, huh? Less work, more money. That way, you wouldn't have to complain about the lack of sleep."

My jaw drops as I stare at her, unable to formulate a sentence when she turns away. Neo crawls over to me, and I automatically pick him up. I cannot believe she said that to me, and even worse? I can't believe I didn't have a comeback.

Silently seething, I go to my room and make sure to occupy her son while she vanishes into the bathroom humming, as if she hadn't just nailed our sisterly casket shut.

CHAPTER NINE

TIA

ALMOST TWO WEEKS have passed since I last saw Blake. I have no idea how I know that. Lately, my mind's jumped from one useless thought to the next. I'm tired, my movements sluggish. I started writing down everything because I keep forgetting things. Warrick's commented on it, so I've made sure to appear sharp at work at least.

As I walk from the subway station toward the bar, my mind a million miles away, my neck prickles. I turn, but in the shadows of the night, I don't see anything. I clutch my purse closer, wishing I had pepper spray—or Blake's number.

I continue walking, but the feeling of being watched doesn't go away. I glance over my shoulder again, seeing a guy hurrying toward me. I gasp, my heart hammering, and brace myself, but he runs past, not even acknowledging my presence. I realize he could've come from anywhere and I wouldn't have seen him.

Placing a hand on my chest, my heart starts to slow, my

breathing decreasing. I'm not usually paranoid like that, but with how tired I am, my brain is sluggish.

The morning after Chloe's awful comment, we made up. I still watch the kids. The alternative is that I catch up on sleep while the kids spend long periods of time alone. I couldn't stand that.

Something's in the air. Work is busier than ever, even during the week. Both Donna and Warrick commented on it, which makes me wonder.

I stare at a tree as I pass. Seeing only one leaf on it makes me pause. What makes the leaves fall off in the winter?

Not hearing anybody approach, I startle when something bumps into me.

"Hey, Tia. Are you asleep again?" Donna grins and links our arms.

"What do you mean? I've been awake at work."

She shrugs, her face pale in the glow of the streetlights. "You're like a zombie, Tia. You don't fuss at the idiots, or get flirty if you think there's more money in it for you. Our regulars have noticed, and I think Warrick's gonna sit down with you soon. Trust me, you don't want that."

I arch a brow. "Why?"

"Because once War sits down with you, it means he's worried, and he takes that very seriously. He'll butt in, constantly asking you if you're okay, if there's something he can do."

That's the last thing I need, and she knows it.

We enter Gun & Shot. Not watching where I'm going, I run into someone, apologize, then step around him.

"Tia?"

The hairs on my arms stand on end, recognizing that voice. I look up, seeing Blake's hazel eyes on me. I smile to myself because the freckles on his cheeks and bridge of his nose seem to be extraordinarily pronounced today.

"Hi," I whisper, my heart skipping a beat. He cocks his head, watching me. I can see the detective in him coming out.

"You look horrible," he mutters, stepping closer.

I close my eyes, almost pissed at him. *Almost*. Truth be told, I'm glad to see him.

It's then I realize I've missed him. We've only seen each other a few times to talk, yet I've missed him.

"You are a true charmer, Blake," I say, turning away from him and taking off my jacket.

He reaches for my arm, his skin on mine sending fireworks throughout my body. "What's going on, Tia?"

I hesitate for a moment, then turn back to him. "I'm okay, Blake. It's just been...a stressful few days." I'm tempted to reach out and brush my fingertips across his cheek, but I know people are watching.

He releases his hold and I walk behind the bar. I grab an apron and join Warrick and Donna, who stop talking to each other when I walk up. I couldn't care less, though.

Hell, besides Warrick, I know Blake will probably watch me like a hawk today, too, so I have to up my game. I grab a glass and pour myself an energy drink. I absolutely love that we can drink whatever we want, as long as it's a non-alcoholic. I drain the glass, then smile.

"You cannot live on energy drinks alone, Tia," Warrick mutters as he passes, taking off his apron. With his shift over, I know he'll make sure we have everything we need, then leave. Donna and I can lock up, then walk together for a bit. Sometimes she walks to the subway station with me, which I appreciate.

"Beer, pretty," a guy orders. Although I've never seen him

before, I don't call him out on it. I appreciate it if they call me by my name or nothing at all.

I walk over to the tap, lift the glass and draw the beer, keeping my whole attention it. On good days, I can look around and see which patrons might walk over and order another one, but today, it takes all my concentration to just hold the glass where it is.

"You look exhausted. Tia, you need to go home and—"

I glare at Blake. "No, I don't need to do anything but work." I don't have the mental capacity to talk to him or be extra nice right now. As much as I want him near, I also want him gone. If that's not confusing, I don't know what is.

―――

BLAKE

Her cheeks are hollow, and the bags under her eyes have bags under them. "You need sleep," I try again, surprised by the intense worry I feel. I don't know why she's so exhausted, but the fact that she ran straight into me when she came in proves how much she's *not* focusing.

Or at least not on the things around her.

She looks up at me, her eyes blazing. "I know what I need and what I don't, so I'd appreciate it if you could just…just…be quiet." Her statement lacks heat, the last word sounding defeated. A lot of things I've come to like about her are absent. The way she's quick to smile, the secret curl of her lip when she argues with a patron.

As I watch her serve people, I realize she has to calculate the total on a sheet of paper instead of her head like usual. The girls tend to only enter the orders into the cash register after the costumer has paid and left.

I make my way back to Kelly, who smirks. "She turned you down, didn't she?" he asks. I roll my eyes.

"I didn't hit on her. She needs sleep. Can't you see that?" I watch her out of the corner of my eye. She leans against the counter behind her, rubbing her temples. I don't think she has a headache, but she wants people to believe that's what's causing the shift in her personality.

I haven't been here much lately. We've been busy, but no matter how many leads we track, how many cold cases we check, we've come up with nothing. The uniforms call him the "Bartender Killer", a moniker I've started using. I know Wolfe would kill me because giving them names makes them an individual, someone who stands out, which just encourages a lot of them.

"I don't watch her as closely as you do because you've basically put a claim on her, so..." Kelly shrugs. "I don't even bother. Can't risk falling in love with her when you are."

I snort, disbelief coursing through me. "Love... What a big word. Especially because neither you nor I fall in love. I don't even think I'm capable of it any longer." Grinning, I lift my beer and take a tiny sip. I'm set on taking Tia home after her shift, so this one beer will be all I'll have.

"I see the way you look at her, Blake. I mean, the moment we walked in, your gaze went to the bar and your lips pressed together when you realized she wasn't here. Don't think I didn't know whom you're looking for."

The denial is on my lips when a crash nearby catches my attention.

"Shit! I'm sorry. Let me clean that up, then I'll replace your order...on the house." Tia kneels near the broken glass, beer most likely soaking her jeans. I'm out of my seat in a flash, crouching next to her.

Her hands shake as she picks up the glass. I reach out and tilt up her chin. "Are you okay?"

She pulls free from my grip and lowers her gaze. "Of course. It was a little heavy, that's all. I underestimated the weight."

That's bullshit. I've seen her carry trays heavier than that. I count three glass handles, meaning there'd been only three beers. "Let me help you. Tia, please get up. You're soaking your jeans."

She lowers her head slowly, staring at her knees for a moment, then meets my eyes. "Oh."

Donna rushes up, a broom and a few dish towels in hand. "Get up, Tia," she orders gently.

"Tia, a word, please?" Warrick stands by the hallway, his arms crossed over his chest.

I grasp her hand and help her up. I feel her grip on me tighten for a brief moment, then she lets go and walks over to her boss.

Being the protector I am, I follow, just in case I need to jump in and defend her.

"You need to go home," Warrick announces gently.

Tia instantly shakes her head. "I'm fine. It was just a... The trey slipped. I—"

"You're starting to cost me a lot more than you make." I know that tone. He's lying, but by the way Tia presses her lips into a tight line, she doesn't know that. "I need you to go home and sort out what's going on; otherwise, I cannot have you here any longer."

Tia gasps, yet I'm not worried. I know it's an empty threat. Warrick would never kick someone out when they need it the most, and Tia clearly needs this job.

"I'll take her," I tell him, and his eyes swing to me, narrowing.

"You've been drinking."

I nod, pointing over my shoulder at the table. "I didn't even drink half of it. I had planned on taking her home anyway, so I'm fine to drive. I wouldn't be offering otherwise."

"No one takes me home," Tia interrupts. We both look at her.

"It's either that or I fire you." His tone softens at her horrified expression. "Look. Go home. Sleep, eat, watch a movie. Tomorrow, you come in for your next shift, okay?"

Her shoulders drop in defeat. I know I should feel bad for her, but I don't. Instead, I'm glad to have a few minutes alone with her.

Maybe, just maybe, I can find out exactly what is going on.

TIA

The moment Warrick lets me know he's not fooling around, I can hardly move my feet. I'm conscious of Blake's gaze on me as I make my way behind the bar, grab my purse, and start pulling on my jacket.

My wrist gets caught in the sleeve. I try to tear it out, but the material doesn't budge. Warm hands grasp my shoulders, then work my hand through the sleeve, pulling my jacket up until it's where it belongs.

"Thanks," I mumble.

Blake leans closer. "What was that?" When I meet his eyes, a yawn escaping me, his expression softens. "Come on."

He doesn't touch me, which I appreciate, even though I want to lean on him for support through everything.

Sucky sister.

Exhausting job.

Loneliness.

"My car's parked just down the street," he says gently.

I nod, still dragging my feet. They catch on a raised section of the sidewalk and I stumble, my mind too slow to realize what's going on.

Luckily, Blake's right there and catches me. I hold onto him as I regain my balance. "Thank you. For everything. Catching me. Bringing me home."

When I sway, he wraps his arm around my waist, as if to make sure I won't fall again. It feels nice.

"How in the world did you end up this exhausted, Tia?"

I smirk. "Only an hour or two of sleep every night."

I feel as if I'm drunk. I nearly giggle, wondering if I'd be excused if I mauled him. You know, like people take pity on others when they're drunk.

I see a car in the distance, but because I can hardly focus and trip over my feet constantly, we have to walk slowly.

"This is where I lost the feeling of being watched," I say to no one in particular when I spot the tree with the one leaf. I feel his body stiffen.

"Being watched?"

I giggle. "Why, Detective Atwood. It's nice to see you. Funny. I left the bar with Blake, but now—"

"Cut it out, Tia," he interrupts, then steps in front of me and tilts up my chin. "You were being watched?"

I cock my head. "No. I *felt* as if I were being watched, but then a guy ran past me and Donna appeared. It was just her."

He glances around, as if picturing the scene, and I grasp onto the lapels of his jacket. "I won't lie. For a second, I wished I had your number so I could've just..." My voice is low as it trails off.

"I'll give my card to you later," he mutters, then presses

his lips against my forehead so briefly, I'm not sure it really happened.

"I'm so tired." The words are out before I really thought them. My eyes threaten to close as Blake's arm comes back around me.

He nods. "I know. Almost there, sweetheart," he assures me, using the same tone I do when I want to calm the kids and make them fall asleep.

When we reach his car and he helps me inside, I grasp his jacket and pull him toward me, pressing my lips against his for a brief second. "I'm gonna pay you for gas for taking me home," I tell him and lean my head back against the seat. If he finds my randomness weird, he doesn't say so.

Through drowsy eyes, I watch him walk around the car and climb behind the wheel.

"Buckle up," he orders. I blindly reach for the seat belt, drawing it around my body and fumbling to snap it closed.

Blake reaches over to help. His fingers against my skin feel nice. I turn toward him a little when he starts the car.

"I don't know why you help me. You shouldn't. I'm no one." Realizing how ridiculous that sounds, I add, "I'm no one to you." *Much better. Less pitiful.*

He doesn't even look at me, his face illuminated by the dashboard. I want to reach out and touch each freckle on his nose.

"I'm a cop. I help people," he replies, and I smile to myself.

"Sure." My lids are heavy. "I'm glad you were at the bar, Blake. I didn't feel like cleaning up the mess I made." I know if I keep talking, I won't fall asleep.

It's a good thing he lives close to my place because, that way, he can park at his own place and I can just walk the rest of the way to mine, not having to give him my address. The last thing I need is for him to know how to find me.

Besides at the bar, that is.

He huffs quietly, but stays silent.

"What?" I prompt.

Warm knuckles brush along my jaw and back up. "Sleep, Tia. I'll wake you when we're close," he orders softly, his voice a nice hum in my head.

"No, I'm gonna stay awake. I'll stay awake." I try to stifle a yawn, telling myself I need to last just a few minutes longer. How long can the drive really be?

When we went to his place after the ball, the drive felt like minutes. I also remember how soft his bed was and nearly sigh, imagining being right there that moment.

I smile to myself. As much as I want it, that won't ever happen again.

Blake

A side glance proves Tia's asleep. Her hand rests on the center console, as if she'd been ready to reach out, then decided against it. I brush my fingertips over her skin and discover that she's ice cold.

I pull over to the side of the road and take off my jacket, draping it over her. I also crank up the heat a little, but not so much that I'll be uncomfortable. I take a detour, driving around aimlessly for at least an hour. Sometimes I'm surprised how peaceful the city can be at this time of night, then I remember that just because we don't see the demons hiding in the shadows doesn't mean they aren't there.

Tia shifts. I pull the jacket back up to her chin, wondering why she wakes all these protective instincts in me.

Besides the fact that she fits the killer's preference, that is.

"Tia," I whisper softly, touching her shoulder. "Tell me your address."

She sighs, swatting my hand away, mumbling in her sleep.

"Tia," I try again.

She just shakes her head, causing me to smile. I glance at the dash, thinking that she probably still has a few hours until someone expects her home, and while I shouldn't take her to my place, I can't help but feel smug concerning the douche she has at home.

Parking across from the building's entrance, I nudge her again, but she just turns into my touch, making my heart skip a beat before I slip out of the car and walk over to her side, opening the door.

"Woman, I'll have to carry you if you don't wake up."

Her eyes open for a brief moment. "Okay," she replies, then moves forward. It takes a second for me to realize that she really wants me to pick her up.

"Walking is out of question?" I joke as she wraps her arms around my neck.

"Carry me, white knight."

The words sound sleepy, sluggish. I smile to myself, glad she's holding on because it makes it easier to unlock the door and call for the elevator. Luckily, we don't see anyone; otherwise, I'd probably have to explain why I am carrying an unresponsive woman around.

Once we're inside my apartment, I carry her to the bedroom and place her onto the bed. "Take off your shoes and jeans," I order, nudging her until she starts moving.

I help her with the shoes, then turn away as she kicks off her jeans, eyes still closed. It doesn't matter that we slept with each other. This is different because I cannot be sure she's aware of what she's doing.

The sheets rustle and I turn around. Seeing her eyes on me, I kneel next to the bed. "Thank you," she whispers and reaches out, brushing her fingertips over my cheek, then my lips. She shouldn't be that gentle with me, yet I don't turn away from the touch.

Instead, I comb my hand through her blonde stands. "You're welcome, Tia."

"I'll see you around, okay? Be quiet. The kids are asleep," she warns me, then turns away, making me smirk. I slip out of my bedroom and walk into my kitchen, my body and mind wide awake.

When my phone rings, I pick up, keeping my voice low. "Atwood."

"You took her home? Blake, what the hell?" Hearing amusement in Kelly's voice, I can't help but smile.

"Well... At least she thinks she's in her own bed. She wasn't awake long enough to tell me her address, and I wasn't going to let her sleep in my car."

Kelly snickers. "Convenient."

I roll my eyes, even though he cannot see it. "We both know that I would've taken her home. Kelly, she has a family, kids, and..."

"You aren't gonna help her cheat?"

That isn't the way I want to end that sentence.

"Domestic abuse comes in many forms. Something at home brought her to the brink of exhaustion. I want her to realize she has options."

I'm a police officer. I can't look past what her significant other is doing to her. Or is it what she's doing to herself to please him?

"Blake, you're in love with her." The statement is matter-of-fact. As much as I'm inclined to deny it, I stay silent. That might be exactly it.

"I guess I need to make sure she leaves the asshole behind." I don't know why I said the words, other than it's on my mind right now.

Kelly clears his throat. "She has three kids, Blake."

"I know, but I'd still help her even if she didn't want to be with me. I cannot let her get hurt over this. You saw her. Hell, when we got back here, I couldn't even wake her up."

He stays silent for the longest time, then sighs. "Fine. I pray she feels for you what you feel for her; otherwise, it'll be weird finding one-night stands to hook up with."

I know he's teasing, trying to make light of a situation. "I don't even want one any longer."

He smirks. "Except with her."

Yeah, but that ain't gonna happen again until I know she's free to be mine, I think to myself.

Kelly and I hang up. I hope I can find some sleep before Tia has to leave. This time, I'm not going to let her slip out on me, no matter what.

CHAPTER TEN

TIA

I WAKE WITH A START. It takes me a moment to realize I'm in bed. I dreamed I was at work, then Blake took me home. I reach for the phone on my nightstand, but when it seems farther away than usual, it settles in that it wasn't a dream.

I look around the room. *Blake's* room. I also feel I'm not wearing pants. Panicking for a minute, I vaguely remember taking them off myself.

I sit up and check the time on my cell. It's only three. I probably only slept a few hours, yet I feel more rested than I have in a while.

I forego my jeans, although I know I should dress and walk home. Instead, I see one of Blake's police hoodies draped over a chair and pull it over my head, smiling when it reaches to my thighs.

I find him sitting in the living room, bent over a file. I walk over quietly, clearing my throat before I brush my fingertips across the collar of his shirt, then settle down on the couch next to him, close enough so our bodies touch.

His eyes are on me, questioning, searching, as if trying to figure out what's going on. I don't know what comes over me, but I cup his cheek and draw him in, not missing the way he closes his eyes, looking as if he regrets the kiss before it even happens.

His lips are soft and strangely undemanding. We've kissed before, but he always owned the kiss, was the one dominating it, but today, he just takes what I offer.

It's a silent "thank you", I guess, and a plea for something I know I cannot have or openly ask for.

"Why are you awake?" I ask.

He rolls his shoulders, as if trying to shake off tension, then starts flipping through the pages of the file again. Blake's thoughtful silence makes me wish I could comfort him, so I rest my head against his shoulder.

He sighs. "What are we doing, Tia? You have kids to take care off and are in a relationship. Granted, he's an ass, but..." He shakes his head.

I finally open my mouth to set the record straight when he points at a picture in the file. A picture of a little boy.

"Jackson Davis and his sister, Lou, were found dead. Abused, mutilated. We found the stranger who did it, but when we chased him down, he pointed a gun at us. He wouldn't put it down, no matter how often I told him to. When I saw his finger twitch on the trigger...I shot him," he explains.

"You are a hero, Blake," I whisper.

He hesitates, then draws my legs over his, pulling me closer. "I killed a man. In fact, I've killed a few. While I know they were cruel and hurt others, I've...I've killed people." His voice cracks.

I run my fingers through his hair. "Is that what keeps you up at night?"

He rests his head in his hands. "Sometimes I dream about the exact moment I shot them, only to find out they were innocent. Other times, I have nightmares where they sit next to me on the bed and tell me what a useless cop I am, that I'll die from a bullet one day. I hear all their voices and..." He lifts his tear-filled eyes to mine. "Nights are hard."

I rest my lips against his shoulder. "I can only imagine," I whisper. I've never killed a person, and I certainly never want to be in that position. Just thinking about it has me shivering. "Tell me about the other people in that file."

It's obvious they are supposed to serve as a reminder to him. I listen as he explains the photos and the cruelty of the crimes. Eventually, he wraps his arms around me, caressing my back.

Cleary, Blake has looked at those pages often. I wonder why he constantly puts himself through this.

"Do all your team members feel the same, Blake? Do they suffer from it? I guess it would be a form of PTSD."

"I don't know. We don't exactly talk about things like that. I should... I had the mandatory psychologist visits after each, but..." He shrugs.

I pull away and arch a brow. "You're not honest with them, are you?" Seeing the ashamed look in his eyes, it suddenly clicks. "If you are, they'd most likely take you out of active duty for a while, right?"

"Being a detective is my life, Tia. I cannot imagine what I'd do if they took away my badge for any length of time. It doesn't matter how many people I've killed or how often I've dreamed about them. I mean, we justify it all with saying we're saving lives, but can we really know if they would've killed again?"

"Blake," I whisper, moving my face so he looks at me, but he refuses to. I cup his cheeks with my hands and climb into his lap, making it impossible for him to focus anywhere else. All I want is to ease Blake's pain.

BLAKE

I don't know why I told Tia all of that. I once mentioned it to Kelly in passing, but that was it. But this heart-to-heart?

It's a sucker punch to the gut because it cements what Kelly and I talked about earlier.

"Blake," Tia repeats, her hands still holding me captive. I finally look at her. "It doesn't matter," she starts. I'm about to protest, but she places her thumbs on my lips. "It doesn't matter if they would've killed again. They had already killed somebody. What *innocent* person would carry around a gun and draw it on police officers? What *innocent* person would do anything they could to get away if they didn't have anything to hide? None, Blake. No *innocent* person would do that."

I swallow around the lump in my throat. "What happens next time if I just think the guy is drawing a gun but there is none? What if I make the wrong split-second decision?"

She brushes my cheeks, her touch tender and soothing. "When do you make that split-second decision?"

I blink. "What do you mean?"

She shrugs. "You corner a suspect. When does Detective Blake Atwood decide to shoot? The moment he reaches into his pocket? The moment he pulls something out of it? When. Do. You. Shoot?"

Licking my lips, I think about her question. "The moment

he threatens to shoot any of us. We are taught to react to the first sign of a risk, instantly deciphering who could be hurt, but... I always hope we can solve it differently. I mean, if I feel my partners' lives are threatened, I don't hesitate to jump into the line of fire, but..."

She's right. Some shoot much faster than I do. Hell, I've gotten injured because I've hesitated.

She frowns. "What makes your life worth less than everyone else's?"

This one is easy. "I don't have a family at home. My parents and sister live far away. It's not like I'd—" When her brows furrow in anger, I quickly stop.

"Wrong answer," she states. "The right answer is, it's *not* worth less. Your life is worth as much as those with kids and a wife at home. I know you have dreams in your life, Blake. You aren't disposable. Think about this." She cocks her head, her expression set. "Kelly, that weird and charming best friend you have, and Will, as well as everyone else on your team, would always prefer you to any scum. From the little I know, I can honestly say I feel confident that if they have to make a choice between your life and that of some fucker who is shady as hell, they'd always pick you." She swallows. "I would, too," she adds quietly.

"Tia..." I don't know what I want to say, but I know I'm glad she's here. I cup the back of her neck and draw her closer.

I know some people don't consider kissing cheating. While I'm usually not in that category, I tell myself that I am today.

Before our lips touch, she presses her hand against my chest. "There's no boyfriend or husband, Blake. I swear," she whispers.

I search her eyes, but there's no hesitation, no doubt, no lie to be found. "Tia, I'm not going to... I..."

She places my palm against her chest, and I can feel her steady heartbeat. "I promise there is no boyfriend or husband I could cheat on. No girlfriend, no wife..." She smiles softly. "Just in case you start wondering about that. If it makes you feel better, we don't even have to do anything, but I'd...I'd like to stay just a little bit longer."

Her heart only jumped once, and that was when she mentioned staying. She licks her lips, and I close my eyes. "I'm not sure I believe you, but by God, please stay. I need... I..."

Disappointment enters her gaze, but it vanishes as quickly as it came, so I ignore the way it stabs at my heart. She has three kids. I doubt she's raising them alone when she works at night.

"I told you what keeps me up at night. Will you tell me what you fear?" I ask quietly. If I cannot lose myself in her, I can at least try to get to know her better.

"Are you asking about my nightmares?" There's a small smile on her lips.

I smile, too. "I'm asking for you to allow me to get to know all about you. What do you fear?"

She's still in my lap, but that's all. We're close, yet not too close. My mind's convinced there is no significant other, but my heart still worries because none of this makes sense.

"Loneliness. This bartender fears loneliness. I... What if I devote my life to people who don't care, who don't appreciate it?"

I cock my head, watching her for a moment, wondering what she's asking. "They're kids, Tia. Of course they don't appreciate it. And being a mom isn't exactly something that—"

"You slept okay when I was next to you, right?" she asks,

quickly changing the subject. I wonder if she's hiding something.

"I did, yes," I admit. She climbs off my lap, grasping my hand.

"Come on. I'm not leaving just yet, and there's no one waiting up for me, so let's make sure you get some sleep. I could use a few more hours myself."

I'm on my feet before my mind realizes it and let her pull me into the bedroom. She takes off my shirt and opens my jeans. I draw her into my arms, holding her against me for a few minutes.

"You're not alone, Tia. Just... Trust me."

I know it's ironic to ask that of her when I'm really not sure I can trust her, either, but when I feel her lips press against my chest, I can't help but feel as if, one day, there will be no more secrets between us and I'll still want her as much as I crave her that moment.

CHAPTER ELEVEN

BLAKE

"FUCK."

I startle at Tia's curse and sit up, wondering what happened, but all I see is her trying to pull on her pants.

"I should've set an alarm. I was sure I'd wake up. I always do. Shit," she mutters, and I swing my legs off the bed.

"I'm taking you home. It'll be faster than you walking." I don't know why I offer, but after last night, I want to see where she lives, see what her morning routine is.

She pauses. "You are?"

I nod and pull on dark jeans, then a shirt and a hoodie. She still wears the one she pulled on last night, and I have to admit, I like how it looks on her. I don't even mention it when she rushes out of the bedroom and into the bathroom. I join her, seeing her brushing her teeth with a fingertip.

I wink, reaching into a drawer. "I got a spare toothbrush."

It's funny how something as mundane as brushing our teeth together makes me think I could do this every damn day and never tire of it. She combs out her hair with her fingers, then pulls it into a messy ponytail. Even though we're rushing, this feels...nice.

Once we're in the car, she leans over and kisses my cheek. "Thank you, Blake. For everything."

"You're very welcome." I squeeze her hand briefly, and then wait for her to tell me where to go.

When she gives me her address, I nod. I don't need directions, knowing my way around the streets, and even before she points out the entrance, I know which one it is because I recognize the two kids sitting on the steps, an older girl and a woman walking out as we pull up.

The car hasn't even stopped before Tia jumps out, stepping toward the four. I can't help but think I should leave, but I'm way too curious about what's going on.

"Auntie Tia!" the little girl greets her, and my heart soars.

They aren't her kids...

"Chlo, I'm sorry. I—"

Tia doesn't get to finish before the woman slaps her so hard, I see all three kids wince. I jump out of the car. In less than two steps, I stand between the woman and Tia, my hackles rising.

"Problem?" I growl.

She glares at me before looking around me at Tia. "You don't turn up because you're *fucking* some dude, making me have to call work and tell them I'll be late because I need to bring the kids to school? Are you fucking serious?"

Tia steps to my side, still holding her cheek. "Language, Chloe. Your kids. Get to work. I'll take care of the little ones," she says. I see her body trembling.

All three children huddle around her instead of their mother, which tells me all I need to know.

She wasn't talking about the kids last night when she

mentioned sacrificing everything for people who don't appreciate it.

She was talking about her sister.

A sister who now steps toward her and raises her hand, which I grab instantly. "Slap her again and I'll take you in," I state, meaning it. I wouldn't think twice about it because Tia's cheek glows an angry red color, which makes me furious.

She narrows her eyes at me, yanking her hand away. "And who the hell are you?"

I give her a malicious grin. "Detective Blake Atwood with the NYPD, and I just witnessed you cause another citizen physical harm. Now, you can either walk away, or we can talk about this down at the precinct."

Tia places her hand on my arm. "Blake, stop. It's okay."

It's not, but I don't say that. The woman in front of me glares at both of us. "I'm off. You can explain to the schools why they are late."

She marches off. I follow her before Tia can stop me. I step in front of her, and she startles.

I lower my voice. "Listen, and listen good. Touch her or talk to her the way you have again, and I swear, I will get you for something. A night in a holding cell might put some things into perspective for you."

With that, I return to Tia's side. I can tell she's trying hard not to cry. The toddler fuses in a stroller the oldest girl holds onto, so I crouch down next to her.

"I'm Blake, your aunt Tia's friend. What's your name?"

I see the mistrust as her gaze goes to Tia standing behind me. Whatever Tia does seems to satisfy the girl because she gives me a smile. "I'm Liv. I'm already grown up and a big girl. But... I'm late for school."

"Which is why we need to go."

I glance back at my car, knowing I don't have car seats.

"Get in, Tia. You hold the little one, and I'll strap the other two into the back."

After everyone's buckled in, I fold the stroller and place it into the trunk, then slip behind the wheel.

Tia's worried expression meets my gaze. "You might get into trouble, Blake," she whispers. I lean over and give her a quick kiss on the lips.

"We'll be okay. Which schools?"

She directs me to Liv's first. I walk the child in, making sure the badge hanging around my neck shows. When Liv wraps her small arms around my middle, telling me thank you, I get a little choked up.

Next, we take Pauli to her preschool. As she wraps her arms around me, I smile. I think I like these kids.

When I climb back into the car, I tilt Tia's chin up, seeing the red handprint on her cheek. It makes me furious. "Why didn't you tell me they were your sister's kids?"

She shrugs. "You were so quick to assume things about me, it pissed me off. Then I figured it didn't matter because…"

I nod. "They are basically yours, except you didn't give birth to them?"

"I'm not free to be anyone's girlfriend, Blake. I might be free a night here and there, but you saw what happened this morning. It's not the kids' fault their mother is…" She sighs. "This whole thing is my fault."

I highly doubt that, but when my phone buzzes in my pocket, I know there's no time to talk about it now.

———

TIA

Had I known that morning would be the last time I'd see Blake for days, I might not have let him drive off without demanding to know when we'd see each other again. I want to explain to him why Chloe was so angry, want to justify her behavior. I know I shouldn't.

As I make my way to work, I can't help but miss him. He hasn't even come into the bar lately, and although I have seen Kelly around, Blake's absence sticks out.

My neck tingles and I rub it. I pinch the bridge of my nose, my mind still on Blake. The night we spent talking at his place was intense. I keep turning my answers over in my head.

Someone bumps into me, and it's only then I realize I'm taking up almost the whole sidewalk. Before I can apologize to the man, he's already walked away. I know I should try harder to focus.

Things at home finally eased up a little. Luckily, having met Blake and hearing his threats, Chloe seems to have woken up.

Granted, it might have also been the screaming match we had when she got home later than usual, blaming me for everything. Thankfully, Warrick had been forgiving when I'd been late that night.

Again, my neck tingles and I glance around, seeing nothing. I stop and turn, just to make sure it's not Donna. Then again, I know she should be at work already, but part of me hopes that's why I feel watched again.

I have Blake's number in my phone this time, but as much as I long for any excuse to talk to him, maybe find out if he simply gave up on me because of my complicated life, I don't want to bother him in case he's busy.

When I resume walking, I spot someone standing outside

the bar, waving at me. My heart speeds up, only to plummet a second later. He's too tall, too broad in the shoulders, and too much a firefighter to be the detective I'm longing for.

"Hi, Kelly," I greet him, and he gives me a smile.

"Tia." He makes a move as if to hug me, then doesn't, scratching the back of his neck instead. "Hi. I wanted to check on you and just... You know."

I smirk. "Are you hitting on me, or are you here because of Blake?"

He laughs, a blush coloring his cheeks. "Technically, I'm on shift, but he's worried, so I promised him I'd check on you. They have a few leads on one of their cases, so he's been caught up at the station. It's easier for me to get away, but..." He reaches out, touching my cheek like a big brother would. "He wanted me to remind you to call him anytime something's wrong, or...just whenever you need it. You're good, aren't you?"

I nod, feeling all warm and fuzzy. "I am. Chloe lets me sleep more and sometimes takes the kids." I have no doubt Blake told him all about what happened, and when Kelly nods, I know my assumption is right.

"How is work?"

I arch a brow. "It's work. People come in, buy beer, I'm nice, they tip me, I growl at them, they tip me more."

He chuckles, then turns serious again. "Okay. Watch your back. Promise me."

I grab the lapel of his jacket, worried he'll leave before I know what's going on. "Tell me what I'm missing. It's just work, Kelly. It's a bar, but I can handle that."

He nods. "No doubt, but it's you getting *to* and *from* work that worries Blake, okay? It's late, it's dark, it's dingy, we're in New York. That's all."

Lowering my head so he doesn't see the amusement in my

eyes, I promise to be careful and thank him for coming. I watch him leave, then slip inside, finding Warrick grinning at me.

"And what's the emergency that warranted a visit by the NYFD?"

I laugh, feeling stupidly giddy. Blake sending someone to check on me means he cares. "Well, unless you call a worried detective an emergency... Blake sent him to check on me. You know, after he took me home, he hasn't been around. I think he worries that..."

"Chloe's hurting you again?"

I nod and tell him what transpired between Blake and Chloe.

"I think it's more that he's worried I don't sleep much, but I got it. I promise."

He nods, then takes a deep breath. "So, business has been really good, and you and Donna are incredible. Between the three of us, we manage to keep this place open every day of the week. I know the last thing you want is more time off, so... To show you and Donna how much I appreciate you both working the way you do, I'm giving you something special and Donna more time off. I hired a college student to come in whenever Donna's off. But here's the best part. You get a babysitter for Neo. She's right around the corner, and three days a week, you can take the little boy over."

I stare at Warrick, my throat constricting. "No, I cannot take that," I whisper. "I'm serious. It's okay. Chloe and I... We have our issues, but I think we're getting there."

He gives me a kind smile. "She's been background checked and I know she's decent, so I insist. I need you here, Tia, because no one handles patrons the way you do. Having found you was the best thing that happened to this bar, so..."

I shake my head, tears in my eyes, then grin. "I have to get to work. You know, my boss might not like me standing around all the time." I go onto my tiptoes and kiss his cheek, then walk behind the bar, Donna winking at me.

Still, as I survey the room, I can't help but wish Blake were here just so I could see him and tell him the good news.

BLAKE

"I don't think that's our man," I tell Will and shift in my seat in the SUV.

We've gotten a few leads because, unfortunately, there seems to be a leak in the station and people have heard about the murders. Although we don't appreciate it, we can't help but be glad about the new information.

These cases have stalled, and while that also means there are no new murders, I can't help but be constantly itchy.

The guy we're currently observing has been seen in the vicinity of the crime scenes, and while he never actually stepped foot in any of the bars, it doesn't mean he's innocent.

Will sighs next to me and reaches for his cold burger. "Even if no one else dies and we know for a fact he was here the whole time, he can still be our guy. But I agree. While he most likely is guilty of being a creep, I don't think he's the *right* creep."

We've watched the guy putter around his apartment for the better part of the night. He keeps locking and re-locking the windows, but that's about it.

"I'm gonna go talk to him," I decide.

It's eleven at night and would be too early to go out and kill a bartender anyway, but we're working on the theory that he stalks them, learning their routines. He won't get that by sitting home all the time. Then again, just because he's home doesn't mean he hasn't already targeted his next victim.

I'm about to open the door, but Will grabs my arm. "It's late. What are you gonna tell him?"

I grin. "Come along and see. I'm just curious what he has to hide."

We cross the street to the three-story house and push inside, ringing the doorbell to our right.

After a few seconds, our guy opens the door and I flash my badge. He doesn't flinch or pale at seeing us, which means he is either cold-blooded or has nothing to hide.

"Officers," he greets us.

"Sir, your neighbors from across the street reported you constantly checking your windows. They find that highly suspicious. We know it's a stupid reason to call anyone in, but the rule is we have to check out every report." I add an annoyed eyeroll for good measure.

Even though there really are no rules for that kind of situation, I need him to believe me.

He nods. "I understand. But what do they accuse me of?" He looks angry, but not like he's about to murder anyone for sending the police to his door.

Will clears his throat. "They're just wondering if you have something to hide," he says calmly. The guy just shakes his head and steps aside, letting us in without even having to ask.

Will and I exchange a glance. I'm pretty sure he's thinking the same. This isn't our guy.

"Everyone should know why I'm like that. I mean, most of my neighbors installed new security systems, but I just don't have the money. Living on the ground floor, I feel better checking the windows repeatedly. You know, with all the robberies around here." He practically falls into his armchair. "I don't have much, but I'd like to keep it. Especially because the chances of me dying during a robbery are so high."

I start to walk around his living room, glancing around. He has movies, most of them of the romantic kind, and some non-violent games.

Hell, this guy might has well have tits and two cats.

"Why would you die during a robbery, sir?" Will asks as I walk over to the window and glance out. The neighborhood isn't the best or the worst. It's one where you, technically, can walk your dog at night without fear of being caught up in a gang war, but one where you don't want to linger while doing so.

The guy clears his throat and shifts in his chair. "Well, what would robbers do with someone who's home? I work from here because I'm an IT technician and a systems administrator. The only time I go out is when I need to grab parts for my computer. Yes, I could order that online, but I'd rather see what I buy. Even then, I'm out... What? Two hours, max, and that's just because my two favorite computer stores are in those parts of New York where they thought the former factories would thrive." He snorts. "All they have there now are computer shops, a hardware store, and bars."

Which would explain why he's been where people saw him. Still, it gives us something to follow-up on.

"Well," I say, making it obvious to Will that I think we can leave, "it's safe to say there are no dead blondes in here."

He doesn't even flinch. "How in the world would I get dead blondes in here? No girl comes here out of her own volition, and I sure as hell couldn't carry any in here. But thanks for thinking I'm strong enough to be able to." He grins, then stands. "This was the nicest talk I've had in a while. Thank you, Officers."

I incline my head at Will, then walk over to the door, stepping out into the hall. I wait until the guy closes the door, then shake my head, chuckling.

"Nope," we say together, then step back out onto the street.

Will blows out a breath. "Okay. So we need to check if he was telling the truth about the robberies around here and the computer stores. My bet? He'll check out."

I sigh. "Yeah, sadly. I'd rather have found newspaper clippings about the murders hanging on his wall."

Will laughs and slips behind the wheel. "Same, but at least there's no need to hang out here any longer. Who knows? Maybe you'll still get to see your bartender tonight."

I advert my gaze, wondering how he caught on to me when I'd tried to be inconspicuous about passing the bar just in the hopes for catching a glimpse of Tia. "Whatever," I reply.

He laughs, starting the SUV.

TIA

It's late when I leave the bar. When my neck starts to immediately tingle, more pronounced than before, I pull out my phone, wondering if I'll wake Blake. Then I realize I don't care—and he probably won't, either.

It rings only once before he answers. "Atwood."

Just hearing his voice makes my heart settle even while it skips a beat. "Detective, I have the feeling you've been neglecting your favorite bar," I say, hoping to sound upbeat and light.

He clearly looks right through me because he asks, "What's going on, Tia? Are you okay?"

I chuckle, glancing around, even though my worry evaporated the second I heard his voice. "I'm fine. Did I wake you?"

He clears his throat. "Will you hang up if I say you did?"

"No, because I know you'd be lying. Your voice sounds raspier right after waking."

"And you called me Detective, which makes me think you wanted to make it obvious you were talking to the police. What's going on?"

The subway isn't far, and I suddenly realize I won't get any reception down there. That means if someone's following me, they could easily grab me there.

"I'm on my way home. I... I don't know. I feel... I'm..." I take a deep breath. "You know, it's probably nothing."

"Where are you?"

I glance around. "Where are *you*?" Because if he's home... I hear a car door slam over the phone.

"I'm in my car in front of the precinct. Where are you?" he asks again.

I glance around. "Almost at the subway station. I just closed the bar with Warrick."

I hear his car start. "Stay on the phone. I'll meet you there and take you home, then you tell me exactly what is going on, okay?"

"Okay," I reply, although I'm no longer sure there is something to tell him. "So, I assume you worked late again?" It's obvious, but I need something to talk about.

"I'm sorry I didn't come by and see you," he says instead of replying, his voice soft, making my insides go mushy.

I clear my throat and stare up at the sky. "I'd be lying if I said I hadn't looked for you to walk through the door."

Headlights illuminate my surroundings. I didn't realize how close the precinct and the bar were. I hang up. He gets out and comes over to my side.

"Hey." He looks uneasy for a second, then shakes his head and steps close, framing my face with his hands and kissing me softly.

When he pulls back, he rests his forehead against mine, his thumbs brushing over my cheeks. "Hey," he says again. This time it's gentle, soft...relieved.

"Blake." I touch my nose to his, steal a tiny kiss, then step back. I know he said he doesn't do serious, and neither do I, but this... This makes me want to try. However, seeing where we are in our lives, I can't help but think this would be all we could be—late-night kisses and stolen moments.

"Come on. I'll take you home." He opens the door and I get in, watching him walk around the hood of the car, then slip behind the wheel. "What scared you?" he asks, pulling the car back onto the road.

Sitting in his car, warmth coming from the heater, I can't help but feel stupid. "I felt someone watching me. Like... When I got to work, I already had that feeling, but there was no one. I just... I don't know. The officers coming in now are all uneasy, and some watch Donna closer than before. Like... Like you'd watch your daughter or something. It's put me on edge."

He takes my hand, brushing his thumb over the back of it before letting go again. "I'm glad you called. Seriously. I was... I missed seeing you. And I'm worried about you. You know, with Chloe and all..."

I close my eyes, remembering what else I meant to tell him. "I'm sorry I didn't make it obvious before that those aren't my kids, and that, you know, I didn't have a husband."

He glances at me briefly, brows furrowed. "Why didn't you?"

I shrug. "Because I was pissed that you judged me and thought I was the type of person to cheat. Then I figured it was the best way to keep you at arm's length. I didn't count on..." I swallow, "count on wanting a repeat performance."

He smirks for a moment, then winks at me. "Which you didn't get because of the lie."

I hesitate for a moment. "Not that day, but maybe another time... I'm going to try and convince Chloe to be home more, and you have a messed-up sleeping schedule, so picking me up after work occasionally shouldn't be a problem, right?"

His smirk vanishes, and my heart settles into an uneasy rhythm. I'm the one who suggested an affair, but I still have no idea where I would find time for a serious relationship, so it's really all I can offer.

"Occasionally, huh?" he asks quietly.

I rest my head back against the seat, my eyes on him. I nod. "I didn't forget that you don't do serious. In fact, I heard you don't even do repeats, so maybe I should be glad that—"

He takes my hand again, squeezing. "Forget what you hear. People like to talk, and men are sometimes worse than women." He smiles briefly at me, then focuses back on the road. "Promise me something, Tia."

Anything. The word is on my tongue, yet I don't let it slip out. "What?"

"No matter what, always call me if you feel unsafe. I don't care what time it is. Next time, walk back into the bar and I'll pick you up there, okay?"

I swallow. "What if it's just my imagination?"

"Call me," he repeats, and I find myself promising him exactly that.

CHAPTER TWELVE

BLAKE

"SUIT UP," Wolfe calls out.

I arch a brow at Will. Another week has passed without a murder or a decent lead, so we've taken on some other cases. Today, we're scheduled to help storm a drug den or something. I didn't ask for specifics.

I grab my Kevlar vest and shrug it on. Checking my gun and putting it into my holster, I nod at Will. Declan, Jimmy, and Nikki are ready, too. The last one is Wolfe, who seems to be on edge.

"We'll get instructions when we get there. Remember, this is not our case. Arrests will be made by the guys from Narcotics."

We all nod, then follow him outside. He, Jim, and Nikki take the lead in his car, Declan, Will, and I in a car right behind them.

My mind is a million miles away, mainly because I've been talking to Tia every night. She doesn't let me drive her home, only calling me when she is finally there. Either way, it eases my mind.

There isn't even much for us to talk about most times, but I like hearing her fall asleep. I wonder how much longer we can lie to each other about not wanting this to be something more.

There is the issue of time. I know she doesn't have much free time during the day, and when we finally solve this murder case and my hours go back to somewhat regular, we won't have many days together.

God, I cannot believe I'm thinking about a relationship when I've done everything in my power to avoid one for such a long time.

"Wonder what we'll be walking into. Might be dangerous," Will mutters from next to me. I turn in my seat, holding his eyes. There's a challenge in them, and I can't help but feel as if he's telling me to text Tia because we don't know what's coming.

Or maybe that's just wishful thinking because I want to let her know I'm thinking about her. Then again, it would probably just worry her. I never check in during the day.

I never check in period.

"I don't care. I've missed the action. Besides, finally catching bad guys again will make me feel as if we've accomplished something. These bartender cases do my head in. I mean, why kill two women, then just stop? Especially when he's sure he killed the wrong ones?" I arch a brow at him. We've been over the same argument time and time again, yet I want to do it just one more time.

"Maybe he's afraid. Maybe he realized one of them was the right one after all. We talked to their families and friends more than once. Whatever he was looking for, maybe he realized he'd found it in the last victim," Will states, indulging me.

Not that I like the idea of him roaming the streets, but thinking there'll never be another victim seems like a good exchange.

Declan shakes his head. "I doubt that." He clears his throat. "Honestly, I don't like the idea of him out there, and neither do you, Blake. Your obsession with a certain blonde bartender is no longer a secret. I won't even lie. If you wouldn't have a claim on her—"

"Shut it, Dec, or I'll punch you," Will says, his tone sugary sweet. I can't help but feel glad my partner has my back.

I smirk. "Even if I wouldn't have claim on her, Kelly would already be barking up that tree."

In the back seat, Declan groans. Next to me, Will smirks. We all know there's no winning against Kelly once he turns on the charm.

"It would be such a waste, though," he points out. "Kelly never claims them for long, and we don't need her broken before—"

"We're close."

I don't want to talk about Tia being with anybody else, so I'm glad when we enter an area that's known to be full of gangs. We haven't had a case here in a while because a few months back, there'd been a horrible shootout between gangs, terrible losses on both sides. While other teams tried to find out who shoot whom, I know no one will ever be prosecuted.

Gang members don't talk.

The mood in the car shifts. Yes, we're only the backup, but that doesn't mean it will be less dangerous. Suddenly, I remember exactly why I never let anyone into my life. Still, when the need arises to text Kelly and ask him to watch out for Tia should something happen to me, I know I'm in too deep.

TIA

I'm on the couch when the front door unlocks, glad the girls are busy in their room.

I stand. "Hey, Chloe. I'm glad you're home," I say and see her wince, as if I caught her doing something wrong.

"I forgot something and wanted to grab it. I thought you were going to take the kids to the zoo today for a few hours since they didn't have school." She seems on edge.

"I was, but Neo started to throw up and I didn't want to be out with him."

"Oh."

I roll my eyes. "Yes, he's okay. Thank you for asking. He found the girls' stash of sweets and ate it all. I'm so glad you're concerned about your kids." I can't keep the sarcasm out of my voice, and she shrugs a shoulder carelessly.

I can't believe how snobbish my sister is sometimes.

"You obviously got it under control, so why should I be worried? Anyway, I have to run and—"

"No, you don't."

She freezes on her way past me. "You don't get to tell me what I do or don't have to do."

I don't want to fight with her, hate the thought, but I know it will happen today. Otherwise, I'll probably never confront her to solve all this.

"Actually, I do. I'm your *big sister* and am tired of you treating me like your personal maid and slave. I've always tried to help you, but it's time you started watching your own kids and cleaning around here. You know perfectly well how to do the dishes and load the washing machine."

I shift Neo in my arms. "I want more time for myself. I need you to cut back on your hours."

Her face turns from pale to red within seconds. "Cut back on my hours? Just because you want more time for *yourself*? Is this about the police guy? You want to neglect your family just to get a roll in the sheets more often? Seriously. If I cut back, you'll have even less time. I work so hard because you asked for Neo to start going to a babysitter and—"

"He's been going to one for a few days," I interrupt.

She blinks. "How?" There's utter shock in her voice.

"You don't have to pay for it. That's the only thing you need to worry about."

A malicious smile breaks out over Chloe's face. "Then there are your free hours. What exactly are we talking about here? Besides, I'm in a hurry."

She tries to move around me, but I step in her way. "I'm talking about weekends. I want you to take your kids then so I can go back to volunteering at the retirement home for a few hours. I miss it. Also, I want to be able to sleep in the mornings. You know... That thing you need to function properly? A few weeks ago, I nearly collapsed from exhaustion. I'm not doing that any longer. I love you, Chlo, and I love the kids more than you can imagine, but it's time you start being a mom."

She grits her teeth, stepping close. I push her back so she won't hurt her son. "Listen, Tia. I know you think you are the most *gracious* woman out there because you helped me when I needed it most, but that doesn't mean you get to go all high and mighty on me. Who pays the biggest part of everything here, huh? I don't think it's you and your lowly job."

I kiss Neo's head and set him onto the floor, just in case. "Knock it off. I pay the electricity. I pay for the groceries. I pay the water bill—"

"You do not. Those are all included in the rent, which I pay."

I choke out a surprised laugh. "You think that's *included* in the rent? Well, it's not, and just in case you don't realize it, you also don't pay all of the rent."

She lifts her chin. "Yes. I leave the money on the kitchen table and—"

"It's a little more than half of it, Chloe, but that's it. I pay the rest from tips and my paycheck. It's why I work all the time. Literally. Also, I pay everything at the kids' school because you never take them there. So, here's the way it's going to work from now on. On the days Neo is at the babysitter, *you* bring the kids to school. *You* get up earlier, fix them breakfast, and be a mother. I know you can do it because you did it until nine months ago. I know you're busy at work, but let's face it. We can make do with one or two less hours and will just buy cheaper clothes."

She grabs the lapels of her coat. "I don't know what you're talking about. I already buy everything secondhand."

I let the lie slide. "Weekends are mine, unless otherwise discussed. Monday, Tuesday, and Thursday, you bring the kids to school and the babysitter. Now, you may go." I sweep Neo back into my arms and head for the girls' room. I think we should at least go to the playground for a little while.

Also, it gives me an excuse to be away from Chloe. Luckily, after a minute or two, I hear the front door close. I finally have peace—or so I hope.

I dress the kids and consider shooting Blake a message, letting him know I finally talked to Chloe and demanded some time off, then reconsider because I never want to interrupt his work or give him the impression he needs to make time for me. I mean, just because I now have more free time doesn't mean he and I will be any better at aligning our schedules than we were before—or that he'd suddenly want more with me.

BLAKE

Narcotics seems nervous. There's a back-up crew of police officers, but they wanted us on the team that goes in first.

I suddenly wonder whom exactly we're going to take down.

"Two of our contacts and the undercover man inside have gone silent. We're going to storm the building and take as many of them in as we can."

Wolfe crosses his arms in front his chest. I hold onto the top of my vest for a lack of anything else to do with my hands. "What if your man just switched sides?"

Conrad, the Narcotics team leader, glares at him, fury making the vein in his neck jump. "He's a good one. If he would have switched sides, don't you think he would've made sure to feed us bullshit information? We haven't heard from him in four weeks. Plus, we have our two missing contacts. No one has seen them in a while, so... Are you in or out?"

We all exchange a glance as Wolfe lifts his chin. "In. Show me the people we're looking for," he orders.

I grin. He insisted we remember this is their case, yet here he is, trying to take over.

Conrad hands us three pictures, and I have to bite back a comment. The gang inside is Hispanic, but the undercover cop is as white as a sheet. I can't believe they didn't find someone else to put in there.

"Didn't have a black guy you could plant?" Nikki snickers. I can't bite back my grin.

"Bates," Wolfe growls, and we all sober.

I check all three pictures one more time, then hand them back. "Got it. What's inside?"

The way it looks to me, I'd say it's an apartment building, not a drug den. Then again, I've seen buildings the gangs totally gutted, taking out as many walls as possible, while still having curtains hanging in the windows. It's all about appearances.

Conrad cocks his head. "Honestly? Apartments on the top floors and some drug labs on the lower ones. We're not quite sure if all the family members are out. A lot of the women are, having brought the kids to school and whatnot, but we have no guarantee. So, there might be civilians inside, even if most of them aren't likely innocent anymore."

An uneasy feeling creeps up inside of me and I arch a brow at Will. He rubs his thumb across the corner of his lips, a clear sign that he's nervous. It's one thing to storm a house full of assholes selling drugs. It's a whole different level having their families caught in the crossfire.

When a dark-haired guy wearing aviator glasses steps forward, I know we all have trouble keeping a comment in. Yes, it's day, but it's also cloudy.

I briefly wonder what Tia is doing. My heart skips a beat because I miss her. I want to see her and kiss her and... I can't believe I'm even considering it.

I might have also tried to work out the argument in my head, wondering how I could best convince her to be my girl.

"Atwood?"

I blink, then blink again, clearing my throat. "Here." Ten faces stare at me, two of them clearly furious. I couldn't care less about Conrad, but Wolfe... "I'm sorry. I'm worried about casualties."

Wolfe snorts. "If you'd listen, you'd know what to expect.

Upper three floors are where the apartments are, so this is where you'll be headed. There shouldn't be many gang members up there, but it doesn't hurt to be careful. You and Hawkes are going with Kephart. He's your team leader while you're inside." He looks around the group. "Anyone else not listen?"

No one else reacts. Still, I can't shake off the reprimand easily. I need to keep my head in the game.

"Okay. We're going in," Kephart says.

I wonder if I should grab a helmet, saying so out loud, but Wolfe shakes his head.

"You're just securing the apartments and making sure the kids and women stay where they belong. You're one of the best for the job because you know how to talk to terrified people. Keep Hawkes away from them or they'll run, screaming," he points out.

I nod, drawing my weapon and following the SWAT team. I didn't even notice when they arrived, then wonder if they've been here the whole time.

Periodically over the years, I've wished I was on SWAT, then remember they run into any building and situation, hoping their gear is enough protection to keep them alive.

The air inside reeks of pot. I can feel Will walking next to me, because we've been partners long enough, and it calms me slightly.

"When we're out of here, I'm going to find Tia, kiss her senseless, then sneak back to her house. I don't care how many kids she has to watch in the morning," I whisper.

He grins. "The moment you stand inside that apartment and see all the toys, you'll run for your life, terrified of making a commitment."

I consider that while counting the flights of stairs we ascend. Two more and we'll be on the first floor of apartments.

Exhaling slowly, I push all thoughts of Tia away. The last thing I need is a distraction. Coming to the door leading into the first hallway, SWAT kicks it down.

My heart accelerates when the first screams and warning shouts erupt as we make our way along our assigned floor.

TIA

The kids are especially fussy today, and I wonder if it is because they heard me and their mom earlier. I buy them ice cream, although I usually try to avoid that, then we make our way to the playground, the girls bickering the whole way.

I watch them, wondering if Chloe and I were ever like that. Ever since she got kicked out, my memories of my family seem to have shifted.

I'm sure some are more nostalgic than they should be, yet I suddenly miss my parents fiercely.

I place Neo into the sandbox and sit next to him, my eyes on the girls as I take out my phone.

I hesitate, feeling as if I'm betraying Chloe by calling up the people who abandoned her, then decide I shouldn't care since she doesn't take my feelings into consideration a lot of the time.

It rings over and over. Just when I consider hanging up, my mother answers, clearly breathless.

"Hello?"

Her voice sends shockwaves through me and I want to cry. I don't even know why. I've been furious with them for years, but now I feel the need to see them.

"Mom," I whisper, and there's a long pause.

"Tia?"

I cannot decide if it's a guess or if she's saying the name of the daughter she hopes is on the other end.

I clear my throat. "Yes. I... I'm..." I should've thought about what I wanted to say before I even dialed.

"Me, too," she says softly, chuckling. "I miss you. Tell me you made all your dreams come true."

My throat constricts. "I'm just calling because... You know... I mean... How did you know..." God, how ridiculous and lonely am I that I feel the need to talk to my mom about Blake? "How did you know it was me?"

She sighs. "I didn't. I was hoping. Besides, I'm waiting for the day you realize the only person Chloe ever thinks of is herself. She's been that way since she was five, so I figured it was you."

I don't know what to say about that, so we both stay quiet.

"Tia, can we climb the wall? Pretty please," Liv asks, Pauli standing behind her, nodding. As much as they fight, they can be so nice to each other when they want something.

I glance toward the climbing wall. Even though it's made for children and there's sand underneath it, I don't trust that thing. Especially because I couldn't watch a toddler and two girls climbing the wall at the same time.

"Not right now, okay?" I tell them.

Liv huffs. "But, Aunt Tia—"

I shake my head. "No buts. Go play on the swing or the slide." I know she's too old for it, but some days, she doesn't mind.

Pauli and she walk away, both clearly fuming, but I don't care. Neo comes closer, crawling into my lap. I draw him against me.

"Was that..."

"Chloe's oldest," I say quietly.

My mother gasps. "Oldest?"

I forgot that she doesn't know about the other kids. "Yes. She has three now."

Neo starts fussing in my arms. I kiss the top of his head. "We'll be going home in a bit. Promise," I tell him.

"Why are you not at work?" Mom suddenly asks.

I stare off into the distance for a moment. "I work at night. I'm a bartender and love it. The kids are off today, so I'm watching them for once." I shouldn't lie to my mom, but even when Chloe is a bitch to me, I want to protect her.

There's a very long moment of silence, then my mom clears her throat. "She still bends people to her will, doesn't she? And you are the worst. She knows exactly what she needs to do to get you to do what she wants. God, Tia. I thought things have changed, but they haven't. If you ever want to get out on your own, call me. We'll take you in any time, but your sister? No. Never."

Then she hangs up. I stare at the phone for the longest time, only realizing I was squeezing Neo when he starts complaining.

When I hear screaming and can't see Liv or Pauli, I jump to my feet and scoop up my nephew before walking around the playground, looking under things, finally realizing they are probably among the people watching whatever is going on over by the climbing wall.

"Pauli, Liv, we're leaving," I call out, placing Neo into the stroller before pushing it over. I scan the crowd for my nieces.

"Where's her mother?" someone asks.

Dread coils in my stomach. "Paulette! Olivia!" There are maybe twenty kids and parents. How hard can it be to—

"Aunt Tia!" Pauli pushes through the crowd, her face wet with tears. "I am so sorry. We should've listened, but I just wanted to climb the wall once. She was being mean. I just wanted to... I promise, I didn't mean to..."

I look at the crowd. *Oh god. Liv.*

I see her lying on the ground, people crowded around her. My ears buzzing, I grab Neo from the stroller, then push through the throng of people kneeling next to Liv. She stares up at me—then starts screaming as if her life depends on it.

CHAPTER THIRTEEN

BLAKE

DECLAN LOOKS AT ME. "You gonna be okay?" I nod, knowing none of this is okay. "We're going to Gun & Shot. Wanna come?"

The thought of seeing Tia is appealing. Even if I wouldn't be able to talk to her, her presence would soothe me. But I'm too raw, too…confused. Seeing her might end in a disaster if I said things I couldn't take back.

"Um… I don't know yet. I'll just wait for the mother, then see how I feel." I clear my throat and force out a smile.

He pats my shoulder and walks out. I stare at the brown chairs by the pale green wall of the waiting room, the tone making me feel sick. Had I checked the rooms properly, the little boy wouldn't be here, lying in a hospital bed right now.

It doesn't matter that he shouldn't have been there in the first place. Whenever you have gang violence, innocent people get caught in the melee.

I throw my jacket onto one of the chairs, rubbing my

hands across my face, trembling all over. My stomach churns as I see the scene in my head.

The boy coming out of nowhere, tears streaming down his face.

The bullet that was meant for me.

Will staring at me for the briefest moment because I'd announced the room was clear.

I go over it again and again—glancing through the room, my gaze sweeping back and forth. How did I overlook him?

"Fuck!" I push my hands through my hair and tear at the strands, wishing something could alleviate the pressure on my chest.

"Detective?"

Anything but her.

I take a second to school my features, then turn to Tia. I have no idea why she's here, but can't decide if it's punishment or relief. Her blonde hair is tied back into a braid, her work shirt showing under the open jacket. Her tight jeans hug her curves, and she is even wearing make-up. She's beautiful, tempting, and yet for the first time since knowing her, I don't want to push her away or hug her close.

All I want to do is talk to her, look at her and know someone's listening.

"Tia."

I give her a cocky grin, then look over her body. Funnily enough, I'm spoiling for a fight and know she'll give it to me. It's not even her fault. I just need an outlet. Then I remember where we are and worry takes over.

"Are you okay? What the hell are you doing here?"

She crosses her arms over her chest, the surprise on her face quickly replaced with anger. "What the hell are *you* doing here? Weren't you supposed to be at work? Are you stalking me now?"

She steps closer, her scent of vanilla and cinnamon hitting me square in the chest. I want to cup the back of her neck and kiss her until she melts against me.

"We helped take down some drug pushers." I swallow hard. "A little boy was hurt. I'm here checking on him."

Her features soften. It nearly makes me blurt out everything I have on my tongue.

If he dies, it's my fault.
I fucked up. Again.
I shouldn't be a cop. I can't even secure a room.

Instead of letting the words slip out, I bring my hand back to my hair, combing my fingers through it. She stares at me. Her lips part, as if she wants to say something, then she clamps them shut again, glancing away.

I take in her profile, her strong features, those kissable lips. I know she's a distraction, but right now, she's all that stands between me and a breakdown. Briefly, I wonder what she'd say if she knew. Would she be ready to help me, or would she just step back, calling me weak?

She sighs. "Liv fell at the playground and broke her arm. It's a compound fracture. Chloe had to leave for a few hours, so I sat by Liv's bed until she got back. Our neighbor, Danielle, offered to watch the other two...just in case you want to accuse me of anything." Tia lifts a brow in a silent challenge.

"I don't, Tia," I state quietly.

She cocks her head, furrowing her brows. "Are you okay, Blake?"

Her calling me by my name nearly brings me to my knees. It makes me long for cuddling on the couch late at night, waking up in the morning and kissing her goodbye before I have to leave.

I clear my throat and give her another smile. "I'm fine, but if you have an idea on how to cheer me up, I'd gladly pretend to be sad." I waggle my brows at her.

She gives me a sugary sweet smile. "I cannot believe you. I mean... What the hell is wrong with you today?" She shakes her head. "You know, I'd love to stay and chat, but I have to get to work." She starts to walk past me, but I grab her arm.

"Two dead bartenders aren't enough for you to reconsider your job?" I know she needs it and won't give it up until something different comes along, but damn if I'm not worried even more about her never making it home.

For a second, she stares at me. I wonder if maybe the talk in the bar hasn't been as obvious as I thought. Then she gives my hand a pointed look and raises a brow. I release her. "I have to work, and you have to remember that this was likely just a coincidence because nothing else has happened." I wonder why I've never told her why I'm so worried about her. "I'm going to work. I'll call you if I get worried, okay?"

She hesitates for a moment, as if wanting me to say something, yet I don't know what that is. She shakes her head as disappointment enters her eyes.

"Well, Detective Atwood, I guess whatever I thought... You know what? Forget it. You most likely will be glad about not having a repeat performance of me being too close." She licks her lips. "Good night."

When Tia steps toward the entrance, I can't bear the thought of being alone. "Tia, why don't you stay? I'm sure Liv would rather have you here, and Chloe could go—"

She spins and closes the distance between us quickly, not stopping until we're nose to nose. "You don't know anything about me, my family, or anyone else I'm connected to. I don't need you to tell me what to do. Never did, never will. Get that through your head." With that, she turns, the automatic doors opening, and is gone.

The shaking comes back, the memory of why I'm here. *If that boy dies...*

I can hardly finish the thought, feeling tears burn my eyes. I lean against the wall, pinching the bridge of my nose, and decide that I'll allow myself two minutes to give in to the pain. Just a few seconds of allowing myself to feel...

It's only when my ass hits the cold floor that I realize this won't be done in just a few minutes.

In fact, once that first tear falls down my cheek, I'm not sure I'll ever be able to stand up again.

TIA

I step toward the door again, having stood there for a few seconds, seething. I have no idea what Blake thinks is going on between us, but the way he just talked to me...

"You know, even if I needed a man, it wouldn't—"

The words get stuck in my throat when I see Blake sitting on the floor, his knees drawn up, his forehead resting on his legs.

"Just go," he chokes out, and all my anger vanishes. I crouch down next to him, feeling the overwhelming need to comfort him, to ease his agony.

I brush my fingertips over the back of his neck. "What's going on?"

"Go!" he snaps, looking up, tears in his hazel eyes. The one word couldn't be more clear. Any other time, it most likely would've jolted me to my feet, but the silent pleading on his face freezes me where I am.

"Blake," I whisper again. "What's going on?"

My fingertips wander over the scruff of his cheek, and he

leans into my palm. My heart breaks for him. I don't care how condescending he is or what an ass he just was. He's clearly broken, and no one's there to ease his hurt.

He licks his lips and closes his eyes. I cup his other cheek and nudge him until he looks at me again. "I know you hate showing weakness, and I'm probably the last person you want to see it, but—"

"You're not," he whispers.

He stretches out his legs and wraps his arms around me, pulling me so I straddle his lap. He buries his face against my shoulder, and I press my lips to his head, holding him tightly.

There's just a small piece of clothing between his skin and mine, so I feel how cold his hands are. A shiver runs up and down my back. "God, Blake. You're freezing," I mutter, swallowing.

"I was supposed to check the room. I did. I looked through it. No closet, nothing to hide behind. Just a small bed with drawers under it and a small dresser. Didn't think the drawers were big enough for a person." He pauses for a moment, sobs escaping his lips. I close my eyes, wondering if I should say something when he continues. "Turns out, an eight-year-old easily fits into a drawer. He was terrified. I…"

Eight. Just like Liv. I shake my head. "Could you have looked into the drawers without risking anyone else?"

"Even before we entered the floor, we were shot at. There was no time for anything."

Imagining Blake being in a situation like that, his life at risk, makes me start to shake, too. I gasp.

He pulls back to look into my face, panic in his eyes. "Did I hurt you?" I feel his grip loosen, but the thought of him letting go makes the lump in my throat grow.

I frame his face with my hands again, temporarily pushing down the fear of anything happening to him. "You didn't,

Blake. I was just... I mean..." A tear rolls down my cheek. "You could've been shot. It could be *you* in that hospital room. I..." I exhale slowly, trying to suppress the feelings that bubble up.

When in the world did I develop strong feelings for him? When did he turn into someone I expect to be in my life? *Want* to be in my life?

He gives me the smallest of smiles. "I had a vest on. I would've been okay. Besides, had the boy not come out of that room, I wouldn't even have been in the path of the bullet."

"The bullet that hit him instead," I whisper, and guilt flashes in his eyes.

"Had I seen him in that room before, I could've led him outside, or told him to stay where he was, or...something."

I arch a brow. He had told me he was there checking on the boy, which meant he was alive. "He's breathing. He didn't die. *You* didn't take him into the building, Blake. You hear me?"

I can't imagine what he's feeling. I try to picture how I'd react if anything happened to either of the girls or Neo, something I could've prevented. It makes me want to throw up.

"Was he the only casualty?"

He shrugs. "Some of the guys were injured. Or maybe killed. I don't know. I didn't ask. I..."

He turns away from me, but I grip his chin, pulling him back to look at me. "What, Blake?"

I get that he doesn't want to talk about it, but I have a feeling he's kept things inside for way too long.

"I couldn't deal with knowing I might have killed someone else. Not today. It doesn't matter that kids die. It doesn't matter that they shot at us first. I just can't... Not today." He shakes his head. His grip tightens before he releases me. I get to my feet, unsure what else to do, and he follows.

My gaze is on his face, his body, but I see the shaking has ebbed and his eyes are clear again. I wrap my arms around myself, torn between wanting to leave and needing to make sure he's okay.

Eventually, he grabs his jacket, the badge around his neck swinging forward. I instantly hate that thing. That damn badge means he, and everyone else wearing one, runs the risk of dying on a daily basis. Even working in a cop bar, I never thought about it until that moment.

"Can I go to work without having to worry about you?"

He nods and blows out a breath, then walks to the desk to tell the nurse something—I assume to inform her to call him with the kid's status. He walks back and answers my question. "Yes, because I'm driving you. Come on."

He walks away without waiting for me to answer. I release a relieved breath because him bossing me around means he's somewhat okay again.

BLAKE

I don't look over my shoulder to see if she follows. I hear her soft steps, almost feel her presence. I don't know what made her come back, what made me challenge her earlier, but regardless, I'm glad she is here.

I didn't realize how much I needed her until she was in my arms, holding me together while I fell apart. I want to draw her into my side, feel the silent strength she offers, but I don't. There's no way to tell if that moment changed anything between us, and it freaks me out a little bit.

I had planned so many different versions of how I'd ask her to be my girlfriend, but none seem to be valid anymore.

Tia deserves a guy who won't have deaths on his conscience.

Uncharted territory is worse than running into a dark room, not knowing how many people might be inside or how big the risk. Finally glancing over my shoulder, I see Tia chewing on her lip thoughtfully. I stop at my car and wait until she steps up next to me. I feel an overwhelming need to pull the lip from between her teeth, but that gesture seems strangely intimate. I'm suddenly terrified of that.

"Why are you driving me? I thought you were set on staying here." Her blue eyes focus on me, and I shrug. There are a handful of reasons, but only one I can really voice out loud.

After all, saying that I cannot stand the thought of leaving her side just yet might send the wrong signals.

Or the right ones, my mind whispers.

"I owe you."

She blinks in surprise. "What for?"

In my book, comforting another human being isn't something done out of the goodness of your heart.

I thumb over my shoulder. "For what you did in there."

She smiles, the gesture gentle. "You don't owe me for that. Not at all. You *do* owe me because you were an asshole earlier, and because you like bossing me around, treating me as if I'm incapable of making my own decisions, but not for this, Blake. Never for something like this."

She closes the small distance between us and places her hand above my heart. For a second, I worry she can tell how it reacts to her, how just her presence speeds it up, but she doesn't comment.

"If you ever need someone to talk to, Blake, at any time of day, call me. I'll listen. No matter what has happened between us, no matter which words have been exchanged.

Don't hurt all by yourself." She swallows. "Besides, I don't have friends I could tell about you, so your secrets are safe with me. Always."

She holds my gaze. I feel the desperate need to kiss her. The problem is, I also want to stay away from her so I don't cause her any pain now or in the future, yet...

I almost give in when her cell rings, causing her to jump.

She fumbles, trying to get it out of her pocket, then pales. "It's Warrick. God, I'm late. I cannot... I cannot lose this job."

I take the phone and answer before she can protest.

"Where the hell are you?" Warrick snaps, a strange mix of relief and fury in his voice.

"She's with me, War," I reply as I unlock the door to my SUV. She slips into the passenger side.

"Atwood? That you?"

I shift the phone from one ear to the other, then open my own door. "Sure is. I'm bringing her over now. Her niece ended up at the hospital and I ran into her there. It was my fault she was held up."

He groans, then takes a deep breath. "I'm not angry. I was fucking worried. She usually lets me know if she can't make it, and..." He clears his throat. "Anyway, bring her over. And, Atwood? Do *not* touch her. I like her working for me, and you ruining that would mean I'd have to ban you from my bar. I know you want more than to just be her friend."

I can't help but grin as I start the car, yet not pulling it out onto the road. I don't want to risk having someone else injured because I'm distracted.

Especially Tia.

"Can't promise anything. Tia's ready to climb into my lap and be *real* nice to me," I joke. She gasps and punches my shoulder, a smile spreading on her lips.

Warrick snorts. "You wish."

I do, but she doesn't need to know that. "What can I say? It's my charm. No one can resist."

"Sadly," Tia mutters.

"Well, I'm glad she's somewhat immune to your charm. Get her here. I'll see you in a bit." He hangs up.

If he only knew how close we've been, he probably wouldn't call her immune to my charm. I hand the phone back to her, finally leaving the parking lot.

"How much does it bother you?" she asks after a few minutes.

I glance at her. "What's that?"

She shrugs. "How much does it bother you that you never took me up on that offer to be in your lap again? You know, back when you turned me down because of your assumptions."

I chuckle. "A lot." Then I sober. "Most of the time, though, I think it's better that way. You and I... We shouldn't go down *that* road again."

Even if my dick twitches behind my zipper, making my pants uncomfortably tight.

I laugh. "I mean, I won't deny that I had blue balls for days after that." I glance at her. "I don't usually fuck women in my bed. In fact, I never take them back to my apartment. The chance for stalkers is too high. It's my sanctuary, and I don't want my one-night stands to show up there. Yet you've been there and... It's already too much."

I don't look at her to gauge her reaction, although it nearly kills me.

"You took me there. I didn't make you," she points out quietly.

I wet my lips, my heart thudding angrily in my chest. This would be the perfect moment to tell her that she's different. Instead, I sigh. "I had no other choice. I mean..." I leave the sentence unfinished because the truth is, I don't have a lie at the ready.

From the corner of my eye, I see her grit her teeth and close her eyes. That confirms Tia definitely wants more from me than she's ready to admit right at that moment.

CHAPTER FOURTEEN

TIA

WHEN I WAKE the next morning, I'm still absolutely clueless as to what had happened yesterday.

First, Blake never mentioned the details of any cases they were working on, yet it has to be something big for him to be so protective. I am sure of that much. Granted, from the talk in the bar, I'd heard bits and pieces of what was going on even before he mentioned it, but whatever had gotten into him the day before must've been mind-changing. Second, I couldn't remember him ever being as annoying as he was last night.

My sister was able to take Liv home. Besides a broken arm, she's doing well. In fact, she seemed happy, as if she enjoyed the extra attention. Well, her mother can give her some more today.

Chloe passes me while I prepare coffee. As much as I looked forward to sleeping in, my brain won't allow it. I'm tempted to text Blake and ask what the hell happened—and why the night didn't end with a smile, like it usually did. Maybe because of what happened with the boy, or maybe because of something completely different. Either way, not knowing where we stand kills me.

It's when my sister grabs her jacket that I snap out of my daze, spinning around. "Where the hell are you going?" I ask.

She shrugs. "Because of your *demands*, I work less than I am used to and can't finish my work. Since you're up anyway, I figured I'd rush in and try to catch up."

I'm about to snap at her when I realize this is the perfect distraction. I nod. "Good. I'll take them to the zoo then. Liv? Pauli? Get ready. We're going to the zoo!"

Chloe blows me a kiss, then she's out the door.

It doesn't take long for us to get ready and walk out. I stare up at the blue sky, wondering why we have perfect weather when my mood is stormy.

The girls are quiet, and Neo falls asleep in the stroller almost as soon as we're out the door. Pauli walks next to me, one hand on the stroller.

I arch a brow at her. "Not excited for the zoo?"

The sisters exchange a quick glance, then Pauli sighs. "Course I am. I want to see some birds."

She usually bugs me to see the tigers and snow leopards, so I glance at Liv. "What's going on?"

Liv swallows as I steer us down into the subway station and pay for the tickets. "We're just... We were kinda hoping to spend the day with Mom, you know? Like... She hasn't been out with us in a while. We love you, Tia, but..." She shrugs.

I get it. I so get it.

"Your mom works hard so we can—"

"Live in a crappy area and go to a school that's dangerous? So you can work in dirty bars and serve old men?" Liv mutters angrily.

Although I'm pushing the stroller, I nearly face-plant on

the platform. I never doubted Liv knew we weren't rich, but I never expected her to think about her life the way she did.

"I don't serve old men in dirty bars."

She glares at me while we wait for the next train. I wish we could keep walking because Pauli suddenly takes my hand, shaking, and Liv's body vibrates with anger.

"Oh please. I hear mom talk all the time."

God, I suddenly need to sit. When the train pulls up, I let out a breath as I maneuver everyone inside. Seeing me, a man jumps up so I can have his seat. I smile at him, then pull the girls close.

"Do you remember Blake? The man who drove you to school the other day?" I ask, and her face lights up. I have no idea what he said inside the school, but he's been her hero since that day.

"Of course I do!"

I shrug. "Well, I met Blake at work." Not quite true, but that doesn't matter. "He's one of the guys I serve. Also firefighters and paramedics. You'd love them." And she would. For some reason, she loves to watch shows about people helping others.

Her face falls. "You're lying," she whispers.

What the hell has Chloe been saying about me behind my back? "I'm not. I'd say you can ask him when he comes around, but... Well, when I have time during the day, he's at work."

Her face falls. "And drinking when you're working. Do you see him every night?"

I need to tread carefully. "Sometimes. He likes to drive me home to make sure nothing happens to me. I work far away from here because the bar is safe. It's owned by a policeman."

Should I be discussing this with an eight-year-old?

She thinks for a second, then turns worried eyes to me. "Tia, do you promise your work is safe? And that...that...that you met Blake where you said you did?"

My heart skips another beat. I should steer the topic away from this, but I have a feeling Chloe has told her daughter something different.

"Where else would I have met him?"

She starts chewing her thumb, and I'm tempted to do the same. "Mom might have... I mean... She says he drove you home that morning because he paid you and didn't want anyone to know."

I start shaking, torn between sadness and anger. How can I fix this situation so the kids don't suffer? "What did she say he paid me for?"

Liv shrugs. "No idea. Are you cleaning his apartment or something?"

I rest my head back against the seat, glad Chloe hadn't gone as far as telling her daughter what she was implying, but that doesn't change the fact that my sister makes me out to be a hooker to her children. I cannot help but think my mom is absolutely right.

Chloe only thinks about herself.

―――

BLAKE

I stand in front of Tia's building, knowing I need to talk to her, apologize, just...see her?

I should've kissed her last night. Instead of bringing up the case, I should've remembered that she's had enough to deal with lately.

A woman about Tia's age comes out of the front door, so I

catch it before it can fall closed. "Hello, ma'am. Can you perhaps tell me which floor Tia lives? Blonde with cute nieces?" I give her my warmest smile, and she cocks her head.

"Are you the one who dropped her off the other day? The cop?" I nod. "Liv hasn't shut up about you. Third floor, three doors down." With that, she keeps on walking.

I make my way up the stairs. The apartment building doesn't look so bad from the inside, yet I still wish it were less...in this area.

I find a door with a colorful handprint right in the middle. I smile to myself, ringing the doorbell.

There's a female giggle behind the door, then some squealing. My heart drops—until her sister opens the door, hair a mess, cheeks flushed, wearing a robe. She's beaming, her eyes glazed over. She looks at me. "Yes?" It takes a moment for her to realize who I am. She draws the robe closer around her body.

"Where is Tia?" I growl.

"Not here." She tries to close the door, but I catch it with my foot and push my way inside.

The apartment is quiet. Too quiet.

"Babe, what is it?" a male voice asks, then everything clicks into place.

Slowly, I turn to Chloe, keeping my detective face in place. "You get dressed, then we go wherever Tia is. You'll be a *mother* while I take her away. I'm off today, so don't expect her to come back," I say casually. I have no idea if Tia even wants to see me, but that doesn't matter.

Chloe crosses her arms over her chest, her robe slipping down and revealing a soft shoulder that I cannot look at without thinking of Tia, wishing she were here right now to witness this. "And what makes you think I'll do what you say?"

A guy in all his naked glory comes out of a door to my right. "What's going on?" he asks. I glance at him, then look back at Chloe.

"Because you don't want Tia to know what you're doing, do you? Why you leave so early in the mornings or come home just in time for her to make it to work. Besides, your daughter was in the hospital just yesterday, and—"

She snorts. "That was Tia's fault. She didn't watch my children closely enough."

I take out my phone, dialing Tia's number. Chloe's eyes widen.

"Blake…" Her voice is soft, disbelieving, a lot of commotion in the background.

"Hey, where are you?" I ask, waiting for Chloe to make a decision. As much as I want to keep this from Tia, especially because it will potentially fracture her world, I need to drive the point home.

"Fine," Chloe whispers through clenched teeth just as Tia speaks again.

"I'm on my way home. I wanted to take the kids to the zoo, but Neo started throwing up. I swear, my rather free day is cursed."

I perk up at that. "Rather free?"

She sighs, as if she regrets saying that. "Warrick gave me today off. I didn't tell my sister because I didn't want her to get any ideas… I'm a horrible person, aren't I?"

"Not at all. Listen… I'm off today, too, so why don't I meet you at your place, then I can apologize for the other night."

Chloe cocks her head, her cheeks aflame with anger, but I don't acknowledge her.

"You don't need to, Blake," Tia replies, yet I know I have to.

"I'll see you in a bit to discuss that, okay?" I tell her, then hang up and look at Chloe.

"Your son threw up. Tia's on her way back. Probably fifteen minutes, max. So..."

I stalk over to the couch and sit on it while naked dude and Chloe stare at each other. She breaks into a frenzy trying to get dressed, her expression worried, as the man runs around and grabs his clothes.

I was right. She didn't have to work nearly as much as she made Tia believe, which made me hate her just a bit more. I didn't think it was possible after she slapped her.

When naked dude is out the door—dressed this time—and Chloe has clothes on again, she glares at me before marching off. I hear her puttering around the kitchen, then she comes back and forces a cup of coffee into my hands, pulls me off the couch, and pushes me through a door.

"You wanna wait for her? Do so in her room."

I look around a room that's hardly bigger than something you'd give a child. There's a bed, pictures on the wall of places I bet she wishes she could visit, song lyrics haphazardly taped across them wherever it suited her.

This room is Tia. My heart squeezes. She should have more space, even her own apartment. If not that, at least her own life.

I sit on the bed, inhaling her vanilla scent that puffs up. I'm almost tempted to stretch out when I hear the front door open. The walls in here are paper thin, which makes me ache for her even more.

I stand, entering the living room again. I see Tia staring at her sister, eyes narrowed. "What are you doing here? I thought you were at work?"

"I forgot my keycard," Chloe lies.

Tia arches a brow. "And you decided to change into

sweatpants while you were here? I'm not buying it, but I'm happy here you're here...." She trails off when she spots me, a dark smile crossing her face. "Now, if you'll excuse me, I have to do what *you* told your kids I do for money."

She doesn't hesitate as she walks over to take my hand, placing the mug on the coffee table. She kisses the kids, then we're out the door.

TIA

I drag Blake outside, then drop his hand and close my eyes. "There was a guy with her, wasn't there?" I turn to him, but he doesn't need to say anything. "*Fuck*. I'm so stupid. I should've known. Should've—"

He cuts me off by framing my face with his hands and kissing me. "I'm sorry about yesterday," he whispers against my lips. "It was exactly..." He swallows. "What happened yesterday is part of why I stay away from relationships. I could've gotten hurt. I could've killed an innocent. That little boy... I..." He shakes his head, swallowing again. "No woman deserves to have my baggage, my fears, the threat of losing me, and yet..." He pulls back enough to search my face. "Yet I want to try it with you. I want to be with you even if it causes you constant worry and makes you hate me at times."

I lick my lips, my heart yearning to just say yes. "I barely have time, Blake. Even if I make Chloe schedule her...affairs differently, I still work at night, and you work during the day."

He shrugs. "I'll take what I can get. I'm ready to make sacrifices, Tia, even if it means picking you up at three in morning to drive you home because it's the only hour I can see you. Please."

I smile. "I have to be at work tomorrow at four. Can you drive me home before that to pick up my work clothes?"

He wraps his arms around me. "Best thing ever." He leads me over to his SUV. I slip in, giggling when he climbs behind the wheel.

"We could just walk through the park, you know," I tell him.

He gasps and places his hand on his chest in mock horror. "I'm not going to leave my precious baby on this side of the park. Besides, the way's too long."

The drive takes no time at all. Once we stumble into his apartment, lips and fingers hungry, I suddenly draw away, remembering I wanted to shower when I got back.

"I need a shower. And I mean that. I had just picked up Neo when he..."

God, this is too embarrassing.

"Come on," he whispers, slipping his fingers into mine and leading me to the bathroom. He gestures to a cabinet. "Towels are in here. I'm gonna grab you some shorts and a shirt, okay?" His eyes twinkle. "You won't be wearing them long anyway."

I turn on the water and strip as quickly as I can. If things go my way, this shower will take quite a bit of time and I won't even need any clothes. The moment I step under the spray, which is much stronger than ours at home, I nearly forget where I am, moaning in pleasure.

I don't hear the door open again, but I feel a draft when he steps in, wrapping his arms around me from behind.

His tongue traces my shoulder and I rest my head back on him, feeling him cup my breasts, teasing my nipples until I'm soaked...and not just from the shower.

Turning, I wrap my arms around his neck, his erection

pushing against my stomach. "Glad you caught on to the silent order," I say.

He grins. "You didn't think I'd let you shower alone, did you? I have to make the most of every second with you. I also noticed you didn't say anything to starting more with me. I need you to say it, Tia. I need to know we're on the same page."

I lick my lips, deciding to test him. "And if I won't do this serious thing with you?"

He swallows and his eyes close. "I'd kiss you, step out of this shower, and let you finish alone. I'd probably sit down with you afterward, talk to you, but... I couldn't touch you anymore. I cannot do casual with you, Tia."

I nod slowly. "Good, because you wormed your way into my heart and there's nothing I can do about it," I whisper, then press myself against him again.

He picks me up, and I wrap my legs around his hips, now feeling him even closer to where I want him. He kisses me as if his life depends on it and presses me against the cold tiles.

For a moment, he meets my eyes, but it's obvious he knows exactly what I'm thinking. "No condom, no sex." He sets me back onto my feet before he kneels and places one of my legs over his shoulder.

"Jesus, Blake..." He trails his finger up my leg until he reaches my core, teasing, then grinning up at me. "Don't give me that smug look."

"I can look at you whichever way I want. Besides... I think you talk too much." Then his lips are on me, my hands gripping his hair.

His tongue teases my clit, his fingers massaging my thighs, making me even more sensitive to everything he has to offer.

"I... I'm..." I think my legs are going to give out, but Blake takes my hands and steadies me as I explode, seeing stars.

BLAKE

Her moans are the cutest thing ever. I'm rock hard, but because her hands are in mine, I cannot ease some of the pressure.

"Blake... Blake..." Reluctantly, I stop when I'm doing and look up at her. "I'm terrified of slipping. So can we please go to your room where I can turn off my brain and just...have you inside me?"

I groan at that thought and nod, climbing back to my feet and pulling her into my arms. She's warm and soft and wet all over.

I turn off the water and wrap her in a big towel, drying her off while kissing her softly. There are so many things I want to say to her, probably should've said before we even started this, but now? No chance.

Wrapping a towel around my hips, I lead her into my bedroom, wondering why it feels as if she belongs here, belongs in my space, when I've not allowed it before.

She pushes me down onto the bed and rips off my towel, dropping her own onto the floor and crawling onto my lap. She reaches for the nightstand and pulls out a condom, then wraps her arms around my neck and pulls me in, her tongue teasing my lips until I open for her.

She pulls away, a smirk on her face, and tears the condom open, then rolls it down my hard erection. Just the feeling of her fingers on me nearly makes me explode.

"I don't wanna wait, even if I know we have all night," she whispers.

I grab her hips, lowering her onto me. She gasps. I hold my breath, my need to thrust into her overwhelming. I don't remember when I've last been this close, this intimate with anyone.

Tia holds onto my shoulders as she starts rotating her hips, slowly moving up and down, teasing me until I can hardly think. "This is not going to last long if you keep...," I gasp, but she just smiles, moving faster, using my shoulders for leverage. My hands on her hips are the only way I can possibly stop her so I can set the rhythm, but do I want that?

She leans back, her rosy nipples teasing me, and I know I don't want it. She is sexy when taking control, and she seems to know it. I lean up and bite one tempting peak. She clenches around me, causing me to groan. I do it again.

"Fuck, Blake..." She pushes me back onto the bed, and I grab her hips tighter, keeping her in place as I move farther up the bed.

The new position makes me slip even deeper into her, and for a second, I wish we could do this without protection. I want to feel all of her, more of her... Everything I can get.

I wrap my hand around the back of her neck and draw her down to my lips so I can decide the rhythm. I moan into her mouth, swallowing all her little noises.

She threads her hands into my hair again. I close my eyes, taking in the way her nails scrape across my scalp and her body moves against mine. This is different than anything I've ever done before, and words that I refuse to voice dance on the tip of my tongue.

I hold her tighter and take her harder until she bites my shoulder on a moan. The pain-pleasure causes me to grit my teeth. "Tia," I gasp, but she just shakes her head against my shoulder.

"Just... Don't stop," she begs.

As much as I want to give her everything she deserves, I fear I can't hold on much longer.

I slip a hand between us and find her clit. She giggles.

"Impatient?" she asks.

I groan. "No... Yes... I mean... God, Tia. You feel so perfect, but now you want to talk?"

She rubs her nose against mine and presses a tender kiss to my lips. "No. Just making you step back from the edge." She sits up again, riding me harder, more intense, as I keep teasing her clit.

"Blake...," she moans and presses her hands against my chest, just barely moving as her insides grip me tightly.

I rock my hips, knowing I just need a few more thrusts. Growling, I come harder than I ever have.

She collapses onto me, and I wrap her in my arms, holding her until our breathing is under control.

Gently, I place her onto the pillows, then get up to discard the condom. When I walk back in, she lazily blinks up at me. "Are you gonna leave the bed if I fall asleep?"

I grin and crawl into bed, cover us with the comforter, then draw her against me. "I'll stay here, but...I might wake you with my nightmares."

She presses a kiss to my chest. "I might wake you for a little fun," she retorts. I smirk, liking that thought.

"You know," I start, drawing lazy circles over her back, "The thought of falling asleep terrified me...then you walked into my life. Thank you."

She's quiet for a moment. "No, Blake. Thank you."

I don't know what she's thanking me for. She gives me everything I need, yet all I can do is take because what do I really have to offer?

CHAPTER FIFTEEN

TIA

I SHOULD BE on cloud nine the following Monday, but the truth is, things at home are worse than ever. While Chloe takes the kids to school on her assigned days, it's obvious there's a strain on our relationship.

I didn't say anything to her about her being home that day Blake picked me up, and neither did she. The girls are quieter, more subdued, and Neo fusses more than ever, as if they can sense the tension.

I try not to let it bother me much, but it's hard when you can tell that things are starting to shift.

The apartment is silent since the girls are at school and Neo's asleep next to me, half hanging off the couch because he'd been standing on the floor while playing on it. I hold onto him with one hand to make sure he doesn't fall. Since he's been throwing up, we decided to keep him home. Feeding him toast and ginger ale seemed to ease whatever is going on.

My phone rings. When I see Blake's name, I answer with a smile. "Hey, Detective Atwood."

"Tia, can I come over? We're headed to interrogate someone in your neighborhood, and I need to kiss you again." His tone is urgent, even though I can tell he's trying to make light of it.

"Where are you?"

Hearing a soft knock on my door, I hang up, placing Neo onto the couch before walking over and opening the door. Blake gathers me in his arms, holding me tightly, and I wrap my arms around him.

"What's going on?"

He presses a kiss to my shoulder before pulling back enough to claim my lips, his tongue teasing mine until I all but melt into a puddle on the floor. He tastes of sugar and coffee. I pull away and grin up at him.

"Had a donut before coming over, did ya?"

"Had one in the car," a voice calls out from the hallway.

I laugh, peering around Blake's shoulder. "Hello, Detective Hawkes." Meeting Blake's eyes again, I brush my thumb over his lips. "How long can you stay?"

He kisses my nose, the gesture tender. "Not long, but Will feared if he didn't come up with me, I wouldn't return."

I cock my head playfully. "Then he's smarter than I gave him credit for."

"I heard that," Will announces. Blake's expression brightens a little, yet I can't help but think there is more going on.

"Hey," I say when he looks past me, clearly trying to figure out how many kids are home. "Tell me what's wrong. I can see it on your face."

He closes his eyes and licks his lips. "I don't know. My gut feeling says something is off, and..."

"And your gut is never wrong."

He nods, looking at me as if he wants to say something

more, then he frames my face with his hands and kisses me, his lips soft, teasing, tempting.

"I'll be at work tonight. Drop by for a kiss before you go home, okay?" I whisper.

He shakes his head. "I'll be taking you home, so it'll be more than a kiss, then I'll crawl under the sheets with you."

I swallow, nodding. I want it so much, but how bad is his gut feeling that he doesn't like the idea of going home alone? "I'll be waiting, Detective."

And I will be. In fact, I can already tell that I'll be checking my phone more than usual, probably driving Warrick crazy.

"Okay." He lets go, then places his hands on my hips again and pulls me into him. "Call me the second you get off the subway. I'll talk to you the whole way."

It's then I realize he's not worried about himself, but *me*. "It this about the dead girls? Because there hasn't been one in a while. I don't think...whatever has been going on is still going on."

Will coughs. "You shouldn't know that much about the case. Fucking cops. Can't keep their mouths shut."

"Actually, that's why I work in a bar, you know. Alcohol loosens the tongue. Yet still... I've clearly missed something." Blake shakes his head, letting me know he can't say anything. "I promise. I'll call you." I go onto my tiptoes to whisper into his ear. "And should I get lonely and think of you, I might call you just to tell you that I wish you and I were alone so I could put my hand down your pants..."

He groans, the tension in his shoulders relaxing. He kisses my neck. "Vixen."

"Just for you," I reply, and he kisses my forehead.

"Good. I'll see you later." He looks over my shoulder.

"Hey, little man." I turn and see Neo looking over the couch, watching us, smiling at Blake.

"Bye, Will. Watch out for him," I call, seeing one hand wave around the corner of the door.

"Will do," he promises, then Blake steps out of the apartment.

I close the door and walk back to where my nephew grins at me widely—before he throws up all over the couch.

―――――

BLAKE

Will punches my shoulder. "Way to ease the girl's worries. We should've just met the fucking suspect."

He's right, but knowing there's a guy living *in her building* who's on the list of assholes who might have killed the bartenders makes me itchy. There's a chance he doesn't know what she does, which is why she's still alive, but...

It was weird. We'd been reading over the files again and saw a name of a witness pop up twice. He'd been at both, had seen "nothing" at both.

We did a quick search on him, but besides the fact he didn't work at his job as a truck driver anymore, we just found his address, nothing else.

Granted, not exactly prime suspect material, but when I read the address and showed it to Will, we knew we needed to at least talk to him.

Will knocks on his door, which is a floor beneath Tia. We both wait with bated breath. We have no idea what to expect, but when he opens the door, his face slim, his body heavy, I exhale slowly.

Will glances at me. There's no way this guy is the killer.

For one, he's not tall enough, and two, he seems too out of shape.

I flash my badge. "Mr. Sinclaire, we're NYPD and would like to talk to you about a couple things. Can we come in?"

He hesitates only a brief moment, then steps aside. "Sure. What is this about?"

I look around, seeing an extremely dirty apartment. I give him a small smile, hoping to not appear threatening. "This is about witness reports you've given near two bars. We—"

"Me? Bars?" he asks. "I don't leave my apartment if I can help it. Got fired from my accounting job because I was getting too big and my boss found that to be a liability."

"Accounting?" Will echoes.

The guy nods angrily. "Yeah. Just because I'm fat doesn't mean I'm dumb. I now do freelance accounting work from home. I..." His eyes narrow. "Wait... It's that other Sinclaire guy, right? The criminal?"

I blink. "Criminal?"

He snorts. "You police officers really ought to do better research. There's a second Dean Sinclaire, not me, who obviously comes to town quite often. Each time he fucking breaks the law, the cops come here." He shakes his head.

Will clears his throat. "Sir, you gave your address when the police took your witness statement near the crime scenes."

He sits down. "Well, I didn't give it. Seems he realized he has a namesake here. I swear it wasn't me. What did I supposedly do?"

Will gives him a brief overview about what's going on. He pales before suddenly jumping to his feet and rushing away. Will follows, then comes back.

"Throwing up. The mention of a dead body clearly didn't go over well," he mutters.

"What are the chances?" I ask.

"Does he look like someone who could do that? I mean, he doesn't even *smell* like someone who leaves his apartment...ever."

Looking around, seeing trash everywhere, I arch a brow. "Can you imagine how much spray he'd need to use to get rid of the stench?"

The man's probably used to the smell, but Will is right.

"Okay, let's talk to his—" The man walks back in, and I clear my throat. "Are you okay, sir?"

"Don't... I... Bodies..." He pales again, and I lift my hands to try and calm him down.

"Look, it's okay. We're done here. Don't go anywhere, just in case we need to reach you, okay? And if you should think of something..." I hand him my card, relieved that this guy most likely is no danger to Tia.

Once in the hall, Will nods toward the doors on the left and right. I nod. We knock, asking around. Indeed, not many of the neighbors have seen Sinclaire in the last months. His apartment is reported for strange odors on a regular basis, but as soon as the landlord shows up, it seems to ease for a while before the cycle starts again.

"Were you tempted to ask about Tia just to see if he recognized her?" Will asks when we're back in the SUV.

I shake my head, although it's a lie. The thing is, if he *is* our guy—which I doubt—I wouldn't want to hint that she fit into his victim profile. "Let's go back to the precinct and see if we can find any information about the other Sinclaire."

He wouldn't have popped up the first time because we did a local search of the address on the report, but I can't help but be curious now. If he is indeed a criminal, we might have someone on our hands who has seen more than he's said—or even done more than he let on.

"Blake, try not to sabotage this thing you have going with

Tia, okay? She seems to be a good one—and, honestly, you're less broody since you met her."

I doubt that, but don't say it out loud. "I don't think we should have this talk because, well... Neither of us is an expert in the whole relationship thing, so..."

Will just sighs, rolling his eyes before starting the SUV, making his disapproval clear.

Even though Tia is safe for now, I can't help but wish I was with her. The uneasy feeling in my gut hasn't eased, and that is what worries me the most.

TIA

The bar's buzzing, as if Blake's nervous energy has carried over, and I have my hands full, as do Donna and Warrick.

It's seldom that we're this busy on a Monday. Hell, Mondays are usually pretty dead, but it seems every cop who isn't working decided to be here. I see regulars, quite a few of them, but there are also more strangers than normal.

"What the hell is going on?" I ask as Warrick walks behind me while I draw another beer. I have a feeling this will be my permanent job today.

He shrugs, his eyes surveying the room. "Honestly? I don't know. Maybe it's the full moon."

Donna rushes around to serve tables, just a few coming up to the bar. Always positive, she seems to be fine with it, her smile bright, her mouth running.

I don't think there's much that can throw her, and I sometimes envy that.

"There's no full moon tonight," Donna chirps as she grabs

the next round of beer from me. I give her a wink, then she's off again.

I should thrive tonight because, hell, we don't have much time for idle chitchat, which means no one will get to see my sassy side—and can complain about it.

"Tia, before you leave today, I need to talk to both you and Donna. Also, I'm gonna drive you to the subway station and—"

I don't lift my eyes from the glass I hold under the tap. "Detective Atwood is picking me up."

I never realized Warrick wouldn't be okay with us dating until the incident at the hospital, and ever since then, I avoided the whole topic with him because, well...our dating was a new thing for us.

"So Atwood does affairs now? I thought the two of you were just friends. I mean, I am fine with it, but Blake..." He shakes his head. "That boy—"

"Stop right there. There's nothing boyish about Blake. I'm serious. I appreciate you looking out for me, but I'm old enough to make my own decisions. As the saying goes, if you gotta be stupid, you gotta be tough." I wink, and he sighs. "I think he just needed the right person to show him what he's doing is not working. Do you know that he has nightmares?"

Warrick grimaces. "Hate to say it, but I'd be more worried if he didn't. So yeah, I guess I knew. Why?"

"If you're done with your chatting, lady, I want a beer."

I look up at the guy, giving him nothing more than a passing glance. He looks like any other guy who's come straight from his boring company job and is absolutely glad he got out.

Warrick nudges me, as if he can sense the bitchy answer on the tip of my tongue, so I force out a smile, take a shot glass from under the bar and pour him a vodka. "Here. On the house, and one beer coming right up," I announce. "Sorry for the wait, handsome." He isn't, but men like it if you compliment them.

"We both know I'm not," he says, his tone much nicer.

I don't even look at him, keeping my eyes on the beer while my mind is on Blake. "Oh please. I've seen worse." The words are out before I realize that maybe he won't appreciate the joke, but he bursts out laughing.

"Noted. Keep the change for that laugh."

When I slide the beer over, he puts a twenty on the bar, takes his drinks and walks away, making me stare after him and his bald spot on the back of his head.

"Thank you, handsome," I call after him.

"Am I handsome, too?"

I whirl around to the guy standing to the left of me and cock my head. "Nope. You have quite the ugly mug. However, you look beat, so what's your poison, firefighter?"

Kelly shrugs, the small smile vanishing from his face as he takes a barstool right in front of where I'm drawing yet another beer. "How about I start off with beer?"

I nod and hand him one, not caring that others might have waited longer. "What happened?"

Shaking his head, he takes a long swallow from his glass, then licks his lips. "I don't know. We had a lot of weird fires. Small ones, when some teen decided to suddenly be a drug dealer, and bigger ones, like when a woman just threw the towel, literally, at the stove, causing a fire that nearly burned down her apartment. Why are people so stupid?"

I cock my head, placing more beers on the bar, which Donna carries to tables. "Blake showed up at my door this morning because he felt weird. Must be something in the air."

He rubs the back of his neck, rolling his shoulders. "I sure hope he is okay."

I don't tell him that Blake wasn't worried about himself, but me. I don't even get to reply because the door opens and a group of young men pour in.

Donna's face lights up, while I can't help but think that we'll have to spend even longer on our feet without a break now.

"Maybe I should close the bar," Warrick mutters.

I furrow my brows. "Why?"

For a long moment, he glances around. I realize there are more people standing than sitting now, their chatter increasing the noise level in the room. Working bars for as long as I have, I don't even notice anymore, which I'm glad about.

"There are too many dangers lurking, too many people we might not recognize later on, and it just... You never know which devil walked in while you weren't looking."

I touch his shoulder. "Nothing will happen, okay?" I smirk. "Even if we have a full moon."

BLAKE

We chase a guy we think might be the right Sinclaire through the streets of downtown New York. I won't lie. I absolutely welcome the exercise, not minding running along the street.

Will and I called in the misunderstanding about the guy in Tia's building, and even as we made our way back to the precinct, Nikki checked and rechecked, finally finding a picture. Because of my gut feeling, and the fact that I knew I should always trust it, we'd gone to all the bars, looking for anybody suspicious.

Most bars were quiet, yet the feeling didn't leave me as we

walked up to Watt's, a bar tucked away between a whole row of clubs that were all closed during the week. There were a few people out, but in the glow of a streetlight, we'd been sure we'd recognized the guy in the picture Nikki had sent over.

The second we'd identified ourselves as NYPD, he took off.

Will hasn't caught up to us yet, but I don't mind. That just means I can be a little rougher with him.

When he stumbles, I all but jump onto his back, both of us crashing to the ground. He grunts while I grab his hands, telling him his rights as I cuff him. The area is dark, the streetlight busted. I can't help my smug smile.

"Running from the police isn't the smartest idea," I tell him just before Will catches up, breathing heavily. "We just had a few questions, then you would've gone home, but I guess you'll be coming back with us now."

Having to interview him will probably hold me up longer than I want, but then again, if the fucking killer is right in a room with me, he's far away from Tia.

As I lead the guy back to the SUV, Will follows. I grin at him over my shoulder. "Getting old?" I tease, but his expression darkens as he joins me and the suspect in the glow of a streetlight.

"Not our guy," he growls.

I blink, then step around the fucker to look at his face. Will is right. The proportions are all wrong.

"Why did you run?" Will asks.

He just arches a brow, and I cock my head. Usually, guys in custody at least sneer, telling us we'll get nothing, but he just stares at us.

I pat him down, finding drugs in his pocket, but not enough to be huge trouble. "Dealer or buyer?" I ask. I know if he just bought, we're likely to let him rot in a cell overnight.

"One night or new lifestyle?" Will crosses his arms over his chest.

"I could use a coffee and a donut. You have some in your car?" It's the first and only thing the guy says.

I push him toward the SUV while Will calls in the bust. A patrol car will soon be there to take in the dude so we can get back out onto the street and look at some more bars.

Technically, I know anything can happen at any bar we've already been to, but I tell myself that the presence of two detectives was enough to scare anyone off for a night.

Once we hand the guy over, I can't help but feel the need to talk to Tia, just for a second. I don't care if she's working, if she should answer her phone.

"You're making me nervous," I hear Will say as I search my pockets.

"Lost my phone," I tell him with a sigh. "Must've fallen out when I tackled him to the ground. With any luck, it's still there."

I jog away before thinking that jumping into the SUV would be faster, or before considering that it might have been found and taken already.

Rounding the street corner, I spot it, moonlight reflecting off the screen. Walking over, I crouch to retrieve it.

Hearing a car engine, I look up, knowing there's no time for me to move. I jump slightly as the car hits me, my body rolling over the hood and windshield, then the roof, finally landing on the asphalt with a thud.

Groaning, I push up onto all fours, taking a mental inventory of my body, finding nothing horribly wrong. I glance up, seeing the car reversing to hit me again, my head hitting the ground this time.

Pain explodes inside my skull, causing a screeching sound to bounce around in my head. Or maybe it's the car hurrying out of there. I try to look around, but something warm clouds my vision. I try to blink it free as I struggle back onto all fours.

My left side is on fire. I place one foot onto the ground, trying to push up, but can't.

I hear the screeching of car tires before...

"Atwood?" I hear the panic in Will's voice.

I nod. "Yeah. Some fucker ran me over. Probably waiting for the guy I tackled," I mutter, my words slow and slurred.

"Yes. Most likely a dealer. What hurts?" He grips me under my arm to help me up.

"I think I just have bruises and a bump on the head..."

"We're going to the hospital. Do you remember anything about the car?"

I force a smile. "It had four wheels." I wipe at my brow, my wrist coming away bloody. "I think I'm hurt."

My thoughts feel jumbled. Before I let Will help me into the SUV, I look around for my cell again. I spot it, crushed into the pavement.

"Tia," I whisper, my thoughts becoming more sluggish the longer I stand here.

"Hospital first," Will says, sounding far away.

I want to nod, not sure my body's following orders any longer.

CHAPTER SIXTEEN

TIA

MY SURROUNDINGS BLUR as I rush to the ER entrance, Kelly standing there.

"Where is he?"

My voice sounds hoarse as he leads me inside. I feel as if I've been screaming for hours when, in reality, I haven't spoken since Will came into the bar, telling me what happened.

"How is he? Kelly, say something!"

He wraps me in his arms as tears stream down my face.

It's midnight. All I can think is we were so close to the day ending without anything happening, his gut feeling wrong. Now we're here.

"He's just being thoroughly checked. When Will brought him in, he had a cut, a lump on his head, and was slurring. They were worried about a head injury."

"My head's fine."

I spin at the voice and see Blake sitting in a wheelchair, a nurse pushing it. His head is a mess, his dirty blond strands covered in dried blood, and there's a butterfly bandage over the cut, the area around it bruised. His shoulder is wrapped, securing it to his body. I hurry over and stop myself a second before throwing my arms around him. I drop to my knees in front of him, unsure if I could touch him or not.

"Man, you're okay," Kelly exclaims.

He licks his lips, ignoring his best friend while his gaze stays on me. "I'm okay, Tia. I promise. Just some bruises, a cracked rib, a dislocated shoulder, and a small cut on my head." He cups my cheek.

I lean into his touch, trying hard not to cry. "When I heard you were at the hospital, I thought…"

"They wanted to keep me for observation, just to make sure my brain was okay, but I signed myself out. I'm not spending the night here."

"I'm taking you home," Kelly announces.

I stand. "Will left the SUV so I could come here—"

Blake's expression hardens. "He let you *drive* here?"

Before I can answer, the nurse clears her throat. "No matter how he gets home, Detective Atwood should not be alone for the next twenty-four hours, just in case he has a concussion."

I nod. "He won't be alone."

Kelly agrees. "There'll be someone with him."

She smiles. "I'll get the discharge papers and the pain medication."

I nod, then feel Blake grasp my hand, squeezing it. "You should be at work."

Turning my attention back to him, I shake my head. "I shouldn't be. Warrick knows why I had to leave."

Kelly squeezes my shoulder, then nods toward Blake. "If you need any help with his lazy ass, call me, okay? Any time."

I nod, and he hugs me.

"Hands off my girl," Blake mutters, trying to get to his feet.

I gently push him back down. "Wait until we're outside."

Of course he doesn't. Once the nurse comes back and hands me everything, he gets to his feet with a groan. Kelly offers to help him into the SUV, but Blake threatens to kick his ass if he doesn't leave. Holding his hands up, he smirks and winks at me before walking off. I feel Blake wrap an arm around my shoulders. He presses a kiss to the side of my head. I close my eyes for a second, allowing the worry to finally fall away.

"Promise to tell me the moment you don't feel good," I beg.

He chuckles. "Promise, but I've had worse. Once, when I was shot, I—"

I hold up my hand, wincing. "Thank you. That's enough. I don't need to know that. You were hurt on the job, and..." I swallow, shaking my head.

He squeezes me tighter as we walk outside, then pulls me against his body, pressing his lips to mine. I can tell it's for my benefit, not his. I cup his cheeks, feeling the stubble under my hands. He tastes of sugar, so I pull back.

"What exactly did they give you in there?"

He laughs. "A sucker. I wanted food, but they didn't want to give that to me. So we compromised."

"I'll cook for you once we're at your place."

His expression turns serious. "You sure you don't want to go home? I don't mind coming with you."

Despite the fact that Chloe would throw a fit, I know that the kids wouldn't leave him alone, and he needs rest. "I already texted Chloe. She knows she has to get the kids ready. We're all settled."

He draws me in again, holding me. I want to ask what other

injures he has, what hurts the most, but decide to take him home first. Opening the SUV door for him, I hear him huff.

"I'm not an invalid, you know."

I shrug. "You're hurt. I need to know I'm taking care of you."

He smirks, then slips into the seat. I help buckle him in and close the door, then walk around to my side and climb in.

When he laughs softly, I glance at him. "What *now*?"

"I don't usually let people drive my car. I did with Will earlier because..."

"Because of your gut feeling?"

He nods. "Exactly. But other than that..." He shrugs, grimacing at the pain. "My car, my wheel."

I grin. "Tough, because it's my car and my wheel right now. By the way, Will went back to the precinct instead of coming to the hospital because he wants to look into that car and the guy you arrested."

Blake shakes his head. "Must be your doe eyes," he mutters.

"Come again?"

"Well, he's already complained about you knowing too much, but then he goes ahead and tells you about what we did tonight. It must be your eyes."

I sober. "Or maybe it was the fact that he was worried sick about you and had to watch me pale before his eyes when he told me what happened. Besides... I think he wanted to make sure you knew he didn't abandon you or didn't care."

He smirks, the corner of his lips lifting just a tiny bit. "I would never think that. We're partners. Also, Wolfe will probably show up at my place."

I pull onto the street. "I don't care, as long as they don't expect me to go anywhere."

BLAKE

I watch Tia tremble. I'm not even sure she realizes it as she putters around my kitchen. I don't mind watching her, but I worry about her breaking down. Then again, knowing she's worried about me makes me smile.

I won't say getting hurt was worth it, but this is nice.
More than nice.
This tells me she's in deeper than she thought.
"Tia, come here," I order as she stirs noodles in a pot.
"I'm good."
"Liar," I whisper.
She looks up, giving me a smile. It's almost convincing. Almost. I cannot imagine how many times she's faked a smile like that.

"No. I'm seriously okay," she assures me, her voice steady. I'd be worried about her ability to lie if I didn't know she only did it when it concerned her.

"Tell me you don't wish you could hug me tightly right now."

This time, her smile is genuine before she turns serious. "I don't want to hug you right now." Her voice jumps and she lowers her eyes.

"Liar," I tell her again, then I hold out my arm for her. "Please."

She places the spoon onto a plate next to the stove and walks over to where I lean against the counter. She carefully wraps her arms around me and I pull her as close as I can. The medication makes every pain in my body nothing more than a dull ache.

I know I shouldn't move much, but I need to hold her. I kiss the top of her head. "I'm okay," I promise her.

"You could be dead." Her voice cracks.

"With you in my life? No chance."

She shakes her head against my chest, then trembles, the shock finally catching up with her. "I thought you were going to die on me. Will said…" She sucks in a breath. "Your words were slurred. I… I…" She grips me tighter, my ribs protesting, but I don't say anything.

"It was because the adrenaline wore off and my body wanted to shut down. Nothing else."

She starts crying silently, her shoulders shaking, and I let my hand slide up her back, cupping the back of her neck before kissing her head "Look at me, Tia."

"In a minute," she mutters.

"Now," I urge. She lifts her face, tears streaking down her cheeks.

I love you.

The words are there, ready to be said. I've never had anyone worry so much about me.

"Jesus, Blake. Don't ever scare me like that again, okay? Promise?"

I want to, but the words get stuck in my throat because that's exactly why I haven't dated anybody. I cannot promise that.

"At least lie to me," she demands, clearly knowing where my thoughts are.

"I promise. No more scaring you."

She nods, then goes on her tiptoes to kiss me thoroughly. She tastes of rosemary. I grin to myself. "Already ate some without me?"

She rolls her eyes. "I needed to taste the sauce to know I seasoned it right. It's not so easy when your mind is everywhere but on the cooking." I watch her return to the stove just as the doorbell rings. "I—"

"Got it," I finish for her, then walk over before she can move. I can open my own goddamn door. It's Wolfe, as expected. He stares at me for a long time, then nods.

"Good."

I step aside, letting him in. I know exactly how hard it is to find the right words when visiting someone from the team who got injured.

"Who has your back?"

"I do, sir," Tia announces, walking out of the kitchen.

Wolfe eyes her for a long moment, then cocks his head. "I've seen you before. Where?"

She lifts her chin. "Warrick's. I've worked there a few months."

"She's also my girlfriend."

Wolfe's eyes snap back to me. "A bartender?"

I grit my teeth, hoping Tia doesn't think he insulted her. He's just making sure he understands things right. The case is now much more personal for me.

She walks back into the kitchen. I look back at Wolfe. "She's safe. She doesn't know about...the particulars of the case. I... I didn't plan this, and trust me, knowing her line of work..."

He nods. "Hard, huh? Knowing what you know, yet not wanting to scare her?"

I force a smile. "Try not wanting to make her angry. Arguing with her about anything is... Yeah." I blow out a breath. "She's felt watched twice so far."

He arches a brow. "Our guy isn't a stalker."

"He isn't, but he's also killed women by mistake. We've suspected him to get smarter, change his MO."

"Mr. Wolfe, are you staying for dinner?" Tia calls from the kitchen.

He smiles at me. "No, thank you. I just wanted to make sure my man here was okay. You seem to have things under control, kiddo. Call me if you need anything. I'll leave my card."

I smirk, wondering what Tia thinks about being called kiddo, but don't say anything. Wolfe steps closer to me, lowering his voice, his expression serious.

"We'll keep your girl safe. You have my word. And the fucker you arrested? Narcotics was actually looking for him. More than likely, his partners were in the car that hit you. We'll find them."

I nod, thankful for the information, mostly because now I can ease Tia's mind. That's all that really matters.

THE BUZZING of a phone wakes me. My head hurts, but when I shift, I feel a warm body next to me, moving whenever I do.

"It's not mine," Tia mutters, her voice sleepy.

"I got it," I reply, but my whole body aches in protest. I knew that was going to happen. Day two and three after being injured are usually the worst.

I look at my phone, seeing two things. One, it's Will, and two, it's three thirty in the morning. Instantly, I'm wide awake as I answer.

"Tell me she's still with you," he says, his voice anxious.

"What?"

"Tia... Tell me she's still with you."

I glance to my side, seeing Tia sit up, one of my shirts draped over her body. "Who is it?" she asks.

Will sighs. "Thank God. They found another body around the corner from Gun & Shot. I was worried she went back to work. I wouldn't have known how to tell you, man."

"She's here," I say, gathering her close, despite my pain. "She's safe." I don't say it for his benefit, but for mine. My heart flips. The thought of how close it was this time nearly makes me throw up.

Tia suddenly pulls the phone from my hands. "Is it Donna? Tell me it wasn't near the bar. Will, please tell me it wasn't Donna." Her voice is urgent, her body shaking again.

"I don't know, Sunshine. I haven't arrived yet. Got the address from Wolfe and needed to know before I got there... I just wanted to be prepared."

I kiss Tia's forehead. "Maybe it's not related, but a crazy coincidence," I mutter. Tia turns on the speaker, then drops the phone onto the bed, curling into me.

"They told me she had a note on her arm, Blake."

I close my eyes. "Call us when you know something more," I tell him, then hit end.

Tia throws the covers off. "I have her number. I need to call her, just to make sure... I don't care if I wake her. I need to call her." She stumbles off the bed in search of her phone. I follow, yet much slower, my body protesting each step.

I make a detour to the kitchen to pop another pain pill, then find my girl standing in the middle of the living room. Just as she picks up her phone, it starts to ring. She looks at me, eyes wide.

"Warrick," she whispers, then answers. "H-Hello?" Her face pales, eyes filling with tears, bottom lip trembling. "Yes. Okay." She hangs up.

I walk over and pull her into my arms, my heart breaking. "I'm so sorry."

I knew Donna, and it hurts me to think someone as

bubbly as she was won't be around anymore, but part of me can't help but think we got lucky. Had I not been injured...

"It could've been you," I whisper into her hair, needing her to understand how close it was.

She shakes her head, stepping out of my arms, anger on her face. "*No*, it *couldn't* have been. You would've picked me up. Donna would still be alive because he would've seen you!" I let her rant, knowing she needs to. She places her hands on her hips. "She would be safe. Why would anyone want to hurt her? And what kind of note was left on her? Wanna tell me?"

"Did Warrick find her?"

I itch to go to the crime scene, be with the team and hunt the bastard down, but I'm even more motivated to never let Tia out of my sight again.

"The guy was probably at the bar tonight." She starts pacing. I sit down on the couch, watching her. "I probably talked to him. Maybe even served him."

She pushes her fingers through her hair, tearing at the blonde strands. "I shouldn't have left, but I was so worried about you. You said something felt wrong... That gut feeling of yours... I couldn't stop thinking about you. Couldn't..." She gasps. "It's my fault."

I shouldn't have shown up at her door when I was vulnerable because she now blames herself for things that were my fault.

"Yeah, you're right. You should've stayed at the bar instead of coming to see me at the hospital," I agree.

She freezes, then spins and kneels in front of me. "No." She kisses my thigh. "That wasn't how I meant it. I couldn't have been anywhere but by your side, but Blake... Had I finished my shift, maybe I could remember someone who stood out. I..."

I draw her onto my lap, gritting my teeth against the way my muscles scream, and kiss the side of her neck. "You'd be dead now." I don't know where the conviction comes from, but it's there.

Had I not been injured, I know with certainty that I'd be hearing about Tia's body.

TIA

"You need to stay home. I'm going to close the bar for a few days. They found Donna's body, and I only have myself to blame."

Warrick's words echo in my head as Blake cuddles me, caresses me, tells me it would've been me.

There's something in his tone that lets me know he's convinced of the fact, and frankly, so am I. Guilt threatens to swallow me, and yet...

"You saved my life." In a weird, twisted way, he did. "I mean—"

"I didn't," he interrupts.

I rub my nose along his jaw and kiss his lips. "If you and I weren't dating, I would have been there. Would I have remembered the guy? Maybe, but I also probably would've been dead. You'd be standing over my body now, another nameless woman, another mark in your files. If you and I weren't a thing, I'd be..."

He cradles my face in his hands, kissing my lips, peppering my cheeks with kisses, then sighs. "It wasn't your time. You'd still have been alive. Maybe you would've left early that night for some other reason. I'm a strong believer in fate."

I pull back so I can look at him. He brushes a curl behind my ear. "We would've talked in the bar eventually, Tia. After I would've spoken to you, there's no way I could've walked away. I'd have started to worry about you. You and I, Tia... We were meant to be in each other's lives."

Hearing the conviction dripping from each and every word makes tears come to my eyes. "You think so?"

He nods. "Yes. Before I met you, I didn't want anyone in my life, but now I can't imagine my life without you. Ask Kelly. I think he was the first who knew how special you were to me. So, as much as I hurt for Donna, I'm grateful I got injured so you weren't at the bar. I'd take all the physical pain in the world over having to find your body in a ditch."

He draws me back against him, holding on tighter than before.

Pain sears through me. "Donna..." I clear my throat. "She was my first real friend in a long time. And if Warrick closes the bar down..."

I'd be out of a job, a friend, and everything else, besides Blake, that gives me pleasure. I love my nieces and my nephew, but over the last few weeks, I've realized they can't be all my life is about.

"Warrick won't shut the bar down. It's a refuge for so many cops. He won't take that away from them. Besides... We know Donna wouldn't have wanted that. She was someone who always said to fight against what scares you and not let it take over your life."

He's right. I saw that in the way she lived life to the fullest. But it still worries me. "I need the bar. I need the regulars. I need that escape."

His jaw flexes. "Maybe we should get some more sleep. Even if you don't have to take the kids to school tomorrow, you'll still have to pick them up at some point, right?"

Before I can answer, my cell rings again. I glance down, blinking. "It's my mother." I look at Blake. "She never calls." I put on a fake smile and answer. "Hi, Mom."

When I hear her sob, my heart squeezes. "Letitia? Thank God! You're okay! An officer called, asking if I knew where you were. He found my number in a file or something. He said you work at a bar and someone is killing bartenders... Chloe didn't know where you were."

I startle at that because Chloe knows exactly where I am. Also... "You called Chloe?"

She sniffles. "Of course. You are my daughter and I needed to know... Oh god, it's all over the news."

I nod toward the TV. Blake turns it on, cursing under his breath. There's a news report running, complete with yellow police tape, flashing lights—and one lonely shoe. Donna's shoe.

"Did you know the girl? I know there are many bars out there, but they wouldn't just call me for no reason, right?"

I bite my lip, unsure if I should lie to her or not. Blake holds out his hand. I furrow my brows, and he nods toward my phone. I hand it over.

"Mrs. Howe, I am Detective Blake Atwood of the New York City Police Department. The officer had no right to call you, making you panic. I promise, that's not the way we do things up here. If your daughter had been involved in this in any way, we would've showed up at your house. Please, trust me when I say she's safe." His gaze stays on me as my mother replies. He nods a few times, then smiles softly. "Trust me. I won't let her out of my sight."

My heart warms. Still, I have a feeling there's a storm brewing.

CHAPTER SEVENTEEN

BLAKE

BEING at home with Tia and *not* able to get her naked drives me crazy. I had hurt worse than I thought I would, but luckily, it only lasted six days. We watched the kids together, which was...nice. There is so much innocence, so much pleasure to be found in the smallest things, I find myself wondering what it would be like to have my own.

Of course, that thought is followed by the ultimate fear of leaving them alone in the world because of my job.

It's eight days after Donna's death, and I'm going stir crazy. God, I wish I could be at work, but Wolfe refuses, and Will doesn't protest. He also doesn't show up to tell me about what's going on with the case. I wonder what they found, what's going on, and wish they'd just let me be behind my desk.

"Warrick's opening the bar tonight."

The words I've dreaded to hear finally come, and my stomach drops. "I hope you don't plan on working. Not after what happened."

She lifts her chin, fire and determination in her blue eyes. The kids play in their room, so I pull Tia into my arms.

"I am going in *because* of what happened, Blake. I need the money, have had Chloe tell me I'm a burden, a liability, and how selfish I am to be hanging out with you as much as I do. You know, because the kids will get used to you, then you'll walk out on us."

I cannot believe that's what's Chloe's been spewing when I wasn't around. She's the last person who should call her sister selfish. "I hope she realizes I won't be going anywhere."

She presses a kiss to my nose just as my phone starts vibrating in my pocket. I grab it and look at the caller ID, my eyes widening as I answer. "Will?" I say, and Tia perks up.

"Blake, you ready to come back in? We want to get you caught up on everything."

"Oh, my god. Yes." It's out before I even think about talking it over with Tia. "I'll be right there." I hang up, curious about what is going on—and worried because I know Tia will definitely go back to work now.

"You're going back to work? God, I'm so happy for you," she says with a tight smile. I know exactly what she's doing. I grab her hips and pull her to sit next to me on the couch.

"Just because you pretend to be happy about me going back after I was injured doesn't mean I can do the same. I still think you shouldn't go to work. In fact, I—"

She places her finger on my lips. "I did my own thing before you came along, and I'll do it now. I'm not going to let a freak scare me. I'm not going to let Warrick deal with everything alone, either. He knew her longer than I did. He probably considered her more than just an employee."

I know she'll go in no matter what I say, and I also know she'll fight me if I try to make her stay home. If that happens, I wouldn't even get the luxury of picking her up tonight.

Besides, I admire her loyalty, no matter how stupid I consider that to be.

"Call me once you exit the subway and—"

She shakes her head before I even finish. "No. He's already killed near our bar. He won't be back. I'm going to be fine. It's just a few blocks. I'll be okay. I promise."

I wonder if Warrick will wait for her at the station. Then again, he probably won't be able to leave the bar while it's open. Rubbing my hands down my face, I bite my lower lip to keep from ordering her to stay home. She holds my gaze, daring me to fight her on this. I'm reminded that she's been fending for herself for years. She's not used to having someone around who cares about her.

I stand from the couch because sitting makes me anxious right now. "God, woman. Promise me you'll be careful. Scream as loud as you can if someone weird approaches you. Kick and fight. Promise me that when I reach the bar tonight, you'll be standing there, a smile on your face."

She stands and steps into my arms. "He kills after closing, not before. Besides, he took a long time between his second and third kills. Cooling off period, right?"

I don't know if that were the case. Maybe he's been sick or out of town. We don't know, which makes this all the more scary.

First two victims were too close together for comfort. We'd seen all the news reports on it. Not because I was curious, but because I'd hoped it would scare her enough to reconsider working for Warrick.

I love the guy, but Tia...

She shrugs as the girls come running into the room. "I'll be fine. You go to work and help them catch the sick bastard. And then... Then we'll deal with everything else."

As if she'd stop working at the bar once everything is safe again.

I kiss her long and sweet. When I pull back and see hardly any trace of sadness in her eyes, I wonder briefly when they'll release Donna's body to be buried, fearing it will give Tia another kick in her stomach.

If only I could protect her, not only from the killer, but the whole pain in the world. I'd give everything just to know she'd never suffer another day in her life.

After all, she's the woman I love, and that means more to me than my own life.

―――

TIA

The kiss Blake gave me before going back to the precinct leaves a bitter taste in my mouth. Not because he's worried about me, but it tasted like so much more than there should be between us.

The last several days have been a flurry of activity, and I dread being alone because I know I'll think too much. Luckily, Chloe walks through the door.

"Hey!"

We haven't spoken much, but I haven't really missed her. It made me realize that we're not really sisters anymore, but people who take care of her kids in shifts.

She gives me a brief smile. "Hello. Where's your shadow?" I think I detect a hint of jealousy in her voice, but decide to ignore it.

"He went back to work. Thank God. It drove him crazy not to know what was going on with the case. And luckily for me, because it's back to work tonight. The kids were okay today, and Neo slept a lot. He might be coming down with something. It he's still sick tomorrow, I'm going to take him to the doctor."

"You won't have to."

I blink, surprised. "Really? You'll be home?"

She shakes her head. "No. Come tomorrow, the kids and I won't be here anymore."

It feels like the floor shifts. "What?"

She finally faces me fully, checking the hallway, but I sent the girls back into their room. Ever since Chloe slapped me, they've been...different, more compliant, as if they thought what happened had been their fault. I watch my sister lick her lips.

"What you've been doing the last several days is a disgrace. Flaunting your sex partner in front of them..." She shakes her head. "You kept him in your room and—"

"I can't believe you. He's my *boyfriend*. What I do in my room and with whom is none of your business, unless I let him wander around naked."

Chloe lifts her chin. "You seem to forget that these are *my* kids and I can decide whom I want around them and whom I do not. Definitely not a cop who reeks of danger and reckless decisions."

I cough, my mind spinning. I feel lightheaded, as if the air I breathe doesn't reach my brain. "*I* forget that these are your kids? You've barely been home the last few months! You cannot be serious. Where exactly are you moving?"

"In with Christian."

I blink. "Your *boss*?"

She finally looks a little uneasy. "We've been so much more than that for a while now. He's well-off, has a house big enough for all four of us, and the kids will have a great nanny. It's outside of New York, but at least they'll be in a better school and no longer in a shitty neighborhood. You should've picked a better place for us to live. If anything would've happened to them..."

My jaw drops. "Who *are* you? I picked this area because it was the only thing we could afford on my paycheck.

She nods. "Exactly. It's your fault for having such a stupid job. Well, now you and your corrupt cop can have all the space to yourself. I'm just here to gather up the most important things and grab the kids, then Christian will pick us up."

"I sacrificed everything for you."

I cannot believe she's spinning this tale to make me out to be the bad one. Blake and I watched the kids, and I know they love him. Neo is much calmer when he holds him, as if the deeper voice soothes him.

"What exactly did I ever do to you, Chloe?"

I wonder what's brought this on. This has hit me out of the blue, leaving me speechless, breathless—and hopeless.

"He comes into your life, all knight in shining armor with his hazel eyes and perfect teeth, thinking he is the only one who knows what's good for you, and you follow him like a goddamn puppy. He may be handsome, Tia, but he's not forever. He's a cop. He likes to take risks. You don't honestly think you can excite him for long, do you? And you neglect your family for him. Don't come home at nights, forget to bring the children to school. I'd say I hope you'll be happy with him, but the truth is, it won't work. You're just not enough. You give up everything for him, and he just keeps on taking and—"

"You know nothing about Blake, his work, or his ethics!" She, who took everything from me until I was so exhausted I could barely walk, dares tell me the only good thing in my life isn't good? "You are as selfish as Mom always said you were. Call me when you come down from your high horse. I love you because you're my sister, and I'll always watch the kids for you if you need me to, but I will not listen to this another second. Be well, Chloe, and tell the kids I love them."

I grab my jacket from next to the door and pick up my boots, glad I'd been ready for work anyway. I put everything on out in the hall, shouldering my bag, then make my way out of the building,

I don't allow the worries to flood in, the fear of what will come. Instead, I pull my collar up, ready to face the world, no matter what.

BLAKE

I don't get to the precinct until ten, but everyone else comes in just as late. They've probably been working on tips that lead nowhere, following suspects who turn out to be innocent. As much as we allowed the whole case to sit when there weren't more murders, everyone now scrambles to find even the smallest clue that can tell us exactly what's going on.

"We hoped to have something, but Warrick said the night of Donna's murder, the bar was crawling with new patrons. Seems kinda organized, but we couldn't find any reason they'd all meet at that bar," Nikki reports. I shift through the much bigger file on my desk.

I've already read it all, my mind trying to make connections. "Warrick is opening the bar tonight," I say, and everyone stops talking.

"I'm not surprised, to be honest. The ME released Donna's body today. There'll be a memorial soon, so maybe Warrick feels as if this would be the proper way to say goodbye. To have people at the bar, drowning their sorrows the way he probably wants to," Jim says.

Nikki stands and leans a hip against her desk. "Does that mean your girl's back on shift today?"

"She is, but there's a police car parked outside. Nothing will happen to her." Wolfe walks in. "Good to see you back, Atwood. You take it slow, you hear me?"

"Sure do, sir," I reply, still caught off guard by the fact that there are uniforms at the bar. "Are we watching all bars?"

He doesn't answer, just vanishes into his office. Declan clears his throat. "Well, no. He did that for you. Will told us how worried you were."

"Blake Atwood finally fell for a woman?" Nikki asks, a twinkle in her eyes.

"Of course, she can't be just anyone, but has to be a girl whose life could be in danger, but..." Declan shrugs.

"I love her. I swear, if anything happens to her..." I blink, realizing what I just said. It's the first time I've said those words out loud, and while she probably should've been the first one to hear them, I don't know how she'd react.

They all stare at me as I shift the files on my desk.

"We got you, okay? Someone will have eyes on her at all times," Declan says, and everyone mutters their agreement.

"So, tell me what I need to know."

There's uneasy shifting. Eventually, Wolfe walks back out of his office. "He knew he had the wrong one when he killed Donna. We don't know when he realized it, but he did. Yet he killed her anyway."

My heart drops. "Do we think he's not just going for blonde bartenders now?

Will stands and walks over to the evidence board, pointing at the first two victims. "With the first two, the message on their arms was remorseful." He points to Donna's picture. "With Donna, the words were angry, like he killed her *because* she wasn't who he was looking for. And there was more fury this time. She wasn't just strangled. After she was dead, he beat her up for good measure."

"The anger implies that he won't wait long before he kills again. He seems to be impatient now," I mutter.

"Exactly what we think," Wolfe announces. "When's your girl getting off tonight?"

I shrug. "I don't know. In fact, I'm not sure she knows, either. There's no telling how busy the bar will be today."

He nods. "Okay. So we have some more reports to run through, then I think we all should go over to Gun & Shot. We all knew Donna, talked to her. There's not much to do today anyway. It might be good to talk to some of the regulars there outside of an interview room. I'm desperate. I don't know what else to do, and the media has started pressing down on all of us. That guy needs to be found. Besides, one of our own is at risk now."

I blink. "Who?"

They all smile at me. "You, man. If anything happens to your girl, we'll lose you. Trust me, we like your hairy ass around here," Jim explains, and my chest grows tight. We've all been in this group for a few years now, but I don't think I've ever appreciated them as much as I do that moment.

"She refused to stay home." I don't know why I even say those words. Nikki just snorts.

"A woman who doesn't bow down to you? I like it. She's definitely cool. I need to talk to her. Let's get these reports finished so we can start the secret undercover questioning the boss wants."

Everyone nods as Nikki hands out files. I start reading, realizing how similar the reports are. There has never been anyone who stuck out, acted weird, or spent time in each of the bars. Hell, with him just seeming to target blonde bartenders, we cannot even be sure what he's looking for.

After all, if it were an ex-girlfriend, wouldn't he know exactly what she looks like?

———

TIA

The bar is even busier now than it was the last time I worked, which keeps my mind off Chloe, Blake, and the hundreds of candles burning on the sidewalk not two feet from the front door.

I cannot even begin to imagine how many people have been here over the last few days, placing letters, candles, and single roses on the sidewalk. When I arrived, I wanted to linger out there, but tears came to my eyes the moment I saw her picture.

The mood in the bar is subdued. Warrick and I take turns working behind the bar and waiting tables. A guy Warrick knows has started to help out, collecting the money, and I appreciate it because it means I can deal with the orders while he makes sure they pay.

I see a guy take a seat at the bar. He's of average height and looks, nothing particularly memorable about him, and even though I'd started to classify our patrons as strangers and regulars, we have more strangers in here than ever before so even *that* isn't anything particularly special.

"What can I get you?"

"Oh, so you decide to talk to me today?"

I blink at him. "Come again?"

He gives me a grin, his teeth crooked and yellow, and his

clothes look worn, as if he cannot afford new ones. "I am here, aren't I?"

"I'm sorry. I'm not following." I force out a grin, even though the back of my neck prickles.

He shrugs. "I'd like a beer. You know, I've been here before, but you were too busy talking to a tall guy with dark eyes. You know, the kind who draws attention. Seemed you know him quite well. So, of course, I wasn't important enough." He doesn't sound angry, but there's something about his words that makes my skin crawl.

Is he talking about Kelly? I rack my brain to try and remember if I'd seen him at the bar before, but I come up empty. I knock over a glass on purpose, needing an excuse to get away.

"Shit," I curse. "Warrick, can you come and take over, please? I need to clean up my mess." I kneel behind the counter, my heart in my throat. Warrick kneels, too.

"There is no mess," he mutters. I shake my head. The glass I knocked over fell on the rubber mats behind the bar, so it didn't even break.

I shrug. "Just serve that costumer, okay? He's... I think he tried to hit on me before and was upset because I didn't talk to him. And that was the night Donna died. Kelly came in, the bar was crowded..." I shake my head. Warrick leans forward, kissing my forehead.

"I got it," he promises, standing.

I enjoy the small escape, even though we're busy, but Warrick doesn't say anything.

"Atwood, guys... What a pleasure. Come on over."

I stand so quickly, I get dizzy, holding onto the bar for a second, then see a pair of familiar hazel eyes meeting mine. "Blake."

"Tia."

"What are you doing here?"

He just gives me a soft smile and shakes his head, letting me know that now is not the time. I want to wrap myself up in him, escape everything that's going on. He seems to be my only refuge.

"Take him to the back for a sec and tell him what happened," Warrick says under his breath.

My brows furrow, trying to figure out what he means, when Blake's expression hardens.

"Wolfe, beer in the back?" he asks. His boss looks at Warrick, then me, seeming to see something on my face. His scowl deepens and... Was that a growl?

Once I lead them into Warrick's office, Blake kisses my cheek. "It's nothing," I say, not sure if that's the truth.

"The killer won't be back," Blake mutters, but I'm not sure whom he is trying to convince.

Wolfe shrugs. "How about you tell us what's going on?"

I swallow. "Honestly, it's nothing." He's not the first freak I talked to, and certainly not the most creepy, but I'm more prickly than usual, and it seems to show.

"Why don't you let the pros decide that, sweetie?" Wolfe says. Blake glares at him for the "sweetie" part as I sit down in Warrick's chair.

"There's a guy in the bar. He said something about me finally wanting to talk to him because I didn't last time. I think it was the night he got..." I look at Blake. "You know... Kelly came in. I probably talked to him and ignored a customer or two, but we've been so damn crowded lately, it could've been any other time. I don't remember him. He's nothing spectacular. Besides... I don't make a habit of checking out guys. I flirt with them until they pay, then I move on. I'm a bartender. Smiles make me money."

Blake cocks his head. "Did he stutter or anything? Anything that would make him stand out?"

"Brazen, pissed off..." I rack my brain to remember his eye or hair color, coming up empty. "His tone was controlled, even, but the way he formulated his words... It made me think he was angry. He looked like he barely survives on the money he makes. I..." I rub the heel of my hand over my forehead. "You think... Do you think..."

Wolfe shakes his head. "There hasn't been evidence of the murderer coming back to the bars after he killed. Besides, he's a coward. He wouldn't have called you out like that. It might have been just someone who was pissed because you ignored him. We'll check up on him and ask Warrick about the surveillance tapes, but you should be fine. Don't worry, okay? I'll go and check the guy out." He nods at Blake and walks out the door.

Blake steps close. "You okay?"

I shake my head, feeling as if my world is falling apart. "Chloe moved out. We had a fight about how I'm such a bad person... God, Blake, I don't know what I'm going to do."

And damn if that isn't exactly the point.

CHAPTER EIGHTEEN

BLAKE

THE GUY WAS GONE when Wolfe got back out to the bar. Warrick promised to help however he could, then decided to close the bar for the night.

Tia sits silently next to me as I drive her back to my place because she doesn't want to be alone right now. I hold her hand, kissing the back of it a few times until she finally gives me a smile.

"You're safe, Tia. Wolfe will make sure of it. The case just got personal."

She furrows her brows and turns to me. "What do you mean?"

"He'll make sure someone has an eye on the bar at all times. You'll be safe no matter what."

She pulls her hand from mine and crosses her arms over her chest. "And the others? All the other blonde bartenders out there. I don't need or want a personal guard, Blake. I want this creep off the streets so everyone's safe. I mean..." She grits her teeth.

"What?" I prompt.

"Just because I got lucky enough to bang a cop doesn't mean I should get what others aren't special enough to have."

Her words are like a punch to my stomach. I'm about to lash out when I realize her anger isn't for me. "What exactly did Chloe say to you, Letitia?"

"Oh... *Letitia*, is it? Was I a bad girl? Did I do something you didn't like, Detective?"

I lick my lips, trying to curb my anger. "What the hell is going on? I mean, yes, you went to work, which I didn't like, but that doesn't mean anything. That's how relationships work. You sometimes accept that the other person has their own mind. And I can handle that, as long as you allow me to make sure I get you back home in one piece."

"My work is *my* business, not yours."

I grit my teeth, angry at this discussion. I check the rearview mirror, then pull over and turn toward her.

"You and I are a thing, Tia. You are my girlfriend, and you mean a whole lot to me. I haven't done this relationship thing in a while, but we're in this together. A team. You'd better get used to it."

Her blue eyes mist with tears. I draw her in, kissing her. My lips are aggressive, intense, but she gives as good as she takes, her hands curling into my jacket. Breathless, I pull back and rest my forehead against hers.

"Blake—"

I place my finger against her lips. I saw the way she was on the verge of freaking out, and know we'll have to talk about her job again, but I won't do that in the car.

Instead, I kiss her cheek, then her lips again. "We'll talk at home, okay?"

She closes her eyes and rests her head on my shoulder.

"Tell me about the case. Tell me what you know," she pleads quietly.

I shake my head. "You know I can't do that. As much as the public already knows, we cannot risk a chance of something getting out, and I certainly won't scare you more."

"They are bartenders. Blonde ones, right? Do you know what he's looking for? Will said there's a note. Tell me what the note says."

I wonder for a moment if whatever she can make up in her head will be worse than the truth, and maybe cause her to fear everything, but then decide that she won't tell anyone about what she fears if she doesn't know the truth. I stall by pulling the car back out onto the road.

"Please, Tia. Don't make me compromise my job, okay? How about you tell me what Chloe said?"

She stays silent for a minute, then sighs. "I don't know what to do, Blake. I mean... I can live in the apartment for a little while longer, but buying food, paying bills... Then the kids... What will happen to the kids?"

I take a deep breath. "She counted on you to manage her family. It was easy for her, comfortable."

"She said I was selfish for dating you. She said..." She shakes her head, her devastation obvious. "You know what? None of it matters."

Donna, us, the kids... She doesn't deserve any of this, yet I have a feeling telling her now that she's the least selfish person in the world will be useless.

"Tia, I mean it. You're damn important to me," I say.

"And you to me. I just need you to understand that some things can't change that fast. Maybe she was right about—"

"I'm pretty sure Chloe wasn't right about anything, Tia. We were with those kids almost the whole day for the last week. The moment they came home from school, we were there. We watched them. We spent more time with them than Chloe did, and we both know that."

She shrugs. "It doesn't matter, Blake. She's my family. I promised her I'd take care of her no matter what, but lately, we've drifted apart. A lot. I think I started resenting her for everything she had. I wanted that nine-to-five job, the luxury of coming and going when I wanted, the nights in my bed. It wasn't supposed to be like that."

As I pull up to my place, she jumps out of the car. I quickly put it in park, then rush around to her side. "You *can* have it. Hell, if that's what you want, you should have it. She has the life she does because you have taken care of her mistakes."

The words are out before I can think them over. Tia's jaw drops. If she wasn't already upset and angry, I know she'd listen, but at the moment, that was possibly the worst thing to say.

TIA

Her mistakes.

I stare at Blake, then shake my head. "I'm sorry, but her *mistakes* are my nieces and nephew, and in case that hasn't become clear over the months we've known each other, they are the single most important thing in my life." Even while I say that, my heart thuds in my chest, letting me know things changed.

He steps in, framing my face with his hands. "Maybe you should take tomorrow off to talk to Chloe and sort this out."

I sigh, looking away. "Maybe I should, but I could also give her a day or two—"

"No. Imagine all the things she'll tell herself in the time you don't contact her. It might make it worse.

"Anyway, let's go on up. I think we should get some food in you, then get some sleep."

I stare at him, then up at his apartment. As much as I want to be with him and pretend today didn't happen—hell, that the last weeks didn't happen—something's nagging at the back of my mind. I step away from him.

"First you say Chloe is wrong about everything, and now you suddenly want me to talk to her? Should I have my own life or not?"

Unease crosses his face as he turns away from me, pulling out his keys. "She's your family. Of course you should talk to her, but you should also have your own life sometimes. Come on."

I touch his elbow. "Look at me, Blake," I demand.

He closes his eyes, sighing. "What?"

I cross my arms over my chest. His eyes dart around because we're standing out on the sidewalk at three in the morning.

"This isn't about Chloe and me, is it? This is about you not wanting me to go back to work."

His jaw clenches. "There's a killer on the loose, so yes, this is about you going back to work."

"I need to be my own person. For that, I need to work!"

"Until he's caught, be *my* person."

While the sentiment is incredibly sweet, I don't think either of us really wants that. "I've had to make money since my parents kicked Chloe out when she was pregnant. I didn't need someone else's money then, and I certainly won't take it now. I'm not going to be a burden for you. You are my boyfriend, not my sugar daddy."

God, maybe we really shouldn't discuss this here, but if I

go up with him and this escalates into an argument, I'll feel caught.

He swallows. "You're not gonna come up with me, are you?"

I look back at the park, knowing I'll have to go around it to get home. Which I know he wouldn't allow. Might as well go up with him and hope for the best. "No, I am."

He lets out a relieved breath, then unlocks the door, letting me enter first. Once we're inside, he draws me against him, kissing me almost desperately.

Hoping he doesn't expect me to roll over and give in, I let him kiss me, then we walk up the stairs together. He opens his apartment door and walks over to the couch, turning on the small lamp next to it, bathing everything in a warm glow.

He looks at me still standing by the door. "Are you gonna take off that jacket?"

I shrug. "Are you gonna tell me to stop working?" I check for his reaction, but the only thing I see is him tightening his jaw. "I mean... Blake, this is my money, my independence. I've always had that, and now I need the job more than ever. I have an apartment to pay for."

My sister doesn't make idle threats. As I think about it, I realized I couldn't care less where she goes, but when it comes to her children? I'm worried what they will go through. Besides, I don't know anything about her boss, which makes me nervous. I eye Blake for a moment.

"What?" he asks.

"Nothing. Forget it," I whisper, and he closes the distance between us, titling up my chin.

"Tell me."

I shrug. "I was just wondering. Chloe's boss, the guy she's moving in with—"

He grins guiltily. "I checked him when I first met him.

Clean. Good guy. I don't know what she did to get him, but he checks out. Is he a douche because he allowed her to stay away from her kids for so long? Yes, but that's his only crime."

I blink in surprise before nodding slowly, yet it doesn't ease my mind. It also makes me wonder if I should see this as a new beginning. "Maybe I should look for a smaller apartment in a better area," I muse.

He pulls me close. "Yes, you should. For sure."

I lean into him, his heartbeat thudding under my ear calming me. "Damn. Your heart sounds as if it's going to burst out of your chest," I grin to myself.

He kisses the top of my head. "It's you," he replies, "and that's a good feeling. I'm used to panic driving my blood, but it's all you. Has been for a while. Thank you for that."

I close my eyes, knowing this truce between us won't last long because as much as he probably thinks I won't go back to work tomorrow, it's not true. I need to be close to him to remember that there is something good in my life.

AS HE CARRIES me to the bedroom and places me softly onto the bed. I hold onto him, eager to have my hands on his skin. It's a weird urgency, one that feels like this could be the very last time we're together.

He frames my face as my hands slip under his shirt and hoodie. I only then notice how cold my hands are. He shivers and laughs, then lifts his arms so I can free him of the clothes.

"Tia," he whispers, his brows furrowing, but I don't let him get any further, claiming his lips while I shrug out of my coat, then discard that and my shirt onto the floor, pressing my bare skin against his.

He groans, his heart beating against mine. I slip my hands

into his jeans. There's indecision in his gaze, as if he wants to say something, but it's the last thing I want because neither one of us will give in about me working.

We're at an impasse, and while I won't give up on him or us, I don't think discussing what happened tonight is the right thing to do at the moment.

He reaches up and cups my breasts through the bra I still wear, teasing my nipples with his thumbs until I ache for so much more contact. My hands wander to his pants, brushing his erection, making him moan into my mouth.

"These jeans need to go," I mutter against his lips. He nods, not stopping me when I open the belt, then undo the button and the zipper.

I look up at him as I crouch, taking his pants and briefs with me. I hold them as he steps out, then stay on my knees.

I kiss his thighs as he grasps my shoulders. "Tia..." I lazily lick up his length from bottom to tip, then wrap my lips around him. "Holy shit."

He curses more, while I hum in appreciation. His body trembles, his hands in my hair. I pull the ponytail holder free, the waves tumbling around my shoulders, giving him something to hold onto.

His grip isn't painful, yet strong enough to make lust shoot down my spine, pooling in my stomach.

I swallow him down before pulling back slowly and repeating the motion. My palms cup his ass, the muscles jumping whenever my teeth graze his length.

"Please," he gasps. "This is not how I want this to go, Tia. Please, let me be inside of you. I need to be... I..." He moans. "Please."

I'm tempted to make him explode this way, precum coating my tongue and urging me on. While his lips protest, his hips don't as they gently rock back and forth, causing the friction he so desperately seeks. His hand cups my chin and tilts it up. I meet his eyes, knowing how I must look with my lips around his dick.

"Some other time, Tia," he whispers, then gently pulls out before helping me back to my feet, kissing me softly, groaning.

I chuckle. "You know, I wouldn't mind—"

"I would. I want to be close to you, Tia. *Very* close." His fingertips brush over my skin with a patience I don't possess currently.

I close my eyes when he dips his fingertips into my bra, rolling my nipple between his thumb and index finger until I grab his arms, needing to hold onto him before my knees give out.

He kisses down my neck and along my collarbone, his tongue following the path his lips dictate, and then kneels. He kisses my stomach as he takes off my boots and jeans, then urges me toward the bed.

I lay down, watching him in the light falling in from the hallway. It's not much, but enough for me to see the passion in his eyes. "Blake—"

I quickly stop as I realize what I was about to say. There's no way telling him how amazing he is wouldn't end in those three words. The words that basically mean "I got you".

Because, ultimately, isn't that what we mean when we say it?

I love you means I have your back

I love you means you can fall, and I will catch you.

I love you means you can be whomever you want to be around me.

"Tia."

It doesn't sound as if there's a world of hidden meaning in that word, but I can't decide if I'm glad about that or not.

When he covers my body with his, I stretch to turn on the

lamp on the nightstand. He blinks in surprise. "Blake, tell me you'll support me if I go back to work tomorrow," I plead, and he kisses my nose.

"How about we talk about that in the morning? Right now, you're naked underneath me, which means I would promise you anything. That's not fair. Not when it comes to this topic. So... Tomorrow?"

I brush my fingertips across his cheek, licking my lips. When he wakes up tomorrow, I won't be here. The answer he just gave me lets me know everything I need to.

―――

BLAKE

Come morning, I'll offer to give her a loan, something to make it possible for her to find a new apartment and quit her job.

I get that she doesn't want to be a burden, but I have high hopes that she'll give in and not work if I take the financial worries off her. The thought of her taking the subway and walking to work makes me sick with fear.

I've seen the bodies. It's too easy to imagine Tia being one of them.

Shaking the thought off, I let my hand wander up her arm, getting caught in her bracelet. I think I remember it from the ball, but I can't be sure.

"What's that?" I ask.

She twists the charms until she finds the Eiffel Tower. "Before we knew about Chloe's pregnancy, I wanted to go to Europe. When I started my senior year, my mother gave me this bracelet to remind me to always follow my dreams and stay strong. After..." She swallows. "After the fallout, I didn't wear it much." She licks her lips. "I thought it would be... I don't know. Unfair to Chloe or something, but this morning, I felt as if I needed an extra reminder to be strong."

I kiss her wrist, feeling her pulse against my lips, then claim her mouth in a passionate kiss. There are things I need her to know, but I know I cannot risk saying them while we're teetering on the edge of a fight.

She wouldn't believe me, would assume I was trying to emotionally blackmail her, and that's the last thing I want.

When I finally tell Tia I love her, she won't be able to doubt a single syllable I whisper.

I reach behind her to unclasp her bra, throwing it to the floor before pulling her panties off. Watching her, I sit back on my heels to grab a condom, her blue eyes wide and hazy with lust. There's infinity in those eyes, and I'll never get tired if trying to learn all her secrets.

"You are so beautiful," I mutter as I trail one fingertip down her chest to her core, finding her warm and wet. She swallows when I brush her middle, then slip one finger inside of her. It's not enough, for either of us, and it couldn't be more obvious.

"Do you mind if we skip the rest of the foreplay?" I ask, my voice raspy. She giggles, the sound breathless and sexy.

"No. I need you inside of me."

I roll the condom on and settle between her thighs, my eyes on hers as I place my hands on either side of her head. I slowly push into her with a groan, finding her tight and wet. She wraps her legs around my hips, pulling me in farther.

"I'm trying to take it slow, Tia."

"I don't want it slow. Don't be gentle right now, Blake."

I rest my forehead against hers, pushing all the way in and pausing, no matter how much her hips urge me to do otherwise. I nip her bottom lip before allowing my tongue to invade her mouth, kissing her like she's never been kissed before.

When I finally move my hips, I nearly come undone right then and there.

People who tell you there's no difference between fucking a stranger and making love to somebody you care about clearly never loved. It's easy to just get to it when you just want to reach orgasm, never seeing the person again, but right now?

I know I'll see Tia again, and hopefully will do so for the rest of our lives. That makes this different, new, more intense than anything I've ever experienced. I move my hips lazily, making sure my body rubs against hers with each new thrust, and swallow all her moans with my lips.

I don't stop kissing her even when she urges me to go faster, take her higher.

I don't stop kissing her when her whole body starts to tremble, her nails digging into my back.

And I don't stop kissing her when she pulls her lips from mine, whispering my name before the waves of pleasure crash over her, her insides clenching my dick. I thrust a few more times, gritting my teeth while I watch the contentment on her face. The pleasure I see, the pure bliss pushes me over the edge, too, and I press my lips against her erratic pulse while I see stars.

This is exactly what life is all about, and I'm not ready to let go of Tia just yet.

―――

SURPRISINGLY, I sleep through the night and don't feel Tia get up. Even before I'm fully awake and check around the apartment, I know she left. I'm furious, more than I can say, yet I shouldn't be surprised. I knew she wasn't going to give in on the topic of her working, and she knew I wouldn't let her go.

I should've seen it coming. I'm a fucking cop. I pride myself in smelling out people hiding something, but for some reason, I'd been sure she'd see my point, would give me a chance to argue with her about it.

I try to call her, but it goes to voicemail. She changed her greeting.

"Don't hate me, Blake. Try to understand. I'm sorry I can't give in, but I'm not sorry you are in my life. I'll see you."

I climb back into bed with a sigh and lean against the headboard, resting my head back, and wonder how in the world I can keep the woman safe when she's not ready to let me.

CHAPTER NINETEEN

BLAKE

> I'm fine. It's quiet at home. Work is the only thing keeping me busy and distracted...unless you agree I can work.

AFTER READING HER TEXT, I throw my phone onto the table, furious. It doesn't matter that there are cops following her basically all the time and that I shouldn't be worried, but thinking how reckless she is...

After she vanished from my apartment that morning, I haven't seen her. I call her daily, hoping she'll tell me I was right, but the truth is, I know she won't.

Kelly said he saw her at Gun & Shot and she looks pale and exhausted. It can't be from watching the kids because Chloe was true to her word.

"She still won't let you bully her into staying home?"

Nikki waggles her brows from across the room, feeling smug. She's been to the bar to see Tia. It makes me feel a little lighter knowing all my team members watch out for her. That doesn't mean I don't miss her.

"I'm not bullying her into anything. I'm sorry if I want her to be alive more than I want her to have a job."

Declan snickers, and Will rolls his eyes, but Nikki sighs and walks over, perching on the corner of my desk. "If there were a killer trailing you, Atwood, would you stay home if she pled with you to do so, tears streaming down her face?" She holds a hand up. "And before you answer, truly imagine it."

I don't need to think hard about that because the image of Tia crying makes me swallow. And still...

"No, I'd be here, hunting the fucker. But that's different. This is my job. I come here every day knowing there are crazy people who want my head. She is a bartender. She doesn't own a gun, doesn't have self-defense training, doesn't have any idea what to do should she be attacked."

Nikki shrugs. "My point is, you wouldn't stop working because she wants it. Why do you expect her to stop working because *you* want it? Did it ever occur to you that maybe, just maybe, you could keep her safe if you weren't being such a dick? You could pick her up at her place to drive her to work, then be there before closing to drive her home." She glances toward Wolfe's office. "He'd understand you being gone for a while, and you'd know she was safe."

I smirk. "Which implies that you, too, think she is in danger. Shouldn't you be on my side? She could stay home, read, take care of herself the way she hasn't been able to since she was eighteen. Just because I could drive her to and from work doesn't mean she's safe during her shift."

Nikki shakes her head and walks back to her desk, clearly giving up.

"He never killed them during shifts, Blake."

I glare at Will. "What makes you think he didn't change his MO? Chances are, he was at the bar the day Donna was killed." And that's the truth because, finally, we think we've identified him.

The guy Tia had described to us, Robert Detmold, was seen in the other bars, too, but never on the evening the victims were found. It makes us believe he's getting bolder.

Every officer and bar owner in New York have been informed about the guy. We have an open warrant because of a parking ticket. Hell, at this point, we are glad about any excuse to take him in and make sure he's off the streets for a night—or ten. Unfortunately, he seems to have dropped off the radar.

"I want to protect her, yet she'd rather risk her life. As soon as she apologizes for walking out—"

"You're a dick," Nikki groans, and I jump to my feet, fury surging through me.

"I want to keep the woman I love safe, and it's clearly the last thing on her mind. It'll just be for a little bit, and I know Warrick would understand."

She stands again. "And has *he* asked her to stay home? To not come back to work? No, he hasn't. He picks her up at the station, yet he doesn't discuss it with her. He could fire her so she'd be home, yet he doesn't because he gets it. So, you tell me who exactly needs to apologize?"

I bite my lip, then close my eyes, resting both palms on my desk, staring down at the badge sitting in the middle of them.

Nikki snickers. "Come on. I can see it on your face. Say it." She smugly crosses her arms over her chest.

I sigh. "You're right. I hate to say it, but you're right. At least I'd be able to see her, knowing for a fact no hair on her was touched. I should go talk to her. We don't have anything but several pictures and—"

Will gets to his feet after throwing his phone onto the desk. "He was spotted in a bar not far from Gun & Shot. Let's go, hotshot."

I grab my badge and my gun, my heart jumping into my throat. If we can grab him, this whole discussion will be moot anyway.

I can feel it. We're close to finally cracking the case.

TIA

I'm tempted to beg Blake to come over. I need to see him, need to talk to him, even if it ends with us sleeping in different apartments in the end.

Just a glance at his face would ease my tension. Warrick keeps shooting me worried looks, and when I asked him why he hasn't ever told me to stay home, he said because he'd worry too much. Besides, who knows when it will finally be over?

The bar isn't as full as it has been the last week, which I appreciate. I chat with patrons, glad when they distract me enough to make my shift pass quickly.

"Basketball is an incredible game," one of our regulars states.

I nod with a pleasant smile while turning my bracelet on my wrist. I should've talked to Chloe, but after she left me a few awful messages, I refuse to take her calls.

I wanted to call Mom, but then I'd have to admit that I wasted my life on someone who didn't appreciate it. I'm not ready for that.

And Blake... If he calls tonight to make sure I'm home, I might pick up just so I can hear his voice. I know he cares, and I understand where he's coming from, but even talking to some of his team, I have the feeling he's never going to give in, and I need the work. Now more than ever because the radiator broke, and since it was my fault, I have to replace it.

Well, not *my* fault, but it turned out the kids hung their clothes on the pipes leading to the radiators, which weakened them until they gave way to the pressure.

Yeah, the landlord's not fixing that one.

I can't even be mad at Pauli because she didn't have enough room for her things in the closet. Also, we were lucky there was insulation around the pipe or we might have gone up in flames.

I rub my wrist over my forehead, fighting off a headache. I don't know what it is, but I feel as if my vision has blurred a little. I lift my water glass and take a healthy swig. It doesn't help much.

Warrick clasps my shoulder. "Need air?"

I nod, then walk out the back, keeping my foot in the door while I inhale a breath of cold air. It's quiet, yet scary in the alley because sometimes I feel as if Donna is right here, shaking her head at me.

My skin prickles, deciding thirty seconds is definitely enough. When I make my way back inside, I do feel slightly better.

I go back to serving beers when a group of men comes in, clearly intoxicated, clearly in search of more alcohol...and maybe trouble. Warrick meets my eyes. I decide to walk over because I'd be less threatening. The second I tell him they shouldn't be in here, I know he'll make them leave.

"Welcome, guys." I pop out my hip the way Donna would

have and plaster on my most contagious smile. "How are we tonight?"

There are seven of them, all heavy around the middle, and at least five of them are married, judging by the wedding ring on their finger.

"You are kinda hot," the first states, and I arch a brow at him.

"And I'm kinda your server. So tell me what it'll be or walk out again. I can do this the easy way or the hard way. Your choice." I'm not out for a fight, and we aren't normally equipped for that, but there's a police car out front—I hope. It's been there the last few nights. I count on those guys helping me should the need arise.

"Easy it is," a dark-haired one decides with a look at his friends, and they all seem to follow his lead.

I put on my smile again and take their order. It's smooth sailing afterward, all of them turning into gentlemen. Once they leave, the last patrons of the night, Warrick and I are both surprised to see a hefty tip for both of us.

Warrick locks the door and we start cleaning, Donna's playlist on in the background.

"So, you and Blake..." Warrick leaves the statement hanging, clearly giving me the option whether or not to answer.

"It's too serious, and I don't think we can do that."

And maybe that's really it. That he's never cared about anyone the way he cares about me—Kelly's words, not mine—seems to have kicked all his protective instincts into high gear. I don't think I'm in that much danger because, as far as I've heard, the guy never returns to the bars he has killed at before. And why would he? Who would run the risk of the police seeing him?

"So Blake's not gonna pick you up." It's not a question, but a simple statement.

I pull out my phone and glance down, not seeing a call or text. I shake my head. "I'll be okay."

He sighs while I tug on my coat. "I'll walk you. Just give me a—"

A loud bang makes us both jump. Warrick curses. "Someone forgot to close the damn bathroom window again. Wait here."

I nod, taking my bag and walking over to the back door. I push it open and lean against the doorframe, letting out some of the stale air. I know I can close the door quickly if I have to.

Retching makes me lean forward and glance toward the mouth of the alley. There's someone on all fours, his body shaking. I put my bag in the door to make sure it doesn't close, then slowly walk toward him.

"Hello?" I call. The retching sounds get worse. "Do you need an ambulance?" I take another step forward, the back of my neck prickling, but not enough to make me stop. If this guy needs help...

Suddenly, he scrambles to his feet. I decide if he's well enough to stand, I can go back. I turn and—

An arm wraps around my neck. I flail and grab at it. Seeing my bracelet reflect the light, I struggle to grasp one of the charms. He turns us, almost lifting me as if I weigh nothing, and starts to walk farther down the alley. I finally rip off the Eiffel Tower charm and bring it back to his face, hoping to hit something soft.

He howls in pain, and I struggle free. I wonder briefly where Warrick is as I run away, my flight instinct high. I glance over my shoulder, my throat constricting when I recognize him, but before I can say something, he reaches out and grabs my wrist, tugging me back, making me lose my balance.

He also tore off your bracelet, I think as I fall, wondering if someone will pick it up and give it back to my mother at some point or if it will be forever lost.

BLAKE

Robert Detmold sits in one of the observation rooms. Every single one of us bounces on the balls of our feet because we want to talk to him, want to be the one to get his confession.

Wolfe marches into the room and throws the file of the dead girls onto the table, but the suspect doesn't even flinch.

"Why am I here?" His voice is subdued, distorted a little because of the speakers, and I lean forward, my eyes on his face.

Wolfe leans back in his chair, crossing his arms, as if he doesn't have a single care in the world. "Tell me about the bartenders."

Detmold arches a brow and snorts. "I didn't fuck that many. I don't know why the police would be interested in that."

We all watch, trying to determine whether he's telling the truth. Then again, he cannot really let on that he killed anyone.

"What were you doing at Monsters?" Wolfe asks.

"Drinking. I keep trying to find a bar that feels like home. You know, one where you walk in and everything falls off your shoulders? I thought Gun & Shot would be a possibility, but they have that snotty barkeep who just talks to a guy if he's hot. I tried it twice. I was sad to see the other one killed. She was a cutie." He shakes his head.

"He has to be talking about Tia," Nikki mutters.

I nod. "He is, although I don't think she is snotty with

anyone. Doesn't matter. He just admitted to having liked Donna and being pissed with Tia. I think we got the right guy." I wish I could get two minutes alone with him in a private room.

Wolfe's palm hits the tabletop. "We're not here for a pleasant chat about bars, asshole. We're here about that!" He opens the file and pushes it toward Detmold.

The pictures of the bartenders aren't pretty, and Detmold licks his lips. "What does it mean that they were the wrong ones?" His brow furrows. "How can you accidentally kill the wrong one?" Then he leans forward and touches Donna's picture. "Such a shame. He should've gotten the other one."

"Bastard!" I jump forward, my palm hitting the two-way mirror. Will grabs my arm, pulling me back. Inside, Detmold jumps at the noise, while Wolfe's shoulders tense.

"He shouldn't have killed *any* of them," he explains, and Detmold leans back in his chair.

"Agreed. But if you kill, it should at least be the right person."

"Come again?"

He shrugs a boney shoulder. "You'll go away for life, for fuck's sake. If you kill, you should make sure it's the right person. I mean, being wrong three times? How the fuck does that happen?" His confusion is genuine, but I don't want to believe it.

"He might be a killer," Nikki starts, "but certainly not of the bartenders." Which means...

The door behind us opens and one of the female cops comes in. "There's a call from a bar. Said his name is Warrick and he needs to talk to Wolfe."

My heart sinks. "Wolfe is dealing with a suspect. I'll take the call."

She nods. I follow her out and to my desk. I can feel the rest of my team hovering.

"Warrick, it's Blake."

There's a long, pregnant silence. I lower my head.

"Bates, tell Wolfe he's not the one," I whisper as Warrick stays silent.

"S-She's...not dead. I don't think."

My ass hits the chair. "What do you mean? Either she's dead or she's not." My hand shakes, my voice catching.

He clears his throat. "She's gone. We heard something and I told her to wait for me. I went back to the bathroom and found a guy sleeping there. It took a while to deal with him, and when I came back out, her bag was near the back door, but she wasn't... I... I don't know why she didn't wait."

"We're coming." I hang up, my mind racing.

"Is she..." Nikki doesn't finish her sentence.

I shake my head, although I'm not sure. "Warrick says she disappeared."

My mind spinning, I grab my vest and gun, shove my badge into my pocket. This isn't how this was supposed to go. I mean, why didn't she wait? Although her bag implies she did.

"It makes no sense," I say to Will as we head outside. I know everyone else will follow. "He's never grabbed anyone before. I mean... Where were the cops?"

I slip into the passenger seat of Will's car.

"There was a shooting three corners away, so Wolfe pulled them away. He'd been sure we had the right guy. I mean... Come on."

I don't say anything, the urgency I'd expect not present. Instead, I dread every second we get closer to that alley, to that bar. "If she is dead..."

"She's not. If he'd wanted that, she would be. But he's

never taken one, either. I... You never know. Maybe she just ran and is hiding to make sure it's safe. Since she left her bag, she might not have a phone, so..."

I rest my head against the window, wishing I'd have seen her today, even if just to tell her to be careful.

I WALK around the building to the alley. The uniforms are already there, the area cordoned off by police tape. There's no body, but even before I step farther into the alley, my heart sinks. Something sparkles, an evidence number next to it.

I crouch down. My hand shakes as I reach out, not touching it, but wanting to.

"A bracelet," Will mutters.

"*Tia's* bracelet, and there's blood on it."

"Maybe it's not hers," Will says. "Maybe she fought. It's not like she was unsuspecting. She knew there was a murderer running around, and she knew he grabbed them in alleys. I think she ran. We should split up and check the area. Maybe there'll be hints."

I look up to see Nikki holding Tia's bag. I don't know why I'm furious suddenly, but it feels like an invasion of privacy. Instead of saying something, I grit my teeth.

"Her phone's in here. It looks like she put her purse in the door in order to get back into the bar. Warrick is looking at the cameras, but..." She pauses, then sighs. "There's a blind spot."

I blink. *He got the fucking things installed after Donna was killed because we had nothing, and now there's a blind spot?*

"Blind spot?" I have an urge to find Warrick and squeeze the life out of him. "*A blind spot?*"

Will grabs me before I can storm off, which I'm grateful for. Beating Warrick won't do anyone any good.

"She clearly saw something. I assume someone asked for help, which is why she hesitated, then walked out, propping the door open with her purse," Nikki adds. "Maybe she's around here somewhere. You should go back to the precinct and—"

"No!" I interrupt her.

Wolfe walks up. "No body. We need to find it so we know what's going on."

It. He's talking about Tia as if she's just another person. "*Her*. We need to find *her*," I correct angrily.

He ignores me. "Hawkes and Atwood, you go right, toward the subway station. Bates, Davis, you're with me to the left. Look for anything. If he was injured, we might find the tiniest smidge of blood. Call us as soon as you see anything."

I take out my flashlight, making sure I won't miss anything. *As if a body could be overlooked so easily.*

I let Will take the wall side so he can check for prints, while I look straight ahead. I wish there was snow because we'd have a better chance of seeing footprints or blood.

The first alley is empty, and still...

"Tia?" I call, my heart erratic, my mind hopeful. "It's Blake." Will and I wait, hearing nothing. Besides a trash bag, there's nothing in that alley.

The second alley has a dumpster and a ladder leading to a fire escape that could be reached if you jumped high enough. I don't know if Tia would be able to reach it under normal circumstances, but filled with adrenaline and fear? Maybe. I walk farther, swallowing before I glance behind the dumpster and inside.

"Tia?" I call again, then glance up at the fire escape. Even the flashlight doesn't show any shadow suggesting anyone's up there.

Third and fourth alley render the same result. I'm about ready to give up and head back to the bar to search for clues, check all the cameras in the area. Not having found a body doesn't make me feel better. If he took her...

We cross a street and look in another alley, our chances getting even slimmer the longer we search. She could've turned into the street instead of going straight, or she could've...

"How far do you think we should go?" I ask quietly, not wanting to sound hopeless, even though that's how I feel. When someone goes missing, I'm usually bouncing with energy, brain running through all scenarios, wanting to get things done. Now I feel oddly crippled, hurt, hopeless.

"Until we find her," Will says with conviction, illuminating a dumpster filled to the brim. A wooden fence sits at the end of the alley, and I'm certain Tia wouldn't have tried to climb it.

"Tia?" he calls.

It's as if I can feel Tia close, can reach out and touch her. Hell, I can even smell her perfume, as if I'd seen her just a few hours ago.

"Tia, it's Will," he repeats, walking toward the mouth of the alley. I stand there a second longer, wishing there was someone around to tell me what to do.

With a sigh, I turn away, hanging my head—and catch a whimper. It's a tiny sound, yet I know I heard it.

"Will," I call and spin. "Tia. Please, it's Blake." Oh god, it can be anyone, even a prostitute hiding, but maybe, just maybe, it's not.

I walk over to the overflowing dumpster and look behind it to where trash bags are piled up. I'm almost about to chalk the whimper up to my imagination when one of the bags shifts.

My flashlight clutters to the ground. I grab bag after bag, my mind reeling when I see blonde strands.

"Leave me alone! I'm not Patricia!" Tia curls into herself as I reach for her.

"It's me. Blake. Tia, look at me. You're safe." *And alive.* Will comes running up. "I got her. Get EMTs here, stat! I have her. God, I have her."

When I touch her shoulder, she blindly tries to hit me and scramble away. "Letitia, look at me. Open your eyes!"

More people appear as Will runs back up. "EMTs on the way. Is she okay?"

At his voice, her eyes snap open and settle on his face before coming to rest on me. She stares at me, as if not sure what she's seeing, then she propels herself forward. I catch her, wrapping my arms around her, telling myself I'll never let her go.

"Are you hurt?" I ask into her hair. I pull back enough and frame her face with my hands, seeing her split lip and a bruise under her eye. Checking the rest of her, I see blood on her fingertips. "Yours?"

"I don't know. I don't know anything. I just..." She starts sobbing. I gather her in my arms again, picking her up.

"We need to look at her."

Wolfe appears next to the EMT who had just spoken. "Everything about her is evidence. Record any injuries and save her clothes so we can check for prints." The guy nods.

When I place her onto a gurney, she hides her face in her hands, still crying. "I just wanted to help. I should've known better. But..." Her words are riddled with sobs. I lean in to kiss her forehead.

"We'll take her to the hospital to determine all her

injuries," a man says, looking at me. "I'm Ryan Maine. I'll make sure to keep my eyes on her."

I nod. "Can I come?"

He arches a brow. "Are you family?"

"Blake?" Tia's voice is small. I step around the EMT, taking her hand. "I got him with my bracelet. Caught him in the eye. He was furious. Find him."

"I want to come with you."

She closes her eyes. "Find him before he hurts somebody else. And find Patricia." She places her free hand over her eyes, as if thinking. "He was at the bar the night Donna died. Balding guy. I talked to him before Will came in and told me you were injured. He seemed nice. They'll..."

She swallows. "Come and see me later, okay? I don't want you sitting around the hospital, waiting. You are needed here."

I lean in and press a gentle kiss to her split lip. "I love you, and I'll be there soon, okay? I'll tell Wolfe what you just told me."

As much as I wish I could ride to the hospital with her, I can't deny she's right. Sitting in that hospital waiting room, I'd probably imagine things that are much worse than what really happened.

CHAPTER TWENTY

TIA

EVERYTHING HURTS, and my memory's riddled with holes. Almost two hours later, the doctor's done will all the tests, a nurse currently assisting me as I take a shower.

I smell like trash, and am glad Blake stayed at the scene. I have no doubt it went against every single one of his instincts, but I couldn't imagine having him around, harassing the doctors and nurses.

Also... I wanted to regain some of my memories. When they loaded me into the ambulance, I didn't remember much of what had happened, but he would have wanted to hear it all.

If they can't find anything on the cameras positioned outside, I won't be able to tell them anything, either. I don't remember much but the balding spot on the back of his head.

And who the hell is Patricia?

"You bitch. You ruined my life, Patricia."

I had startled at that. *"My name is not Patricia,"* I had choked out, his hands around my throat.

"Lies. They call you Tia, but I know that's short for Patricia! You are the reason my life was as it was!"

No amount of telling him that Tia wasn't short for Patricia had helped, but finally, I'd found a last bit of remaining strength and had managed to hit him in the bleeding eye first, then knee him in the groin. I'd run blindly, just wanting to be away from him. It hadn't taken long for his footsteps to echo behind me.

As the hot water runs down my back, more memories come back. I can feel the trash bags against my palms, the stink in my nose. It probably won't ever fade, but I survived.

Oh god, I survived.

When my knees threaten to give out, hands steady me. I look at the nurse gratefully.

She dries me off, then provides me with a hospital gown before leading me back to the bed. I slowly sit down just as Blake walks in, clothes in his hands and face drawn into a grim mask that melts off the moment he sees me. With a groan, I get back to my feet. He gathers me in his arms.

"Hey," he whispers against my neck. "I brought you one of my sweatshirts and a pair of sweatpants. Figured you'd feel more comfortable in those."

And he'd be right about that. I pull the sweatshirt over my head before leaning into his arms again. "I'm sorry," I admit against his shoulder. He picks me up, placing me onto the bed.

"Careful. She has a broken rib and bruises all over. He also tried to strangle her," the nurse says.

Blake nods. She glares at him before coming over to the bed. "I'll be back in a few minutes with your painkillers and something to help you sleep." She pats my head gently. "Try to rest up. You can give your statement in the morning."

I glance at Blake and see his badge shining around his

neck. I can't help but smirk. It must've been obvious to her that this isn't about the statement, but the nurse clearly cares more about her patients than statements the cops need.

"Thank you," he says politely, then waits until she's out of the room before he leans in and kisses me softly, making me wince. "Sorry," he mutters. "I thought I'd lost you, Tia. I need to apologize. Had I just allowed you to work and not fight you on this, you would've been sitting inside the bar, waiting for me to show. You wouldn't have been tempted to wait by the back door." Guilt drips from every single syllable, and I shake my head.

"Maybe I should have stayed home. I just didn't think he'd be back. And why tonight? He wasn't even in the bar."

"It was tonight because the unit out front had to respond to a shooting not far away. He was lucky, that's all." He swallows. "He was just lucky."

I cup his cheeks and press my mouth against his, even though the cut on my lip hurts. I just need the contact. "I missed talking to you. Had you called tonight, I would've answered, then you would've been there."

He takes a deep breath. "I wanted to drive you home tonight. I was set on it. But then we caught the guy who scared you a few nights back, and... I thought you were safe."

"Blake?" I make him meet my eyes, waiting until I know I have his full attention. I lick my lips. "I love you, too. So much."

At first, I thought I'd just imagined those words, but when the EMT got into the ambulance with me, he shook his head and mentioned how intense my boyfriend and I looked.

He smiles, then kisses the side of my head. "I—"

The nurse comes back in, interrupting him. By the time she walks out again, I'm so drowsy, conversation is pointless.

Blake sits on the bed and holds me, humming me to sleep, making me feel protected.

———

BLAKE

Once Tia is out like a light, I slip from the bed and walk to the small park behind the hospital to call Will. The team went back to the precinct to check clues because the trail is still so fresh.

It does help that we have pictures of him now, as well as a name. Bernie Jenkins, thirty-four, in the system for most of his life, abused and beaten as a child. Any other person and I'd feel sorry them, but not him. His mother was a druggie who sold him in exchange for a high. However, only a year after giving up her five-year-old son, she got her shit together, married, and had a daughter.

I don't know his motives for killing, but I'm positive he'll tell us all about it once we—

"Are you with the bartender who got beaten?"

I look up at the nurse who'd joined me just outside of the door. Her eyes flicker to my badge. I arch a brow. "Yes. Can I help you?"

She wrings her hands together, then clears her throat. "I was with her when the doctor checked her injuries. She mumbled something about stabbing her attacker in the eye. Well..." She swallows. "There's a guy in the ER who has an injured eye and scratches. Said they were from his cat."

My heart in my throat, I hold out my phone and show her the picture of Jenkins that Will sent me earlier. "That him?"

She cocks her head, studying it before she answers. "He's

covered in dirt and looks rattled, but yes, that's definitely him."

How fucking stupid could one person be?

I grasp the nurse's shoulders. "Okay, listen to me..."

She swallows. "Shelly."

"Okay, Shelly. Go in there and quietly tell your colleagues that they need to be aware there is a dangerous man in the ER. Put him into a room and draw the curtain, telling him the doctor will be with him shortly. I'll come down and keep an eye on the room to make sure he doesn't run. Most importantly... Act normal, okay?"

She nods and her chin wobbles. "H-How dangerous?"

I don't want to lie to her, so I just smile. "Let's pretend you didn't ask that. Just make sure he's away from other people. You are responsible for their safety."

Her small shoulders straighten and she nods. "Yes, Detective. I'll make sure he's shielded away."

I give her a warm smile, then watch her walk away before pulling out my phone. "He's here," I tell Wolfe. "A nurse just told me he's in the ER."

"Stay put. Do not, under any circumstances, go near him. We don't want this guy to walk free because you lose your patience with him. You hear me, Atwood? It won't help Tia. Your lady will be traumatized for the rest of her life."

I don't tell him that I think she already is. "I told the nurse to put him into a room away from people. I'll just keep my eyes on the room to make sure he stays in there."

I hang up after Wolfe confirms, then walk inside to tell the nurse assigned to Tia to keep any eye on her and not let anyone not authorized into her room. Blowing out a breath, I make my way down to the ER. The area buzzes, even though it's only five in the morning. I spot Shelly. She nods toward the room right across from us, making sure I know she put him in there. The curtains are drawn, just like I ordered. I lean against the wall behind the nurses station, crossing my arms over my chest. Part of me hopes he decides to run just so I can tackle him to the floor, but Wolfe is right. Anything that would risk this guy not spending the rest of his life in jail would be a stupid to do.

I don't know how much time passes before Wolfe and the rest of them walk through the door. Shelly had gone in twice, telling Jenkins there'd been an emergency and he'd have to wait a little longer.

It feels like hours before Wolfe leads Jenkins out of the room in cuffs, reading him his rights loud enough for at least ten people to hear.

"I'm going to come with you for questioning, but—"

Will shakes his head. "Stay here. I'll keep you updated. Try to get some sleep. I have a feeling once Tia is discharged, she won't be as calm as she is right now." I nod. "And, Blake?" I look up. "Call Kelly. He heard about the whole thing but couldn't leave his shift yet."

Again, I nod and walk back to Tia's room. I slip inside, still finding her asleep, and pull out my phone, opening my messages. They are all from Kelly, and it strikes me that maybe someone should inform Tia's parents. I type a message to Will and get an instant reply that they've already been called.

Finally, I dial Kelly, who answers after the first ring. "Fuck, Blake. How is she?"

I keep my voice low. "Bruised and battered, but alive." He exhales slowly, making me chuckle. "You really would've snatched her up had I not claimed her, huh?"

Kelly snorts. "Of course. I meant that, but the second you warned me off, she shifted into something like my little sister.

I love her like I would a sibling. When I heard there was police at the bar…"

"She fought him off and got away, Kelly. She protected herself. Also, believe it or not, he came into the ER with an eye injury. Wolfe just took him in."

A surprised laugh leaves Kelly's lips. "There are so many hospitals he could've gone to, so many that would've made more sense, and he picks the biggest?"

"He killed three girls…wrongly killed two of them… I don't think he's very bright. I gotta go. Take care, okay?"

After he promises to stop by later, I hang up, pulling a chair to Tia's bedside and holding her hand.

TIA

I blink my eyes open, having to squint in the blinding white light. Even in the confusion of my surroundings, Blake's presence stands out.

"You're here, so that means it wasn't just a horrible dream," I croak out, and he presses a kiss to my wrist.

"We caught him, Tia. He's behind bars," he whispers and brushes a blonde strand behind my ear, his expression tender.

I suck in a breath. "Did you? For real?"

He nods, then helps me up as I struggle to sit. My mind's still a little sluggish, but I know it's only the remnants of the medication I'd been given.

"For real. You are safe. You and everybody else in New York. I have no doubt that the media will soon want to talk to you. After all, you're a survivor."

I nod. "Will I have to face him in court?"

Blake shrugs. "Honestly? It all depends. If he confesses,

it'll be an easy case and there won't be any need for testimony."

I close my eyes and exhale slowly. "I would do it, but..."

He sits next to me on the bed and wraps an arm around me. "I know, but you won't have to. I'm pretty sure Wolfe will invest everything he has to get the guy to confess."

I rest my head against his chest. "I wonder what makes a person kill three people like that. I mean..." I shrug. I can't wrap my head around it.

Blake stays quiet, and I look up at him. "Don't you want to be there to hear what he says?"

He hesitates only a second before shaking his head. "I couldn't care less why. I'll find that out soon. It won't make a difference if I hear it now or tomorrow. However..." He trails off as the door opens, Nikki walking in.

"Good to see you, Tia," she says with a smile, walking over to hug me. I've talked to her a couple of times at the bar. She is a tough woman, but when she pulls back, I see relieved tears swimming in her eyes. "I swear, when Blake said Warrick called him, I thought..."

Blake takes my hand, as if trying to remind me that he's still here.

As if I could forget.

She clears her throat. "I thought it was over." She glances at Blake, then back at me. "I'm here to take your statement."

Blake shifts. I draw him closer, cuddling into him. "I expected this. Are you ready?" Seeing she's not holding anything to take a statement with, I look around for a pad and a pen.

She nods. "Go ahead. I'll be able to remember it."

Blake grins. "She's recording it with her cell. It's why her hands are in her pockets."

Nikki blushes. "Okay, fine. My memory is not that good, but Wolfe asked me to record it."

"I'm sure he told you to *ask* her if you could," he mutters.

Nikki glares at him. "Shut up, Atwood. I just thought she'd be more relaxed if I didn't tell her I was recording this. That's all. Besides—"

I lift my hand. "It's okay. Just let me get this over with, okay?"

They both nod. I try to sort my thoughts as Blake tightens his hold around my shoulders. "I'm not sure if it will be in order or if I will remember everything. I opened the back door of the bar and saw him on the ground, retching. I wanted to help, but then recognized him. He grabbed me. We struggled. He called me Patricia over and over. I panicked. I mean, I knew what was probably going to happen…" I shake my head. "Somehow, I was able to grasp a charm from my bracelet and got him in the eye. I don't think I really hurt him. It might have just been more surprise than anything."

Blake snorts. "Oh, you hurt him, Tia. We arrested him in the ER."

I stiffen, and Nikki shoots him a furious glare. "His eye needed treatment, which he got in one of our prison cells. What happened then?"

I tell them about the struggle on the ground, him trying to strangle me, kicking and hitting him, then me running.

"Maybe I should've turned down one of the streets, but I didn't think. I kept moving, then I heard something crash behind me. I didn't turn back to see if he was following me. I turned into the alley, saw the trash, and hid." My breath hitches. I squeeze Blake's biceps without realizing it.

He pulls my hands away and kisses my knuckles, then looks up, his hard gaze on Nikki. "We know the rest. I'll write my report later."

I reach out for her, grasping her fingers to make sure she looks at me. "Thank you. All of you. For coming to help me. For looking out for all of us."

She nods, glancing at Blake. "I'll be back when Mr. Grumpy is not on shift, then we'll talk, okay?"

The door flies open and Kelly rushes in, carrying a chocolate cake and some milkshakes. He frantically searches for a place to put everything down, then wraps his arms around me.

He mutters something, but my wide eyes are focused on Nikki, who gestures for Blake and her to exit the room.

"You got her?" he asks, and Kelly nods. I think he might be the only one who is actually allowed to stay alone with me right now.

―――

BLAKE

I close the door behind me, hoping Kelly will watch out for Tia. Worried the shock will catch up with her, I nearly rush back inside.

God, I should be there. I *want* to be there. All the time. I rub my forehead, realizing how serious I'm about her.

"Okay, I assume you know why he did it," I say.

Nikki walks to the wall across from me and leans against it, slowly slipping down until she's sitting on the floor. I walk over and stand next to her, then copy her, staring up at the white ceiling.

She sighs. "I'm not dating her, yet I've been fucking worried about her. I mean, I've talked to her a handful of times, but…" She shrugs.

I can't help my smile. "She buries herself underneath your

skin before you even realize it, doesn't she?" It happened to me, and I know Kelly feels that way.

"She's different, for sure. I think the whole team would've hurt for you had she...had..." She swallows.

"What do you know, Nikki? What was his reason? And why the wrong ones?"

Nikki bites her lip and clenches her jaw. It's her tell.

"Just spit it out. I can handle it."

She shakes her head, dark hair falling around her face. "After hearing the reason, Wolfe punched a hole in the wall. Will nearly climbed over the table. Do you know that the guy was such a weak shit, it took less than ten minutes to get the whole story out of him?"

I nudge her with my shoulder. "What story?"

She is silent again, and I curse under my breath.

"Okay, calm down," she mutters. "So, his mother was a druggie and a whore. She never knew who his father was, and when he was five, she sold him for drugs and he landed in the system. We're talking horrible childhood. Abuse and beatings, starving and whatnot. You know. The typical story."

It is, yet he didn't strike me as someone who'd been broken by the system. Besides that, there's no excuse to ever turn into a murderer. "Sob story, check," I mutter.

"So, at seventeen, he starts buckling down in school because he wants to get out of the shitty cycle. Pulls himself together, decides to forgive the mother he barely remembers, and moves on. Yada, yada, yada. Years pass. He gets a boring job at a boring company and lives in a boring apartment, but he made it. He beat the system.

"At thirty-seven, he decided to look for his mom. A year after she sold him, she cleaned up her act. She went back to school, got her high school diploma, started college, worked, met a guy, married...

"Anyway, it takes a few months before he gets her address, then just shows up at the house. She doesn't let him in, but mentions a daughter who's a bartender because she likes studying people's psychology. Her name is Patricia, and he figures she's between twenty-three and twenty-eight."

"That's quite a gap," I mention, and she nods.

"He says he was furious, wanted to get inside to see the house and the new, better life. She didn't let him, but he spotted blonde hair on her clothes. His mother had red hair, so he assumed—"

"She was blonde," I finish, flabbergasted. "Because his life had been shit and he'd been through hell, even though he pulled himself out, he decided she deserved to die?"

Nikki shrugs. "He said he snapped, but regretted killing the wrong ones. He wanted to stop, but then he was at Gun & Shot and heard someone call Tia. He waited for her that night. He thought she was the right one."

I snort. "Tia said he'd called her Patricia. So Donna died because he was furious Tia didn't come out of the building?"

For a long moment, Nikki is quiet, then she shakes her head. "He honestly thought it was her. Said when he realized it wasn't, he just figured since he started, why not finish?" She stops again. I hear her swallow. "He didn't have anything but an age range, a name, and one blonde hair. He didn't think she deserved a good life because he didn't have one. That's all. That's his reasoning. Here's the kicker... We found out Patricia isn't even blonde. The hair was from his mother's best friend. Three girls are dead because of...nothing."

I rest my head back and wonder if it's better to not let Tia know that. "Is there *any* reason any of those murders should be excused?"

She shrugs. "Abuse, rape... I mean, at least we'd have a

reason. It just seems so much more senseless now." She looks at me. "Are you going to tell Tia?"

I climb back to my feet and help her up. "I don't think she needs to know. How would you feel if you went through something like that for no other reason than jealousy and deep-seated hatred?"

I'm about to step back into Tia's room when Nikki grasps my arm. "Imagine reading it in the paper instead of your boyfriend telling you."

I close my eyes, deciding that she has a point. "Thank you," I murmur, and she punches my shoulder.

"Take care of her, or I'll kick your ass. If she managed to wrap you around her little finger like that, she's a good one."

I don't say anything to that, but realize she's the only one who could've managed that.

After all, Tia is it for me. There won't ever be anyone else I'd be ready to give up everything for.

CHAPTER TWENTY-ONE

TIA

"I'M FINE, MOM."

I don't know how often I said that exact sentence since my mom waltzed into Blake's apartment and basically took over. I wanted to call her the minute I was out of the hospital, but I hadn't.

I'd been too worried what she'd think or say, too much a mess, and with Blake being there twenty-four/seven, I'd also had enough of people hovering.

She told me Wolfe had called her after finding her number in the records. He'd decided my family should know, and the moment my parents had heard what happened, they'd come to see me.

"I know you're fine, but you almost died."

I didn't, not really, even though I know it was what Jenkins had been after. The bruises on my neck are gone, and when I look into the mirror, I tell myself it was nothing but a bad dream.

Except for the nightmares and panic attacks when I least expected it.

My mom brought my nieces with her, and while my father sits on Blake's couch, the girls run around, singing and giggling. I don't know where Chloe is, and I'm too afraid to ask, but I do know there are way too many people around right now.

I slip away when the focus shifts to the girls, hoping no one notices, and walk into Blake's bedroom, looking out over the park. It's dark, yet I know exactly how it looks.

"Want me to kick them out?" Blake's voice is soft as he comes up behind me and kisses the back of my head, hands massaging my shoulders.

I hesitate for a moment. "I'm sorry we're invading your apartment." I considered going back to mine after I was discharged from the hospital, but just the thought of being alone makes me want to tear my hair out. "I should take them back to—"

"Move in with me, Tia. I know this might seem rushed, but you keep me sane. I want to do the same for you. It's obvious Chloe is not going to come back. Be honest. That apartment means nothing to you, right? You wanted to keep it because it held your nieces and your nephew, but now there's nothing left."

He's serious, his tone saying it all, and I turn in his arms. I want to. The need is like a living, breathing thing inside me, but I'm terrified of this becoming too serious, too soon. It's not even me I'm worried about, but *him*. It doesn't matter that there's something else playing into this question, too.

"I've never lived on my own, Blake. I moved out of my parents' house and in with Chloe. I know how to deal with someone who depends on me, but I have no idea how to live with a person who is absolutely used to doing things for himself. What if you start resenting having me here because I complain about your socks lying around?"

He laughs, the sound carefree, and draws me into his arms. "I don't let my socks lie around. And I haven't lived with anyone in quite some time. I don't know how to share an apartment with someone I love, but I know it won't be a problem with you because I'm more worried about *not* having you here. I don't even care if I have to pick you up from the bar all the time."

There's a hitch in his voice. The immediate danger is gone, but that doesn't mean walking the city at night is safe.

He takes a deep breath. "Look. Forget I said anything. You and I can just go back to how it was, and then, in a couple months, I'll ask again. I won't give up until you're ready. Now, six months from now, a year from now... I'm confident in you and me, Tia. I can wait."

I blink. "I didn't say anything."

He lightly captures my lips, teasing them open before stroking my tongue for a moment. "Exactly," he whispers against my mouth.

I shake my head, my eyes watching my hands dance across his chest. "I didn't hesitate because I don't want to move in with you, Blake. I hesitated because, for the first time in my life, I realized I can think of myself, do things for myself. It makes me wonder if..."

"If?" he asks, tilting up my chin.

"I love working at the bar, but I was always sure I'd give it up for a day job when the kids were old enough or Chloe took part in their lives. Bartender wasn't what I had in mind when I graduated high school. I disliked a lot of the bars I worked at, but bartenders get better tips than waitresses. However..."

Blake gives me a soft smile and kisses the tip of my nose.

"It's different with Warrick." He says it as if he expected the revelation to hit me sooner rather than later.

"Yes," I admit. "That bar has become like a home to me. People care. I know you guys. I... It's..." *A fucking mess.*

He nods. "You said you didn't stay quiet because you didn't want to move in with me, so I take that as a yes? We can figure the rest out later. For now, working at the bar is safe. I know Warrick misses you." His eyes twinkle as a small smile tilts his lips. "The help he hired isn't as good as he'd hoped."

I cock my brow. "Help?"

"Kelly. He stands in a few nights a week while Warrick trains someone." We both grin.

"We agreed I'd be back on Monday."

Gathering me in his arms, I feel him sigh. "I know. And you know what? I think it'll do you good. If not... You can always quit. We'll figure it out."

I press a kiss to his chest. "I know. You probably should go back out there before my mother thinks you and I are doing things no child should do when their parents are in the apartment. I'll be right out."

He kisses my forehead, brushing his thumb across my cheek, then walks out of the room I lean against the window sill, exhaling, a smile on my lips.

BLAKE

I'd been worried about her going back to work, but the moment we got home from the hospital, I realized it was exactly what she needed.

But she hadn't wanted to. I am someone who swears facing your fears is the only way to overcome them, and seeing

Tia wince whenever someone approaches or mentions the bar breaks my heart.

Warrick didn't think she'd want to go back, but I know it's necessary, even if it's just once.

Closing the bedroom door behind me, I startle when I spot a shadow. "How is she?"

Tia's mother is unlike anything I expected. I don't know why, but I'd been sure she would be an older version of Chloe. Selfish. After all, why else would you cast your daughters out because one of them was pregnant and the other supported her?

But then, when she'd come in and wrapped her arms around Tia's neck, I'd realized she's more an older version of my girlfriend.

She'd made the girls leave home because she'd hoped Tia would eventually see that her sister wouldn't ever be able to think of anyone but herself. Even when she was pregnant the first time, deciding whether to keep the baby, she'd thought only about what an abortion or putting the baby up for adoption would do to her reputation. Cassandra said when she'd suggested abortion to Chloe, she had told her mother she'd rather *be* a bad mother than have someone *say* she was.

I don't understand the logic, and I did briefly wonder why she never told Tia, but I know Tia was blindly devoted to her sister's kids, up until a few weeks ago, and probably wouldn't have believed her mother anyway.

"I don't know," I answer. "It's not like we've had much time to talk. After all, you arrived soon after we got home." I wink and give her a smile.

She slumps against the wall, scrubbing her hands down her face. "I shouldn't have let this go on for as long as it did. In the beginning, I thought... I was sure they'd be back. Then I started to feel guilty because I didn't call them. I know Tia wanted to prove that they wouldn't fail. She's stubborn like that. But Chloe..." She swallows. "I wanted her to grow up and be responsible. I knew she had a good job. I didn't think Tia had sacrificed almost everything for her. I failed both my daughters."

I lick my lips and glance over my shoulder, wondering if Tia's listening. I step closer to her mom. "As a cop, I see a lot of shit. If it's taught me one thing, it's that sometimes nothing the family does helps someone become a good person. Chloe hasn't replied to my message yet. She gets one more day. If she doesn't show up here by then, I'm not going to ever let her back into Tia's life."

Tia's mother cocks her head. "Shouldn't that be *her* decision?"

I grin. "You let her make her own decision once. We see where that led."

She laughs, then quickly sobers. "To you, Detective. It led her to you. I know the path was a long and winding one, but I think she was meant to be here."

I close my eyes, my chest aching with the truth of her words. "You know, in the long run, she probably saved my life. She certainly saved my sanity." I nudge her back into the living room. "I didn't think there was anybody out there who would want to be in this apartment and watch me leave every day, knowing I might not come back."

She arches a brow. "Do you now?"

We cross over to the kitchen, and she waits while I pop open a beer. "Yes. It's not about that one time I possibly won't come home. It's about all those times I will, seeing her standing right here, a smile on her face because I am the best part about her day—and she mine."

And it's true. I know there might be a day I don't come home, or someone knocks on the door to tell her I've been injured, but I also realize that once you know what you have waiting at home, you are more careful.

The thought of jumping into a dangerous situation in order to get the bad guy suddenly doesn't seem so appealing anymore. I know I'll still risk everything to save someone else, but catching someone at the cost of my own life?

No way. Not anymore.

Unless it's someone out to hurt Tia.

Tia's mother grins. Before I can reply or do something unexpected, like hugging her, the doorbell rings.

I roll my eyes. "Probably Kelly, who finally gave up the idea of being able to find someone like Tia," I mutter. "Excuse me."

The moment I open the door, I sure wish I hadn't.

While I know it will be healing for Tia to see Chloe, part of me wishes she wouldn't have come. I don't know what I'll do if Tia decides that she needs to jump in and help Chloe again.

"I'm sorry." Those are the first words she says. I watch her face, realizing she means it. She looks pale, and when she lifts her hands to brush some strands of hair out of her face, I see them shaking. "I don't deserve to be here, and I know my mother won't be happy, but...I need to see Tia. I just..." She shrugs. I consider telling her to wait out in the hall.

Then again, I don't think I'm ready for Tia to be upset if she hears I made Chloe wait out here. I step aside and let her enter, conscious of the silence in the living room. "She's in the bedroom. First door on the right down the hall."

Chloe nods. I watch her walk over to my bedroom, wondering if maybe, just maybe, I should follow her to keep Tia out of harm's way.

TIA

The bedroom door opens. I shake out of my thoughts and the worry about the future. "I'm sorry," I say as I turn. "I lost—" The words get stuck in my throat when I see Chloe standing there.

"Hi." Her voice is small, yet I ignore that as excitement jolts through me. I've seen Liv and Pauli, but Mom didn't have Neo with her.

"Where is Neo? I need to hold him and hug him and—"

She shakes her head. "He's not here. I left him at home. The guy I hope will turn into his father someday is watching him. I... Can I sit?"

I stare at her, wondering if she realizes we are in a bedroom. "I..." I rub the back of my neck when the bedroom door opens yet again and Blake peeks in, wearing a scarf and his coat.

"We're gonna take the girls for a walk and some hot chocolate down the block. Do you want anything?"

Gratitude warms me at this thoughtfulness. I give him a soft smile, hoping he understands my silent thank you. "No, I'm good. Have fun, okay?"

He nods, then vanishes again, leaving the door ajar. I nod for Chloe to walk ahead into the living room. She does, unwinding the scarf from her neck, then unbuttons her coat. I point at the sofa, offering her a seat.

For a long moment, I wait as she stares at me. When she doesn't say anything, I get impatient. "I'm surprised you're here. I was shocked when Mom and Dad brought Liv and Pauli over, but she won't tell me what's going on, so..." I shrug. "How about you give me something?"

She clasps her hands in her lap, then looks at them. "I've been a horrible person. To you, to my kids, to everyone.

When I started dating Christian, he didn't know I had kids. When we fell in love, I had to admit to him… You know, when you started taking back your life…" She swallows, her voice catching. "I had to watch the kids, so he wondered if I was dating someone else. I told him they were mine. He was furious for a few days, then told me to move in with him. I think Blake hates him, considers him an asshole, but…" She looks back up at me. "He didn't know I made you watch my kids while I lived my life. Christian didn't know I was the worst mother possible while you made sure I had the best kids possible."

She pauses for a moment, releasing an unsteady breath, then continues. "We had a lot of late-night talks. He told me I needed to call my mother and make sure she was involved in the kids' lives. After all, she's their grandmother. Whether or not I wanted to let her into mine was my choice, but…"

"She didn't want that," I finish.

Chloe nods. "I have a long way to go because…" She blows out a breath, tears forming in her eyes. "Mom said I ruined your life, and it's true."

Those words propel me forward and make me fall to my knees in front of her because one, it was my decision to let her treat me how she did, and two, because I know she means what she says, sees what exactly went wrong between us. "You didn't. You couldn't have treated me the way you did had I not—"

"You did it for the children, Tia. You knew they would've been in trouble had you left me to my own devices. I was stupid. So stupid. And I don't know why I didn't see it until Blake's boss called me and asked if I knew you'd nearly died."

I stare at her. "*Wolfe* called you?"

A smile flickers over her lips. "Doesn't like me very much. Between what someone named Warrick told him and what your boyfriend said about me, he didn't get the best impression."

I bite back a comment about her having heard me say the name Warrick several times, and decide it's not worth the trouble or the fight. "I'm sorry."

She lifts her eyes to mine. "No, *I'm* sorry. You were exhausted. I didn't know what that felt like, until I checked the mirror this morning. After having heard you were nearly killed, I... Christian asked me if I was happy now. Happy that *Wolfe* called me about you being hurt, and not you or even Blake. He only did after the worst was over. He asked me if I realized that meant I wasn't part of your lives. It knocked me flat on my ass." She laughs, the sound shaky. "Literally. I slid down the wall and cried. He kissed my head and said it was time I realized that while he loved me, I needed to be the person he fell in love with. Like I have two personalities, you know? Maybe I do. I have the bitch I am, then the perfect sister, employee, and woman I pretend to be."

I lick my lips, unsure what to say. She cups my cheeks and rests her forehead against mine. "No more pretending. I'll work on being exactly what I always pretended I was. Can you believe I'm doing homework with Liv? I never knew math could suck that much."

We both have tears running down our cheeks. "I know. I've been doing her homework with her since she started school."

"I'm sorry, Tia. I'm so sorry."

I swallow around the lump in my throat. "So am I," I tell her. She falls to her knees onto the floor, her arms wrapped around me.

"Christian is working on finding you a better apartment in a nicer neighborhood. He has connections and—"

I pull back. "No need." I smile. "I'm moving in with Blake."

Her eyes widen in surprise, then she beams. "God, you're happy with him, aren't you?"

I shrug. "He makes me feel whole."

Hell, I didn't even realize I needed that until that exact moment.

BLAKE

There's a new peace in Tia's eyes. When we came back, we saw the sisters embracing on the floor, crying. While it had taken only a few minutes to get Tia's family out of the apartment afterward, I haven't asked her what Chloe said.

She walks into the bedroom, her hair down, face shining with the lotion she probably put on. Her eyes roam my chest, linger on my tats, then meet my eyes.

I fucking love the way her eyes always slightly widen as if she cannot believe I'm hers. I guess it's exactly what I feel each time I look at her.

"No idea how I deserve you," I whisper as I draw her into my arms.

She lets me kiss her for a moment before she stiffens and her face clouds with worry.

I pull away and cock my head. "What's wrong?"

She takes a deep breath and starts to turn away, but I tighten my grip on her. "Uh-uh. You stay where you are." I'm worried, and a million scenarios run through my head, starting with Chloe saying something awful to her.

There's a tiny smile on her lips, then she wets them. "So... Moving in with you..."

"You already agreed," I remind her, my stomach dropping. I didn't realize how excited I was about the idea until that moment.

Tia nods. "I know."

"Letitia...," I growl, and she chuckles.

"If you call me Letitia, I know I was a bad girl." She smiles, but it's weak, unsure. I grip her shoulders and gently push her down onto the bed, then kneel in front of her, taking her hands in mine.

I kiss her knuckles and feel her tremble. Her eyes fill with tears. It causes me to swallow. "Tia..."

She cups my cheek. "You were terrified of sharing your life with someone. I mean... We both know it's why you tried to keep me at arm's length," she starts. I bite my lip to keep myself from interrupting her. "I didn't think I'd find anyone to be with. I wanted to, but I didn't think I deserved it until I knew the kids were okay. Everything with us was—"

"Right," I say, then bite my tongue.

"*Perfect*," she corrects. "I don't care what happened, or if we fought a lot, but being with you was...*is* everything I ever dreamed of. The way you look at me, the way you hold me... I have no idea if we're ready for this. I mean, I know..." She takes a deep breath.

I sit back on my heels, staring up at her, my heart pounding. "You're pregnant..."

Tears fall freely. "They told me at the hospital. I think they actually said it twice, but it didn't register until the day we left when they reminded me I needed to find an OB/GYN. After what happened, I didn't have enough mental capacity to think about it, and now..." She chokes out a sob. "I'm sorry, Blake. I didn't think it was possible, have no idea how it happened, but it did, and... Shit."

She doesn't want it. It's like a blow to my stomach, even

though I never wanted a child. The thought hadn't occurred to me until I met her, and even then, it had been nothing but a fleeting glance at a future I never wanted to think about.

But I suddenly wonder why it hurts so much for her to not want to go there with me.

"If you don't want it, Tia, I'll raise it alone." The words are out before I even know I think them, and my heart breaks when I realize that would mean she won't be in my life.

She stares at me, her brows furrowed. "Alone? Don't want it? I'm... What? I've wanted this baby from the second the thought settled in. I mean, I forget about it whenever panic sets in and thoughts overwhelm me, but... It'll be different in a few weeks when..."

I cannot even imagine what it must be like for her, struggling with the memories and a pregnancy all of a sudden. She probably goes from high to low and back again constantly.

I stand and sit next to her, drawing her into my arms, kissing her hair. "You'll be okay. We'll be okay. I..." I gasp. "I'm going to be a dad."

We're both quiet, then I stand, beaming. "I'm going to be a father. I didn't know I wanted to be, but... Tia... This... Oh god."

She looks up at me, shocked, then relief floods her features. "This apartment is going to be too small. And we're going from nothing to..."

"Everything. I know." Maybe I should be scared, but I'm not. I don't even know why, but I cannot find it in me to be terrified.

Especially because she'll be a great mom.

"What if I can't do this, Blake? I like the bar. I like you. I like us, but we really didn't even get to be an *us*. And... A child. I know it'll be perfect, but... I..." She buries her face in her hands. I can't help but laugh.

She peeks through her fingers at me. "My misery amuses you?"

I grin, shaking my head before drawing her into my arms. "No, but I never thought I'd be the calm one."

She giggles. "Me, either, but I'm glad it's that way. This is unexpected, but it's going to be okay, right?"

I nod. "It'll be perfect."

And that's something I believe with all my heart.

EPILOGUE

TIA

BLAKE LEANS OVER and kisses my cheek as the sun crawls into the room. It's Saturday, the first time in weeks that we're going to have a quiet weekend. After I finally went back to work, life changed.

Chloe helped me move into Blake's place, but we didn't stay there long. There wasn't any room for a nursery, so a bigger apartment was mandatory.

Blake also decided it needed to be in a different part of town, closer to Gun & Shot.

His hand caresses the baby bump I can no longer hide. Six weeks have passed since I found out about the pregnancy, and while it took me a few days to get used to the idea, he'd been excited from the beginning.

It wasn't that I didn't want children. I just hadn't expected it to happen so soon. Blake calls it a blessing because focusing on the baby helps keep my PTSD in check.

I always thought that was something only soldiers or cops had, but I soon realized any kind of trauma can cause it.

"Morning," he mumbles against my neck, his lips traveling over my shoulder before he bites my earlobe. "You look radiant."

I roll my eyes and turn my head so he can see me. "You don't know that."

He nods. "I do, because you always are. All the more lately." He presses his lips against mine, the touch tender, distracting, while his hands sneak over my body to cup my breasts. I instantly swat them away because I'm very sensitive there now, and as much as he appreciates the growing size, I can't handle him touching them.

Yet.

He swiftly moves, hovering over me without putting his weight on me. "How are you feeling about a little..." He waggles his brows.

While I like the idea of us together, I'm not sure my morning sickness has finally stopped. I don't have it every day, but the mornings I do are the worst.

"Blake..." His fingers travel inside my panties before I can protest, and when he skims them over my clit, my legs fall open and all my doubts disappear. "Oh god. That feels good."

His playfulness vanishes and his hazel eyes turn dark with lust. I love the way his gaze roams over my body, a little more appreciative every time. "I love you," he whispers, then leans in to kiss me, pushing two fingers inside my core at the same time. My hips buck off the bed, needing more friction.

Pregnancy is fun. You go from not wanting anything one second to wanting it hard and fast the next. And we definitely reached the wanting it hard and fast.

"More," I beg.

I laugh as he stands, pulling down his pajama pants and stepping out of them. Then he lifts my leg, kissing my ankle as he pushes my panties out of the way and positions himself at my entrance.

The morning sun makes his skin glow, and I lick my lips at all the peaks and valleys that make up his handsome body. I reach out, brushing my fingertips over his skin while he pushes into me, his movements even and slow. I urge him with my hips, but he doesn't give in.

Instead, his eyes remain on me while he builds a slow, steady rhythm that drives me wild. He grasps my hand and brings it to his mouth, kissing the palm before letting his lips wander to my pulse. I bet he can feel its erratic rhythm.

"Perfect," he mutters, my body on fire. His slow thrusts hit the right spot inside of me, and I moan.

"Blake," I whisper. "Please... Just a little bit faster. I need..." His thumb rubs my clit. "Oh god, yes!" I quiver as an orgasm races through me, making my legs tremble and my body clench him.

"Tia," he gasps, quickening his pace. He's beautiful, his muscles shifting underneath his skin, trembling as he comes inside of me, cursing under his breath.

When he's spent, he falls onto the sheets next to me. "Going slow," he pants, "is harder than anything else. I feel like I ran a marathon."

I chuckle and lean over to kiss him, ready to get up and clean myself, but he pushes me back down. "I'll be right back," he assures me, then vanishes into the bathroom.

BLAKE

As I get a washcloth to clean Tia up, I smile into the mirror. Everything is just perfect. Warrick decided to extend the bar's hours and is now open for lunch, with Tia as the shift leader. She's responsible from eleven to eight, and he takes over after that. No more late nights for her, and she still gets to work at the bar.

Also, we now have an amazing apartment only thirty minutes away from the bar and the precinct, and I...

I stare at myself in the mirror for a second, wondering if something has changed about me, but the guy looking back at me looks relaxed, more so than I can ever remember being.

"Blake?"

"Coming," I call back and return to her side, cleaning her up.

She cups my cheek, the softness in her eyes nearly making me fall to my knees. She's been my salvation, my angel, and I don't think she knows it.

"Have a panic attack in there?" she asks.

I furrow my brows. "Panic attack? About?"

She shrugs. "Us." She gestures to her stomach. "This. Everything."

I lean in to kiss her shoulder, humming against her skin, then pull back, her blonde her shimmering in the morning sun. She's incredibly beautiful, and she's *mine*.

I shake my head. "I looked at myself in the mirror, wondering if I had changed, if I look different now that my life is complete. That's all. There are days I cannot believe I'm here, feeling what I'm feeling."

I take her hands in mine, lifting her left one to my lips. If she notices that I kiss her empty ring finger, she doesn't let on.

"So you're happy?"

I know exactly what she's asking. She knows I was afraid of anything serious because I know more than one cop who never made it home, but...

"I love you, Tia. I didn't know why people were in relationships, but I know now. You taught me. You showed me that it's worth it. Yes, I might be injured because that's a risk we take, but I *will* be back. As long as my heart beats, I will be back here with you. You got that?"

She nods. "I do. Do you?"

I smile, then draw her onto my lap, thinking maybe I should've gotten dressed before having this serious conversation.

"I do. And each time I look at you, I know that won't change. You are my girl. You aimed the gun. You fired the shot. You hit my heart...and it's the best feeling."

I can tell that she wants to say something, but she just rolls her eyes. "Can you make me pancakes? And Chloe and Christian asked us over for lunch."

I nearly groan. Things between her and her sister are still strained, but they're working on it. Things between me and Chloe? I'll call them civil. As long as I feel stress between them because Chloe hasn't made amends, I'll not go easy on her.

"Pancakes it is," I decide and kiss her nose. I lift her off my lap and place her back onto the bed, then pull on sweatpants.

"Almost as hot as naked," Tia hollers as I make my way over to the kitchen. I can't help but grin to myself.

Hell, this is the life.

THE END

ACKNOWLEDGMENTS

I guess I should start with thanking (or cursing?) Blake Sevani and Reggie Deanching for having shared that pic on FB and inspiring a while damn book around it. I am SO in love with it still (you know, it a cool and calm way because I'm all cool and calm, and not giddy AF).

Jay Aheer, you are an effing genius. The cover you created was practically on the first try and I love love love everything about it.

Josephine, you helped me through all those plot holes, danced around the puddles I created with my writing and helped me make sense of things I didn't even knew needed sense-making. You are such a big influence on my writing and I'm grateful every damn day.

Lina and Lainey... I love you and the way you love me. You two make me smile when I'm not sure I can, and you fangirl when I need it the most. Lainey, your support has been tremendous and I can never pay you back. <3

Aimie... I wish I could hug you. You had to listen to me over and over, hearing all the same complains and yet, you still stood by me. Thank you. Jesus, I don't know what I'd do without you.

Jamie, you make me want to be better, want to stick to my routines and even if you don't realize it, that helps me so much. <3 Thank you for being as driven as you are because it drives me, too.

To my betas, your feedback mattered so much. I changed a few things, shifted some scenes around, and I'm glad you enjoyed that story.

To my readers, old and new, I hope you'll enjoy this book and will fall in love with Tia and Blake the same way I did. Thank you for purchasing this book, for having cone through it, for having taken your time to read my words. You make my world go round.

xoxo,
Sam

ABOUT THE AUTHOR

Once upon a time there was a young girl with her head full of dreams and her heart full of stories. Her parents, though not a unit, always supported her and told her more stories, encouraging her to become what she wanted to be. The problem was, young Sam didn't know what she wanted to be, so after getting her A-levels she started studying Computer Science and Media. After not even one year she realized it wasn't what her heart wanted, and so she stopped, staying home and trying to find her purpose in life. Through some detours she landed an internship and eventually an apprenticeship in a company that sells cell phones. Not a dreamy career, but hey. Today she's doing an accounting job from nine-to-five, which mainly consists of daydreaming and scribbling notes wherever she can.

All through that time little Sam never once lost the stories in her heart, writing a few little of them here and there, writing for and with her best friend, who always told her to take that last step.

Only when a certain twin-couple entered her mind, bothering her with ideas and talking to her nonstop did she start to write down their story - getting as far as thinking she could finish it. Through the help of some author friends, and the encouragement of earlier mentioned best friend, little Sam, now not so little anymore and in her twenty-seventh year, decided to try her luck as an Indie author. She finished the story of the first twin, Jaden, and realized she couldn't ever stop.

So, it really is only after five that the real Sam comes out. The one that hungers for love, romance, some blood, a good story, and, at the end of the day, a nice hot cup of Chai Tea Latte.

And if the boys are still talking to her, she'll write happily ever after.

Contact the author:
www.samdestiny.com

Reader group: https://www.facebook.com/groups/DestinysMorningstars/

Printed in Great Britain
by Amazon